CANTRELL

OTHER FIVE STAR WESTERNS BY T. T. FLYNN:

Night of the Comanche Moon (1995)
Rawhide (1996)
Long Journey to Deep Cañon (1997)
Death Marks Time in Trampas (1998)
The Devil's Lode (1999)
Ride to Glory (2000)
Prodigal of Death (2001)
Hell's Cañon (2002)
Reunion at Cottonwood Station (2003)
Outlaws (2004)
Noose of Fate (2005)
Dead Man's Gold (2006)
Gunsmoke (2007)
Last Waltz on Wild Horse (2008)
Shafter Range (2009)
A Bullet for the Utah Kid (2010)
Travis (2011)
The Resurrection Kid (2012)

CANTRELL

A WESTERN DUO

T. T. FLYNN

FIVE STAR

A part of Gale, Cengage Learning

GALE
CENGAGE Learning·

Detroit • New York • San Francisco • New Haven, Conn • Waterville, Maine • London

GALE
CENGAGE Learning

LIBRARY OF CONGRESS CATALOGING-IN-PUBLICATION DATA

Flynn, T. T.
    [Novels. Selections]
    Cantrell : a western duo / By T.T. Flynn. — First Edition.
      pages cm
    ISBN-13: 978-1-4328-2705-2 (hardcover)
    ISBN-10: 1-4328-2705-7 (hardcover)
    I. Flynn, T. T. Strangers talk or die. II. Flynn, T. T. Cantrell. III. Title.
PS3556.L93C36 2013
813'.54—dc23   2013014016

First Edition. First Printing: September 2013
Published in conjunction with Golden West Literary Agency
Find us on Facebook– https://www.facebook.com/FiveStarCengage
Visit our website– http://www.gale.cengage.com/fivestar/
Contact Five Star™ Publishing at FiveStar@cengage.com

Printed in Mexico
1 2 3 4 5 6 7 15 14 13

ADDITIONAL COPYRIGHT INFORMATION

CONTENTS

★ ★ ★ ★ ★

Strangers Talk or Die

★ ★ ★ ★ ★

I

Jeff Parker moved north out of Mexico with two fast pack mules on a black night as thunder rolled and rain poured from the heavens. He was on the run with gold bars worth $44,000, loaded on the mules. He rode with guns ready, knowing sudden and violent death threatened from now on.

Jeff had waited years for the big gamble. It had broken squarely under his nose two nights ago, and he'd tackled it the hard way. He'd known it was the hard way, too, by the bitterness on Fat Sam Scoby's florid face as they talked by lamplight in the sweltering *hacienda* room. The thick iron-studded room door had been bolted as they talked. The one small window, high in the massive adobe wall, had been set with strong iron bars and covered with a red-striped Indian blanket. But Fat Sam had kept his hurried words low, furtive.

"You're the only honest one in the *hacienda*," Fat Sam had said thickly. He was in a hurry, sweating with greed and apprehension. Death or worse would be at Fat Sam's heels in an hour or so. "I've been watching you," Fat Sam had admitted past the smoky lamp. He was cornered, jumpy. He knew his own gunmen for what they were. "You've got a head. You use it, Parker. It's got to be you tonight."

That was when Jeff had guessed Fat Sam might know who he was. The knowledge tightened him inside. Scoby would have put a bullet in his back if this greater trouble hadn't struck suddenly. Jeff had let it lie between them and looked past the lamp into Fat Sam's eyes. "What makes you think I'm that honest, mister?"

Fat Sam had shoved pudgy fingers through thinning gray hair. He had cursed in thick fury. He was in trouble. He was helpless. It ate at him like acid. "You'd better be honest," Fat Sam had growled. "I'll hunt you down if you ain't."

Jeff had let that lie between them, too, without comment. Fat Sam had waited a moment, elbows on the table, eyes searching, perspiration beading his broad face. Then: "There's twelve gold ingots, worth about forty-four thousand," he said finally. "I melted 'em myself, one at a time, out of gold coins. They hide easier in bars. You'll get three of the twelve for taking them north across the border. How about it?"

Jeff had started a cigarette. Inside he had been tight, heart pounding as an idea took shape and built. "What makes you think I'll make it across the border?"

Fat Sam's strong white teeth had gleamed for an instant in the lamplight. "No one would figure Sam Scoby would trust a young maverick like you on a deal like this. If they stopped to think I had gold to get out tonight, they'd be watching for me to carry it." Fat Sam had put a big clenched fist softly on the table. "That's why I was warned." Behind the fat face a fox's brain worked. "They meant to flush me out on the run with anything valuable I've got." Scoby's teeth had gleamed again. "I ain't so dumb. I'll map you a trail you never knowed existed. It'll put you on enough water to keep going. It'll keep you outta sight clean acrost the border. How about it?"

Jeff had sat there, letting Fat Sam sweat. Slowly, past dribbling cigarette smoke, he'd casually inquired: "If you don't get across the border, who gets your nine bars of gold?"

Scoby's mind was not fat. "You get acrost to where I tell you. I'll be there. How about it?"

Even then, in that sweltering locked room in the ancient

hacienda, Jeff had guessed Scoby was certain the gold would start north in Jeff Parker's care, and not because of the wealth Parker would get out of it. Scoby had guessed who Parker was. You could almost admire a man who thought fast enough to use his worst enemy in getting out of a tight spot.

The sweltering silence had dropped about them while Jeff pulled on the cigarette and Fat Sam watched him. Suddenly Fat Sam had laid a warning finger over his mouth. He had come out of the chair, moving around the heavy table.

Jeff marked the absolute silence in which the man moved. Fat Sam was like an animal—big, deadly, silent. Deep in the man some animal sense of danger had quickened. Jeff turned slowly in the heavy, carved chair, watching Scoby move the greased door bolt without a sound.

Fat Sam's two holstered .45s had the low-slung ease of a master gunman. But his pudgy hand reached to a knife in a plain leather sheath. A knife ground from a hardened steel file to hair-slicing keenness. Fat Sam had jerked the door open. His hand had seemed to flirt the knife almost carelessly through the opening. There had been a gasp. A startled man, standing with an ear to the door, had straightened convulsively.

It had been Dongo Steadman, a lean, scarred gunman with cold sly eyes. Steadman had stood there in greasy leather riding pants, hatless, eyes bulging after the one strangled gasp. The knife had buried itself in the side of his weather-burned neck. While Jeff had looked, Steadman had torn the knife out. A spurt of jugular blood had pumped out after it.

Fat Sam yanked a gun as Steadman seemed about to lunge at him with the bloody knife. Then Steadman had swayed forward like a drunken man, blood spurting. He'd dropped the knife and grabbed at his neck as he stepped forward. Fat Sam had moved silently as Steadman staggered through the doorway. Steadman had reeled to the left, holding his neck. Sightless, dying, he'd walked into the adobe wall, recoiled a step, stood stupidly, breath bubbling in his blood-filled throat. Then Steadman's knees had buckled. He'd fallen and rolled over with his cheek flat on the floor while life spurted away. Fat Sam had caught up the knife and wiped it on a leg. He'd looked along the dark hall, closed the door, slid the greased bolt silently, and shoved the knife back in the leather sheath.

Scoby had ignored the last bubbling sounds as Steadman died. His pinpoint eyes had studied Jeff, who sat smoking without expression. "How about it, Parker?"

Jeff had nodded. "I'll take your gold north, mister."

Now lightning flamed across the black heavens. Thunder crashed through the howling wind. The big black gelding Jeff rode snorted and had to be forced into the lashing rain.

The riders back toward the horizon before dark had probably not been Fat Sam's gunmen, riding after Fat Sam's gold. If the *hacienda* men followed, Fat Sam had warned, they'd probably take the short cut across Black Barranca, which even Jeff could not pass with two loaded pack mules. They'd try to head him off here at Little Woman Pass. But those riders back in the distance meant trouble, too. Armed men trailing the pack mules wouldn't be apt to lay up during the storm. Scoby had guessed it might happen. "If word gets back that two pack mules are heading north fast, somebody will start wondering what's traveling in the packs," Fat Sam had said. "Smoke up that trail until you're out of it, Parker. You won't have a chance if they catch you."

Fat Sam had said something else as he helped throw a hitch on the last mule pack in the patio, hidden from prying eyes. Scoby's other riders had been out scouting. The dead man still lay where he had fallen. There was blood all over the body. "If you meet horses in charge of a man named Big Dutch, tell him Sam Scoby said the moon looks bad. Dutch'll understand. Tell him to swing west by the salt lakes and travel to Luis Diego's *rancho,* if he can make it. Or take a chance on turning back with what he's got."

"That all?"

Fat Sam had cursed. "Tell Big Dutch I backed the wrong bunch of politicos. The other side is in. Tell 'im we're through at this place. Then push on fast before Dutch starts wondering what's in your packs. He ain't a safe man to get ideas."

Scoby had been hurried and sweating about his gold bars and his own thick neck. He'd said more just then than he realized. Jeff had filed it away against the time he'd need it.

The blue-white sheet lightning was awesome. Jeff swore at the flashes and tried to see what was behind and ahead in each moment of blinding glare.

The mouse-colored mules were spooky. They fought the braided rawhide lead ropes. Jeff damned the whole mule tribe, spat cold rain out of his mouth, and damned himself for a mulehead. He was gambling, big and risky. He was almost certain to get killed. In the cold sheeting rain a man could think only of the worst.

Lightning struck off to the right in a mighty rip of fire. Thunder tore the night apart. The black gelding shied, then lunged ahead as Jeff yelled reassurance.

He had to yell to be heard. He was deafened by the thunder, and almost spooked himself. A taste of brimstone seemed to come in on the sheeting rain. Then suddenly, as lightning flared again, the devil himself seemed to be waiting ahead on a big white horse.

Jeff fought the mules and gelding to a halt and wished it were the devil lurking ahead there in the storm. A man might outtalk or ignore the devil. That white horse looked like the big Arabian stallion stolen out of California by Long Steve Willard.

When Scoby and his gunmen scattered from the *hacienda,*

Long Steve must have become suspicious. Perhaps he'd found Steadman's body. Willard must have ridden the short cut across Black Barranca to reach this trail that cut to the border through Little Woman Pass. No need to wonder what was on Long Steve's mind. He'd kill first and search the mule packs later.

Jeff grinned thinly in the howling storm. He wore an old slicker. A black sombrero was jammed down hard on his ears and tied under the chin. The storm drove under the broad brim into his streaming face. He had jerked up the saddle carbine. He levered a shell and waited for more lightning.

A ripping flare cut the sky off to the right. The white horse was still there, its rider peering toward the black gelding and pack mules. Jeff thought he saw pale light spurting where the white horse stood. It had to be a gun flash reaching toward him, its sound lost in the thunder. He fired, levered the gun, and waited, wondering if Willard had other men close.

Lightning gutted the clouds behind him. Jeff fired, fast, and the darkness came down again. It was a queer, delayed gunfight. But it was death, too, cold-blooded, deadly. Shots wasted in the howling blackness might leave a gun empty the instant when needed. Through more lightning Jeff fired again. This time he sighted a seething mass in the night beyond the white horse.

The hills came in here, bare, rocky, cactus-studded. Somewhere to the right, not far away, should be a deep cutbank arroyo that the rising trail had been skirting before dark. Sand-soupy water would be roaring in that arroyo, death to anything that blundered in tonight. To the left, a rocky slope climbed steeply to a high knife-back ridge. Anything moving before the storm would be funneled this way. Lightning showed the white horse running in closer. Beyond it a mass of riderless horses were racing down the trail in a wild, uncontrolled wave.

Long Steve and Jeff fired together. Willard's bullet seemed to brush Jeff's ear. The blackness fell hard, then leaped into light again. The white horse was galloping closer, saddle empty. The stampeding wave of free horses was rushing nearer. The black gelding sensed terror in the night and bitterly fought the bit.

Jeff reined hard off the trail, yelling at the mules. Thunder shook the ground. Lightning gleamed on tossing manes and wild, staring eyes. The mules barely cleared the living flood that rushed over the spot where the white horse had been advancing.

Jeff felt sick. Long Steve's body must have been pulped under that torrent of hoofs. The same thing could have happened to him. Jeff guessed they were horses for Sam Scoby, heading south with the storm. Yells cut through the storm as riders followed. In the lightning glare, Jeff sighted slicker-wrapped figures passing like wet phantoms. Riders trailing Parker would be hit by that wall of running horses. Jeff grinned at the thought, waited a few minutes, and headed on.

He was in the badlands north of the border at dawn. Muddy water still roiled in flood-scoured arroyos. Jeff rode far up one twisting arroyo, keeping in the shallow water, where tracks would vanish. In a blind pocket holding more cactus than sparse bunch grass, he dried out all day, resting the horse and mules. He gnawed cold strips of jerky rather than risk fire, and he catnapped. At dusk he went on.

Three days later he brought the pack mules into the little rail-side town of Pelona and dismounted behind a small wind-scoured railroad station. Pelona was a few adobe and sun-bleached frame structures beside the shiny rails. It was a shipping point and not much else. But it had a railroad station for express and telegrams.

The taut station agent's eyes widened when he saw the contents of the four rawhide sacks Jeff Parker lugged in. A look at Parker, unshaven, dusty, bone-lean, obviously just off a long, hard trail, stopped the agent's questions, if any. Men like Jeff came into lonely border towns like Pelona, stayed briefly, said little, and vanished. Questions were not healthy. The agent issued two express receipts while Jeff wrote a telegram to an Ed Bellows at El Paso: ACES UP AT PARADISE.

The agent scanned the telegram without comment.

A run-down general store across the dusty road from the station had a post office in the back. Jeff bought two envelopes, sealed an express receipt and brief note in each one, addressed them also to Ed Bellows, and mailed them.

He rode north out of Pelona at sundown with the pack mules. There had been no sign of Fat Sam Scoby in Pelona. Jeff had had a shave and a bath at a barbershop and had lingered over a big steak in a fly-specked little restaurant. He'd thrown the dirty trail clothes away, keeping only the slicker and black sombrero. In one of the mule packs he'd brought was a gray broadcloth suit and a spare pair of high-heeled boots. He'd bought a new shirt and black tie at the general store. Now he was dressed up, gun belt buckled under his coat, carbine in its saddle scabbard.

If Scoby had gotten out of Mexico, he should be waiting several hours ahead. After about an hour of steady riding, Fat Sam had said, he was to leave the road to the right, following wagon ruts that started at a cluster of four cottonwood trees just beyond a wide dry wash. Night dropped, topped with starlight. Everything was as Scoby had said, even to the meeting spot at a small adobe ranch house with a pole collar on the west side and a windmill behind.

Jeff heard the windmill creaking slowly in the night breeze. He sighted cottonwood trees around the house. He stepped down and tied the mules to a mesquite clump and rode on. No lights were visible. A horse nickered in the corral. The house had no porch. Jeff rode close at an easy walk. No dogs barked. No one hailed him.

The front door was standing open, framing solid and silent

blackness inside. Jeff dismounted, keeping the horse between himself and the open doorway. He waited a moment. Nothing happened.

He drew the handgun from under his coat, cocked it, and rested the muzzle on the saddle, lined squarely on the doorway. He spoke almost casually, but in the quiet his voice carried. "Put the gun away, Scoby. I'm riding light."

The silence dragged out. Then Scoby walked out the dark doorway, carrying a double-barreled shotgun. The man had short legs and a massive torso. It gave him a kind of nimble, waddling walk. It made his advance almost sinister as he moved out in the starlight, not trying to hide the shotgun.

"Buckshot, I'll bet," Jeff commented across the saddle. "I guessed you'd try it. Take your finger off that trigger, you fat, gut-shooting thief. Blowing my belly open won't get you nine gold bars, let alone all twelve of them, like you figured."

II

Sam Scoby didn't deny it. He stood a moment, thinking it over and then began to curse. "That's what I get for thinking any man was honest," he grumbled. "I paid high, you ingrate pup. I give you the chance to get crawling with money. More money than a dirty drifter like you will ever get hands on again. But you got to grab for it all!"

"Looks that way, doesn't it?" Jeff Parker agreed.

"Stand there behind that horse, you damned bum. There's light enough to see them legs. I'll give you buckshot through both knees. I'll blow you down to size and watch the blood pump outta your stumps. I got both barrels cocked and lined on your legs. This is Sam Scoby promising it."

"Fat Sam Scoby," Jeff corrected. "You want my legs . . . or nine bars of gold?"

Fat Sam stopped raging. It was like he'd been talking outside his real thoughts all along. He stood with legs braced apart, head forward alertly on the thick neck.

"Sounds like you're trying something," he offered mildly, sounding puzzled. "Speak it out. I know how a young feller gets ideas. I throwed a few twisters myself when I was young. Let's hear what you got to say."

"Not much," Jeff said. "But it might do you good to hear it. You tied in with the wrong politicos across the border. You had a couple of the wrong men killed. When things blew up around you, you had to bust off fast on the run."

Fat Sam chuckled. "I sure busted. Made it, too, and drawed 'em off your trail. Rode all night and all day, slapping saddle on six different horses. And all the time I was thinking of an honest young feller named Parker, heading north, easy and safe, with good times ahead for both of us." Fat Sam sounded puzzled. "Now you talk different. I don't get it, son. I sure don't."

Jeff laughed softly. "You will," he promised. "Stand and listen, Sam. I've got it all planned for you. You're heading to Paradise to tell what happened down in Mexico. You'll bunch up with Hardy Cantwell, his brother, Bob Cantwell, and old Ben Cantwell, the big crippled loafer wolf himself."

"Know a lot, don't you?" Fat Sam said sourly.

"Old Ben Cantwell'll give you orders for what next," Jeff said across the saddle. He had the gun hammer thumbed back, ready. Nine bars of gold hanging over Fat Sam's greed might not be enough to hold him down.

"Your belly'll get knotty with envy of old Ben and his boys," Jeff guessed. "You'll think you're a better man than any Cantwell. But you won't say so. Your greasy smile will reach back to your ears. You'll take your orders from the Cantwells, as usual, Sam, like the fat thieving dog you are. Am I right?"

He heard the breath Fat Sam sucked in. Anything might happen, now. Fat Sam spoke in a choked voice, sneering. "You're loaded with big talk. Like peyote working in you. Or maybe marijuana. It's that gold eating at you, ain't it? Got you drunk as a sotol-swigging peon on pay night. Anything else to shuck off your chest while I let you stand there flap-jawing?"

"I'm coming to it when I get you baited down to size," Jeff said. "You've been studying me for months. I've been studying you years, Sam. Every wolf has met a bigger wolf. Ben Cantwell is your big wolf. Old Ben Cantwell fanged you back into the pack a long time ago. After old Ben was crippled with buckshot loads from a sawed-off scatter-gun that night the Sullivan Ranch was burned out, Hardy Cantwell and young Bob Cantwell kept you back in the pack. Is that right?"

Scoby stood motionlessly, finger on the shotgun trigger. His voice came through the dim starlight, thick with satisfaction. "I knew damn' well I was right about you. Only one outsider could be sure about those shotgun loads that crippled Ben. I wasn't there. But I've heard it from the boys who were. The feller who used the scatter-gun and got away knew about it. Only him."

"That's right, Sam. Only him."

"John Sullivan and his oldest boy were killed that night," Fat Sam said with thick satisfaction. "There wasn't a witness to swear they didn't open up first on a couple of friendly Cantwell neighbors riding by, and were surprised at it when another bunch rode up and joined in the fracas."

Jeff agreed evenly: "That's what the sheriff heard. That's what the sheriff agreed happened. There wasn't another witness came forward to say different. You know why, Sam?"

Fat Sam said smoothly: "The only other Sullivan was a dirty-nosed brat the Cantwells thought had gone off with his mother on a visit. Took me a lot of studying after I hired you down there in Mexico, Parker, to remember you favor just a mite that John Sullivan who was killed years ago."

"A little like him," Jeff agreed. "I hope a lot like him, Sam.

21

There wasn't a witness to that night because the kid's mother wouldn't let him talk. It looked like Ben Cantwell was dying from that dose of shot the kid gave him. A dirty-nosed kid wouldn't have had a chance against the Cantwells and the sheriff and that snuff-eating old judge, Timmons."

"Wouldn't have took the sheriff or judge," Fat Sam stated. "The other Cantwells would've mashed that kid quick as they could reach him."

"They didn't reach him," Jeff said across the gelding's back. "The kid's mother let Horse Riley take over the Sullivan place and run a few cows and spend most of his time off hunting wild horses. She took the last Sullivan kid back to her folks in Wyoming. She died up in Wyoming, Sam. The Cantwells killed her the night they shot her husband and oldest boy. It just took her longer to die."

Scoby wasn't interested; he spat. His chuckle was malicious. "Ben Cantwell would go crazy if he knew the Sullivan kid had crippled him for life. He's bad enough now when the old pains hit him. He starts thinking how the feller who did it is loose and happy. Sets him crazy. I've seen him foam and beller out until even Hardy and Bob walked wide of him. Old Ben would give plenty to have a shotgun lined on them legs like I've got this gun. He'd pay high to hear how I made a crawling cripple outta you."

"Nine bars of gold, Sam?" Jeff taunted across the empty saddle. "You're too yellow-bellied a thief to chance it. Ben will give you buckshot in the back if he ever guesses you held out on him a little at a time."

Fat Sam said viciously: "I should've killed you when I guessed who you were. I knew you meant trouble! But damned if I thought you'd steal when I trusted you. You going to hand over them nine bars of gold like we agreed or do you get shot up now?"

Jeff waited until the slow-creaking windmill was the only sound in the night. He saw Fat Sam's blurred figure bulking behind the shotgun. Death hung on an uncertain hair between them.

"Sam, you're here tonight because you weren't with the bunch who killed John Sullivan. There were eleven in that bunch. Six are left, Sam. I've got a Forty-Five cocked. Want to take a chance you'll get me and never see that gold? Or will you gamble?"

"Meaning?"

"Ride on and tell old Ben Cantwell how you got run out of Mexico. If you see me at Paradise, I'm one of your hands out of Mexico. That's all you know."

"You'll get your head blowed off. That'll be the end of my gold. Me, too, maybe. Where's my gold, damn you?"

"Safe, Sam. All you've got to do is sweat like a fat thief and hope I don't get killed. Got a better idea?"

Scoby began to swear again under his breath. Then he fell silent, thinking. "Five of them Cantwell men who shot up the Sullivan Ranch are dead," he said slowly. "Each one got killed throwing lead at a stranger he tangled with. It always happened a long way from Paradise. Each Cantwell man drawed against a better stranger. You wasn't that stranger each time, was you?"

"Ask them."

"They're dead, damn it."

"We've all got to die, Sam. Why not gamble you'll spend that gold before you die?"

Sam Scoby muttered: "You'd be safe until the Cantwells guessed who you were. It might work for a little while. I got to take the chance." The shotgun swung slowly over in the crook of Fat Sam's arm.

After a moment Jeff holstered the Colt. "We'll split here, Sam. Don't get ideas about a gun or a knife at my back making me talk. It'd only cost you one way or another. I'm worth money to you now, Sam."

Fat Sam wheeled back to the house. He had the look of a fox's brain thinking hard. Jeff stepped up onto the black gelding and left without illusions. Sam Scoby hated him to the death now. Greed held Scoby in. He'd try to find a way around it.

On the third day Jeff rode out of the mountains through Upper Gunsight Cañon. He skirted the plunging water at Devil's Drop, passing across dangerous slanting rimrock. He worked down the treacherous descent beyond, using the old Indian trail, now obliterated in many spots. Two Rabbits, an ancient Mescalero Apache, had shown him the trail into this deep pocket cañon when Jeff was nine. At the bottom he was on Sullivan land—his land. Gunsight Creek foamed in the crooked sheer-walled lower cañon. The past moved in with somber memories. Finally late afternoon sun on mountain-rimmed Paradise Valley burst into view.

To the east the mountains drew in close to Paradise town. West full eighty miles to the Mustang Hills lay Paradise grass and the different outfits, Jack O'Lantern, BXB, Broken-Bit, RS, Lazy Hat, and the Cantwells' Skeleton Creek spread, with the well-known Cross-Bone brand.

Jeff looked out over the valley, his thin dark face rock-hard. He had one pack mule now. The other had fallen a thousand feet from a treacherous ledge. Mule and black gelding were gaunted and trail-worn. But they pricked ears before Jeff heard brush crashing off to the right. Horses galloped his way, skirting the stone cliff that faced the valley along here with broken talus at its foot and thickets on down the slope.

They must be wild horses that Horse Riley had broken or was holding, Jeff guessed. He heard a man's distant shout. Then the first horse, a glowing chestnut stallion, burst out of thick juniper brush not fifty yards away and stopped short, blowing. Jeff leaned forward, eyes narrowing at the unmistakable Cross-Bone brand. The big horse bugled and plunged on down the rough creekbank, splattering water and crashing up the other brushy bank. More horses followed, eight or ten, racing after the leader. All branded Cross-Bone. All Cantwell horses.

Then a girl rider raced out of the thickets like an old brush hand. She wore jeans and boots, leather jacket, gloves, and a flat-crowned gray hat tied down against the raking brush. She hard-reined her bay at full gallop toward Jeff and pulled up rearing, demanding: "Who are you? What are you doing here?"

Jeff picked off his hat impassively. "Passing through, ma'am. Name of Parker." He tilted his chin after the horses. "This Cross-Bone land?"

She had long slim legs, a brown healthy freshness, long-lashed eyes that looked directly, without subterfuge. "This is the Sullivan Ranch." Her regard weighed him. "Riding toward the valley road?"

"That's right, ma'am."

She put a hand to the neck of her sweating horse. "You came out of the cañon. This is the only way in or out."

"If you say so, ma'am. Are you Miss Sullivan?"

"I'm Beth Riley. My uncle rents this ranch, and who are you, mister? What are you doing back in here?"

"Was that your uncle I heard call?"

"That was Bob Cantwell." Beth Riley turned her head, listening. "He's coming."

Jeff sat watchfully as Bob Cantwell galloped up to them. Years back this Cantwell had been a stringy youth. He had the same look now, thin and long and reckless, different from the bull-build and hard power of his older brother, Hardy Cantwell, and old Ben Cantwell.

He pulled up on the other side of Jeff's horse, eyeing the

trail-worn mule and gelding. "Mister, how'd you happen to be back in this horse pasture?"

"He came out of Gunsight Cañon," said Beth Riley on Jeff's other side. "He said he was riding to the valley road."

Cantwell's grin got tight. "Gunsight's a blind cañon. A man don't go in there to reach the valley road."

Jeff said politely: "I'll move on if it don't suit you folks."

He had guessed it was trouble when he sighted Cross-Bone horses on this land. But even now it didn't seem bad trouble. Bob Cantwell's brusque—"No you don't!"—was surprising. So was the grab the tall man made for his gun.

Jeff had an instant's dismay that Horse Riley's niece was close at his right, in line of fire. His fast reach to the holstered Colt was instinctive. Once more a Cantwell was ready to kill on the same land where the Cantwells had killed that bloody night years ago. He'd wanted it to happen differently and had no choice now. Jeff saw chagrin strike Bob Cantwell's face as Jeff's gun cleared the holster before Cantwell's did.

Beth Riley spurred instantly and hard. Her horse plunged against the black gelding. Her hand dragged Jeff's gun arm down. She got both hands on the arm and clung while their horses snorted and wheeled.

Jeff guessed he was a dead man because of her. He had time for an instant of silent bitter fury against her and Horse Riley, who had turned the ranch over to the Cantwells. Bob Cantwell held fire, spurring close, also. Jeff's upflung left arm only partially blocked Cantwell's slamming gun barrel. It came in above the ear and knocked him weak, helpless. Cantwell's order had a blurred vicious sound. "Drop it!"

Jeff let the six-shooter fall. He caught the saddle horn and steadied himself.

"Get his saddle gun, Beth!" Cantwell said loudly.

She dismounted and picked up the six-shooter and Jeff's

weathered black sombrero that had been knocked off. Then, quieting her horse, she leaned against the saddle for a moment, as if needing support. "Someone would have been killed," she said in a stifled voice.

Bob Cantwell said harshly: "I'll take this gun-pulling tramp to the sheriff. He's a horse rustler, more'n likely. Hand me his guns, Beth!"

He rode behind Jeff's horse with six-gun cocked, thrust Jeff's short gun inside his belt, and took the carbine Beth Riley handed him. "Catch up that mule rope and ride!" he ordered Jeff.

Beth Riley held up the black sombrero. Jeff took it silently. Still silent, Jeff reined to the straying mule and caught the lead rope. The worst of the dizziness had passed. He felt blood oozing on his left ear from a scalp gash. Cantwell kept close, his gun ready. Beth Riley, in the saddle once more, spoke uncertainly. "Bob, he might be able to explain."

"He'll explain," Cantwell promised flatly. "Beth, you ride on home and forget it."

She sat watching as they followed Gunsight Creek down.

"Swing up the valley!" Cantwell ordered presently.

"It won't take us to the sheriff at Paradise," Jeff said over his shoulder.

Cantwell cursed him. "We're riding to Skeleton Creek. We'll find out there what brought you around Gunsight Cañon."

"A man doesn't rustle horses with a pack mule," Jeff reminded.

"Rustling, hell. Rustlers know better than to take Cross-Bone horses. We hunt rustlers down and gut-shoot 'em ourselves if it takes months. Cross-Bone horses are safe. You're a damn' stock detective, ain't you?"

Jeff grinned thinly. "So that's what put you edgy? The lady said you were a Cantwell. Any relation to Ben Cantwell?"

"He's my old man."

"I've been working for Sam Scoby. Mean anything to you?"

"You're a liar. Scoby's in Mexico. Been settled there for years."

"He got unsettled. Run out by a new bunch of politicos. Scoby's heading this way."

Bob Cantwell's silence had a sullen threat. Jeff didn't look back. "I think you're a liar!" Cantwell finally said explosively. "How much do you know about Scoby's business?"

"He paid well."

"Close-mouthed, huh? We've loosened closer ones. You've made a play about Sam Scoby. Stranger, you better be right. Ride faster!"

They met two more riders on Cross-Bone horses. Bob Cantwell ordered one man to bring the slower pack mule. The second fell in with them on a fast slant across the far reach of Paradise Valley.

Twilight fell as they reached Cantwell grass, with foothills rolling ahead to the dark basalt cliffs and the soaring forested slopes of Big Black Mountain. Skeleton Creek spawned in one of the forbidding cañons darkly slashing into the mountain. Where the snow water rushed out among wild hay meadows, Ben Cantwell had built his Skeleton Creek headquarters.

Night came down. The starlight was bright as jaded ponies brought them to the big horse corrals, adobe outbuildings, and great main house that Ben Cantwell had started building shortly after his trail wagon and handful of hard-faced riders had appeared in the almost empty Paradise country.

Jeff's father had come along a little later and worked for Ben Cantwell for a time. Cantwell had come to the valley without cattle and only a trail remuda of fine horses. He had been a Kentucky man by way of Texas. His few heavily armed riders had been surly, close-mouthed, keeping aloof from outsiders.

They stayed apart from the new hands Ben Cantwell hired.

Ben Cantwell, a young giant in those days, had been surly and close-mouthed, too. He had seemed to have a lot of money. There was money to buy land from the Spanish grant holder who had once owned an empire, of which Paradise Valley was a small part. Ben Cantwell had money to fence, build, and hire men. Money for anything the new Skeleton Creek Ranch needed. He had built a fort for a house. His armed fence riders had been harsh with trespassers. But when Cantwell rode out, uncrossed and unopposed, he could be jovial and friendly. Paradise town, growing in those years, had quickly felt Ben Cantwell's domination.

A judge friendly to Cantwell came to office. A member of Cantwell's original crew became sheriff. The rest of the original small, armed band had gradually drifted away. Ben Cantwell himself had often been away for long periods. That knowledge had been part of Jeff's boyhood. He had never been to the Skeleton Creek Ranch. Now his first impression was threat booming through the night in the savage challenge of huge mastiff dogs. A gate appeared in a high woven-wire fence. The dogs, big as panthers, were clamoring beyond the fence.

Bob Cantwell cursed them back and opened the gate from the saddle. He warned: "Stay on your horse until I get down. No stranger lights at the house until these damn' dogs are warned back by a Cantwell."

The fence enclosed acres around the massive fort-like house. Corrals and outbuildings were beyond the wire and dogs. The Cantwell rider left them at the gate and rode on outside the fence toward the bunkhouse.

Jeff looked at the shadowy dogs that ran with them toward the dimly glowing windows of the big house. Fence and dogs were not arrogance and power. They suggested fear at Skeleton Creek. It brought a kind of satisfaction with a tighter feel of danger. Fear at Skeleton Creek made suspicion worse, and this was Old Ben Cantwell's stronghold where Cantwells did as they pleased.

Bob Cantwell dismounted in front of the house. He warned the dogs back, lashing at the nearest with a quirt and cursing them. He drew his gun.

"Walk in, stranger . . . and God help you if you ain't what you say."

The windows had seemed dimly lit because they were heavily curtained. When Jeff opened the thick, solid door, bright light struck out. Brass wall and ceiling lamps seemed to flood each room with light. The curtained windows and glaring light inside heightened the sense of fear here at Skeleton Creek.

Bob Cantwell's gun muzzle prodded Jeff into a long, log-ceilinged room with bare floors and elegant rosewood furniture that must have come long ago from some manor east of the Mississippi. And hate was in the big room. Hate in the silence their booted feet and soft-jingling spurs disturbed. Hate in the suspicious stare of the hunched, gray-haired figure in a wheelchair at the other end of the long room.

A gun holster was strapped to each arm of the chair. A cocked six-gun was in the man's hand as they entered. Danger ran like needle pricks over Jeff, although he'd known for years he'd face this man again someday.

There he was—Old Ben Cantwell, no longer the bull-powerful man who had led his armed riders to John Sullivan's place long ago. The big-boned frame was there, the big jaw and broad shoulders. But the beef and muscle were gone. Grayish skin stretched over the large bones. Glowing eyes were sunken under bristly gray brows. The heavy thatch of black hair had become a gray mane. There he hunched, and it might have been only last night that Jeff, a frightened boy, was sighting the double-barreled shotgun through shot-torn moonlight. Ben

Cantwell on a plunging horse had been a cursing, vindictive target that had reeled when the buckshot blast let go.

The cocked gun lifted a little as Bob Cantwell's gun prodded Jeff toward the wheelchair. So vivid was the past that Jeff was certain Ben Cantwell must know him. Then the old man's harsh demand reminded him that a dirty-faced Sullivan kid wasn't supposed to have been with his father and brother the night of the raid. Old Ben Cantwell was talking to a stranger now.

"What's this?" Ben Cantwell threw at them.

"He was at the mouth of Gunsight Cañon with a pack mule," Bob Cantwell said. "Ever see him before?"

The sunken eyes bored suspiciously. "There's something about him," Ben Cantwell muttered. He moved restlessly, peering from under the bristly gray brows. Pain made him wince. He shouted: "What's a stranger doing around Gunsight Cañon? Ain't you man enough to make him talk?"

Bob Cantwell's grin was bitter, with no warmth for the gray-maned figure in the wheelchair. "I thought you'd want a look," Bob said. "He claims Sam Scoby got run out of Mexico and is heading this way."

"He's another lawman, you fool. Got to be if he comes talking about Sam Scoby. Why didn't you kill him like the others? Damn you for a jelly-backed pup."

Bob answered sullenly: "Beth Riley found him. She was there with us."

"What of it, you love-sick fool. She won't make a Cantwell woman if she can't see a man killed."

"What if Scoby *is* coming?"

"It's a trick!" Old Ben could grin like a gray-maned death's-head. "Lock him in the barred room. Get men to the Sullivan place, and to town, and up and down the valley. Maybe more strangers are sneaking around. Make sure that Riley girl doesn't talk. We'll see what's behind this."

Bob growled to Jeff: "This way."

The room was a cell with a strap-iron door and barred-window slits high up. It held a crude bunk and an old chair. Bob Cantwell clanged the door shut and shoved the key in his pocket. A wall lamp outside the bars cast light on his glowering regard.

"Want to change your story?"

Jeff had started a cigarette. "Scoby will be along."

"He'd better."

Bob Cantwell walked away and slammed a heavy plank door at the passage end. Jeff held out his hand. It was steady. The barred slits overhead let in the deep barking of the big dogs outside. And Fat Sam Scoby presently would peer through the strap-iron door, knowing one word of denial would be enough.

Jeff switched his thoughts to Horse Riley, who had turned the Sullivan place over to the Cantwells, making an unexpected trap. A slow anger built as he thought about Riley and the girl, and how she'd spurred close to help Bob Cantwell. Everything now hung on Scoby. It had been a gamble from the first. Jeff grinned ruefully as he sat on the bunk edge and pulled off his hoots. Fat Sam would settle it one way or another.

III

A thin shaft of morning sunlight was in one of the high wall slits when Bob Cantwell, gun in hand, unlocked the iron door and took the prisoner to the kitchen to wash and eat. The cook was an old-timer with fierce white mustaches and a gun at his hip. He loaded a tin plate with beans, steak, and cold biscuits, poured strong scalding coffee, and walked out of the kitchen in silence.

Later, with surly grace, Bob Cantwell provided a razor and stood watchfully while Jeff shaved. "How'd you come up from Mexico?" Bob demanded suddenly.

"Little Woman Pass, Pelona, and straight across the mountains," Jeff said, not turning from the small mirror on the wall.

"Meet anyone?"

"It's empty country."

"Which way did Scoby ride?"

"Not with me."

"Why'd you head this way?"

Jeff scrutinized his clean face in the mirror, grinned faintly, and wiped the razor on the soiled towel. "A smart man like Scoby will get going again. He'll be a big man someday. A man like that always needs good men along. He said to head this way. Sounded as good as any other place."

"We'll see what Scoby says," Bob Cantwell said.

The late afternoon sun was in the back window slit when clamor of the dogs at the front fence announced someone approaching the house.

Jeff heard the entrance and muffled voices in the long front room. Feet scuffed on the passage floor. Old Ben Cantwell's wheelchair, pistols holstered on each arm, rolled to the strap iron door. Bob Cantwell and Fat Sam Scoby were behind.

Jeff leaned against the door side, pulling on a half-smoked cigarette and eyeing Fat Sam's broad face and massive torso on the short nimble legs.

"Going to join me, Sam?" Jeff asked through the bars.

Fat Sam planted himself in front of the door. He was covered with trail dust and needed a shave. He wore the two guns and the knife he could use so expertly, and he stood for a moment, head forward on the thick neck, enjoying what he saw.

Ben Cantwell snapped: "Well, how about it?"

The house wasn't hot, but beads of perspiration appeared on Fat Sam's thick upper lip. The venomous pull of his avarice went across his face. Behind him Bob Cantwell stared narrowly.

Old Ben Cantwell exploded: "Where's your damn' voice?"

Fat Sam's sigh was barely audible, regretful. "Good thing I got here quick, Cantwell." Fat Sam's wide smile was almost painful as he turned. "You near killed one of my best men."

"Small loss, if he ain't any better than the fat fool who messed up everything across the border," Ben Cantwell snarled, wheeling the chair around to leave. "Get set in the bunkhouse, Parker. If you can bust horses, there's work in the morning."

"I'll take my guns back and ride to town," Jeff said, stepping out when Bob Cantwell unlocked the door.

"We're short-handed."

"Hire more men then. You had your fun locking me up. I'll take my fun in town."

Ben Cantwell wheeled away in the chair without answering. Bob scowled after him. "Sorry it happened, Parker," he said grudgingly. "We're careful about strangers these days."

"That's your business. I'm with Fat Sam." Jeff grinned bleakly at Scoby. "We stay close, don't we, Sam?"

Fat Sam said: "Mighty close." His look behind Bob Cantwell's back was venomous. He walked along in brooding silence when Bob Cantwell took Jeff out past the dogs to a gate in the back fence. Bob turned back to the house. Jeff chuckled as Scoby headed for the horse corrals with him.

"I thought for a minute you'd decide a dead man was worth more than nine bars of gold."

Fat Sam swore under his breath. "What are you up to?"

"Fun in town right now."

"Fun, hell. You're stirring trouble. You'll get blowed over the range and I'll lose that gold."

"Try to stop it, Sam. You can't spend a corpse. I'll give you orders when I need you."

"Orders?" Fat Sam choked and began to swear under his breath.

"Keep thinking about the gold, Sam, and what'll happen if

Ben Cantwell hears you had him unlock the man who put him in that wheelchair."

"It ain't worth it," Scoby said hoarsely. "I should've killed you at the start. Should've pulled the trigger at Pelona."

"Look at that fence and the dogs," Jeff suggested. "Lights burned in the house all night. They're afraid in there."

"Afraid, hell. That's old Ben's smart brain. He's a roosting turkey in that wheelchair for any who's got a grudge against him . . . and plenty has. Hardy and Bob are away a lot. Old Ben sits there a-thinking and a-planning, smarter than he ever was because he's got the time to think. But he ain't taking chances."

"Like you and me," reminded Jeff calmly.

"It ain't worth it," Fat Sam said again as they stopped at the peeled poles of the corral, with two men sauntering toward them from the bunkhouse. Fat Sam made an angrily futile gesture. "I ain't sure what you're up to. But you're bucking Ben Cantwell. He always comes out on top. It could have been easy for you and me. Plenty money, good times. . . ."

"Your good times are waiting, Sam," Jeff assured. "Just make sure I'm not bucking you, too. It'd be hard to tell who would come out on top then."

Fat Sam took it in silence as the Cantwell men drew near. When Jeff rode off past the strong fence and challenging dogs, Fat Sam's broad unshaven face was set in thought. Some idea was working deep in Fat Sam's mind.

Jeff had noticed it as he led the gelding out of the corral. The feeling of danger was stronger now. Fat Sam Scoby was more dangerous than the Cantwells. Far more, for the thin uncertain thread of Fat Sam's greed had to be trusted.

In the long slant of the afternoon sun Jeff reached Sullivan land again, his land, each roll and swell clear in memory. He held the gelding in a long lope to the grassy flat between a serpentine loop of Gunsight Creek and a low brushy ridge.

There was the small adobe house with vine-covered front porch and the little fenced grape arbor his mother had planted.

The slender figure stepping out to a buckboard and sorrel team in front of the house might have been his mother. It was Beth Riley. She saw him and waited, wearing a neat print dress today and her black hair up behind her ears. She spoke as he swung down and removed his hat.

"We drove to town looking for you," Beth said. "You weren't there."

"Did you think the Cantwells would bother with jail," Jeff asked evenly, remembering her part in the trouble yesterday. "Why didn't you try Skeleton Creek and see Bob Cantwell, too?"

Beth flushed and turned as a man came out of the house using one crutch. He stopped at the porch edge, a stringy, gray-mustached man with a livid scar welt on the left cheek from grizzled hair to chin. The drawling voice was straight out of the past. "Howdy, Johnny Sullivan."

Jeff tightened, poker-faced. Beth Riley showed her silent astonishment.

"I'm Parker, mister."

Horse Riley chuckled. "You had on knee britches last time I seen you. But I remember how you could get a horse down into Gunsight Cañon. Beth said she met a handsome young stranger bringing a pack mule outta the cañon, and couldn't find mule tracks going in. I guessed Johnny Sullivan was home."

Her face red, Beth protested: "I didn't say handsome."

"Good-looking," corrected Horse Riley.

She continued indignantly: "You didn't mention Johnny Sullivan."

"I'm close-mouthed," Horse Riley said calmly. "Not a word to Bob Cantwell about this."

"Why not?"

"Things you haven't been told. Step inside, Johnny. Beth was going to put the team up."

Beth drove the team on around the house in almost hostile silence. Jeff followed the limping man inside, anger gone. Horse Riley had been tall and whipcord tireless, a dead shot, wild as the wild horses he hunted. He sank awkwardly into a wire-braced chair and drawled: "My foot hung in a stirrup and I got dragged over rocks. Laid out two days before they found what was left, like Beth wrote you for me."

"I've been on the move . . . didn't get any letter," Jeff said, looking around the room, remembering.

"Well, you know now. You've seen I'm renting grass to the Cantwells. Beth come from Nebraska and nursed me. But we run short on money. I had grass to sell and I sold it, and let the devil balance things later." Riley sobered. "Maybe the devil has started to collect."

Jeff nodded. "I've been working for Sam Scoby down in Mexico."

"That skunk? I wondered where Fat Sam had lit out to." Horse Riley had ridden everywhere after wild horses. He knew outlaw trails, range feuds, trouble everywhere. He said now dryly: "You couldn't need money bad enough to be riding for Scoby."

"No," Jeff admitted.

"I can guess the rest," Riley said slowly. He shook his head dubiously. "I've guessed Scoby never cut off from the Cantwells. And the Cantwells are bad medicine, Johnny."

"Better call me Jeff Parker, so you won't slip in front of someone."

"Sure, sure. Anyway, I'll talk straight. Old Ben Cantwell is crippled and ten times as mean. His boys are full-growed and dangerous. They're set solid at Skeleton Creek. All horses now. They raise a few and sell and trade horses from California to east of the Mississippi."

"From Mexico to Canada," Jeff added. "Most of their business is away from these parts."

"Studied them, ain't you?"

"Kind of."

Riley leaned forward. "I knew your mother before she married. She wouldn't want you killed on account of the past."

"This was home," Jeff murmured, looking around. "The home she wanted to keep. I'm home now for her. Will the Cantwells let me stay here peacefully?"

"Can't say," Riley admitted after an uncomfortable moment of hesitation.

Jeff crossed his knees and built a smoke. "You know damned well they won't," he said mildly. "My father learned some of Ben Cantwell's business while he worked at Skeleton Creek. Years later he let Cantwell know it. That same night they killed him in the doorway there." Jeff pointed to the floor in front of the chairs. "He lay there dying and told my brother and me what it was about. My mother took me away and told me never to think of it again."

"So you been thinking about it ever since," Riley guessed. He was dubious again. "They ain't a bunch to fool with, son."

Jeff stood up restlessly. But his words had hard emphasis. "Ben Cantwell is a horse thief. Not a cheap thief, who gets hanged by some local posse. If any men get hung in this business, they maybe never even heard of the Cantwells. But Ben Cantwell is pulling the strings. The horses are passed along into Mexico. A couple of days' ride away the men pick up a bunch of fine Mexican horses and start north to a point a long way from where the stolen bunch came from. The Cantwells do business everywhere. A man never gets a chance to find his stolen horses and say a Cantwell touched them."

"Sounds bigger than I ever guessed," Horse Riley admitted, frowning.

"I've puzzled out Ben Cantwell's horse-thief trail for years. Cantwell was a horse thief when he settled here. The hardcases who rode in here with him scattered out to spread the business all over the West. They headed up horse-stealing gangs of their own which tied in with Ben Cantwell's big plans."

Riley was fascinated and doubtful. "Can you prove all that?"

"Not in court. Every trail breaks off clean before it leads to Skeleton Creek. Kill a few of their rustlers, hang some more, and new ones are riding in a month."

"Sounds like you bit into something too big to chew."

"It's a bite," Jeff conceded. "I've been riding for Sam Scoby in Mexico, tallying stolen brands and finding where they went. But that still didn't lead back to the Cantwells."

Horse Riley stood up awkwardly, limped to a wall cupboard with his crutch, and took out a bottle and two glasses. He balanced on the crutch while Jeff poured for them both.

"Johnny Sullivan's come home," Riley said, and put his drink down to that, and looked at Jeff quizzically over the empty glass. "You sure hated Ben Cantwell to take his trail for years."

Jeff denied it. "I'd have come straight in a long time ago to kill the Cantwells, if it was just hate. The night my mother died she got me to promise I wouldn't try that. I was scared and crying over losing her. I'd have promised anything." Jeff put his empty glass down. "I didn't promise the law wouldn't get the Cantwells for their thieving, killing tricks."

Horse Riley limped back to his chair. "And the horse-thief trail won't lead to the Cantwells. Have you given up?"

"Sam Scoby got run out of Mexico and headed here to Ben Cantwell for orders." Jeff's slow smile lingered. "Fat Sam brought me straight to the head of horse-thief trail. Your niece and Bob Cantwell almost dropped a loop on me yesterday. Bob

Cantwell thought I was a stock detective and took me to Skeleton Creek. But Scoby showed up today and made it all right." Jeff's thin smile turned reflective. "I'm smack on the horse-thief trail now. I'm Scoby's man, waiting for Ben Cantwell's orders. I'm squatted at the mouth of the old he-wolf's den where I need to be."

"You've denned a grizzly and given him your throat," Riley said bluntly. "You ain't got Ben Cantwell. He's got you. You never can be Johnny Sullivan at home now. They'd kill you quicker than they did your father."

Jeff finished a cigarette with a twist of the end, and was blunt in turn. "I didn't know you had a niece. She can set the Cantwells on me any minute."

"She won't. Beth got friendly with Bob Cantwell while I was flat in bed, not caring what happened. Bob is a catch for any girl in the valley. I've let it drift and kept my mouth shut. I'll talk to her."

"Bob Cantwell means to marry her."

"Damned if he will," Riley said harshly. "I'll head that idea off quick."

Beth Riley's cool sarcasm came at them through the open front door. "Now will you, Uncle Jim?"

"Oh, oh. We done it," Riley muttered.

Beth's quick step crossed the porch. She stopped resentfully inside the doorway. "I heard that last. Now you two tell me what I'll do or won't do."

"Get the chip off your shoulder, honey," Riley advised. "And first off, you listen again . . . the Cantwells can't know this is Johnny Sullivan. Not a word about it to Bob Cantwell."

"Bob should know Johnny Sullivan is back under another name," Beth said coldly. "Back to open up the old trouble between the Sullivans and Cantwells. Bob's told me about it. This means trouble for all of us."

"Now look, Beth. . . ."

"Uncle Jim, you can't give me orders."

"Hogwash, honey. I aim to give you a load of the truth."

Jeff said: "She won't believe you. A girl in love. . . ."

"Gits bucked off her hoss sense," Riley finished disgustedly. "But Beth ain't in love. Not with a Cantwell. Damned if I'll have it."

Beth whirled to the doorway. Her angry steps clicked across the porch and headed around the house.

Jeff said bleakly: "The devil's riding now. She means to see Bob Cantwell.

Riley came awkwardly out of the chair. "I'll handle her. You riding back to Skeleton Creek?"

"I'm heading to town. Is Jake Gibbons still sheriff?"

"Jake was too much of a Cantwell man for some of the new folks that settled, They voted in Bill Trotter last year."

"Don't know him."

"You ain't missed much," Riley said cynically. "Trotter likes the job and don't mean to offend anyone. Someday he'll have to sight his guns or back water to keep friends, and it'll kill him to decide."

"Is he honest?"

"Far as I know. Now lemme get after that fire-tempered gal afore she starts a blaze."

"I'll tell her good bye," Jeff said.

He rode around the house. Beth was approaching the corral gate with a coiled rope. Yesterday his interest had leaped at sight of her. Now her slim angry figure was more dangerous than Fat Sam Scoby. But she was pretty, very pretty.

Hat in hand, Jeff reined up beside her, his thin weather-dark face somber. "You're wrong," he said slowly. "But you'll ride to Bob Cantwell no matter what your uncle says."

"I will if I choose to," Beth snapped.

Jeff nodded. "Yesterday you saved Cantwell's bacon by grabbing my arm. He wasn't fast enough. If you're in love, think again before you egg him on for another try."

Beth swallowed. "You'd kill him?"

"You guess," Jeff suggested soberly, lifting the reins.

Beth was pale and silent, the coiled rope forgotten in her hand, as he rode off. He saw Riley crutching from the back door, and lifted a hand. He rode across the creek, threaded silver-gray *chamisa* bushes, and from the first rise looked back.

Beth was a far-seen, slim figure at the corral, facing her uncle. Jeff looked at them for a long moment and rode on.

Paradise was a small town of adobe, frame, and a few brick buildings, of wagon yards and outlying corrals, a lively town from the valley trade and small mines scattered back in the mountains. The Paradise House was a rambling two-story frame hotel whose long chair-cluttered verandah fronted the main street and served as a meeting spot for all who came to town. Half doors at the north end of the verandah opened into the big cool hotel bar.

Jeff emerged from the bar at mid-dusk and took one of the verandah chairs in the pooling shadows. A solid-looking man in a worn black suit, gun belt under the coat, presently dropped into the next chair, and bit the end off a cigar.

"Got your telegram from Pelona," said Ed Bellows from El Paso. "Aces up finally, huh?"

"How many with you?"

"Two men, camped below town in the hills."

"Not enough."

"You 'n' me make four."

"Not enough."

Bellows lit the cigar and flipped the match over the verandah rail to the walk. "Got to be," he said briefly. After a moment he added: "I bought the sheriff a drink this morning. Told him I was after Handy Bill Hicks and Little Buck Weaver, worth a thousand apiece, dead or alive, for bank robbery and murder. Which they are and I want 'em," said Bellows reflectively. "Only they're in Utah. But two thousand reward got the sheriff interested in helping a stranger."

Jeff watched a group of riders lope into town. A quietness about the new night had a glassy feel of waiting. The feeling was in himself, Jeff guessed, tightening for the showdown after all these years. His own voice evened in warning. "The Cantwells have killed strangers lately they thought were stock detectives. It means a bullet in your back if the sheriff talks. Don't count on him against the Cantwells. He wants no local trouble."

"So?" After a moment Ed Bellows growled: "Where's your aces in this?"

"One ace, Fat Sam Scoby." Talking low, Jeff sketched what had happened. He broke off, listening to the beat of a single horse coming into town, fast.

"That rider must need a drink bad," Bellows murmured.

The running horse held the middle of the dusty street until it swung hard over to the hotel hitch rack.

"Cantwell man," Jeff said, peering through the last light. He stood up and moved along the verandah rail.

It was the lanky straw-mustached man named Regan who had fallen in with Bob Cantwell on the ride from Sullivan land to Skeleton Creek. He ducked under the hitch rack to the walk, saw Jeff at the verandah rail, and stopped.

"Come for you," Regan said, grinning and fishing at his vest for tobacco and papers. "Scoby says to git fresh horses at the livery an' git back fast."

"Why?" Jeff asked.

"Scoby needs you. I'll git a couple of drinks an' meet you at Kidder's Stable."

The Cantwell man pushed through the bar doors, and Ed Bellows came to his feet and inquired softly: "This start it?"

"Seems so." Jeff hitched absently at his gun belt. "Fat Sam was trying to figure a trick. This might be it."

"What kind of trick?"

"I have to find out." Jeff scanned the street, not really seeing it, still thinking hard. "Trouble isn't likely here. Better move your men to the Mustang Hills at the other end of the valley. They're rough, good hiding. Boracho Cañon is good. You'll have daylight when you get that far. Look for a red-banded cliff on your right and follow it back into Boracho. I can get there after Fat Sam shows his hand."

"We'll be there," Ed Bellows promised.

Regan reached the feed barn while Jeff was saddling another black horse in the pungent dimness under a high-hung lantern. He liked a black; it blended with the night. This horse, well-fed, rested, was the pick of the stable. Regan said so as he saddled a dun. "Wisht there was two like that 'un."

They left Paradise at a brisk trot, Regan going taciturn as his drinks wore off and the horses struck a long lope. Regan would not know Fat Sam's plans anyway, Jeff guessed. He tried to put himself in Scoby's place, thinking like Scoby. Each try came against old Ben Cantwell, hunched in the gun-hung wheelchair, hating, scheming.

They passed riders, a buggy, a buckboard or two heading to town, then suddenly on them in the starlight was a racing horse and rider who pulled up sharply.

"Parker?"

"Here!" Jeff replied, wheeling in close, not trusting his ears. "That you on a horse, Jim Riley?"

"I can ride if I'm boosted up," Horse Riley answered, peering past Jeff. "Who's with you?"

44

"Regan from Skeleton Creek. Sam Scoby sent him into town after me."

Regan put his horse close, too, suspicion rasping in his remark. "Nobody said you two knowed each other."

From habit Jeff marked Regan's gun poised near the holster. Things he'd been wondering about cleared up as Riley snapped: "Scoby, hell! You're being baited to a trap, Jeff."

Regan's gun hand moved fast. "That's a damn'. . . ."

Jeff's gun muzzle barely cleared the holster and spewed flame. Regan's horse swung violently away. Regan's gun went off harmlessly. Regan was bowed over, clutching the saddle horn as he swayed and tried to hold on.

Horse Riley jerked and leveled a carbine, then lowered it as Regan slipped over and fell heavily. His horse shied off and stopped with dragging reins.

"Saved me from killing him," Riley said harshly. "That was a fast gun, Johnny."

"Jeff Parker's the name," Jeff responded automatically. "A Cantwell man always drags a gun when he's cornered."

"This one won't ride again," Riley said. "And it won't matter what I call you, if you don't dust outta these parts tonight."

Jeff was dismounting. "So Beth took her ride to Skeleton Creek?" he said bleakly, and made sure the Cantwell man had dropped his gun.

"She didn't," Riley denied. "But Scoby got to our place all tore up by Ben Cantwell's man-eating dogs. He was holed with a bullet, too. Said Ben had him shoved out to the dogs. He fought 'em off with his bare hands, made it to the gate, and climbed a white hoss tied outside the fence. This man had already been sent for you. Scoby circled on the mountain and made it to our place. He said to tell you the Cantwell boys won't want the law up Skeleton Cañon around daybreak or later."

Jeff said explosively: "Those wolf dogs! What else did Fat Sam say?"

"That's all that made sense," Riley admitted. "Scoby raved like a crazy man about dogs eating him alive. He drank whiskey like water and keeled over. Beth dragged him down in that little dug-out cellar under the trap door in the kitchen. I turned his white horse loose miles away and come on to find you."

"A white horse," Jeff said under his breath. The man at his feet had stopped groaning. Jeff bent over him. "Dead."

"He drawed first," Riley stated. "But you better not get locked up while the law thinks it over and Ben Cantwell takes a hand."

"Can you ride on?" Jeff inquired.

"All night, if I don't have to climb down."

"A man named Ed Bellows will be riding this way through town with two friends. He needs to know this." Jeff holstered his gun. "I'd also tell him the sheriff might come out after that two thousand reward tonight if not told anything else."

"Two thousand reward on the Cantwells?" Horse Riley blurted.

"Leave that to Bellows," Jeff evaded.

"Meet you at the ranch," Riley said briskly. "Drag that dead buzzard over behind the sage. He won't mind."

The ranch house windows glowed softly as Jeff's spurs clinked to the door.

He rapped twice. "Jeff Parker, ma'am."

Beth Riley opened the door. She held sewing, and in the lamplight her hand was unsteady as Jeff walked in. Beth looked out the door and asked: "Where's Uncle Jim?"

"Gone on to town, ma'am. Where's Scoby?"

Beth closed the door. She was pale and her wide eyes had a kind of stunned appeal.

"Ben Cantwell was here, riding in a buggy hung with guns.

Armed men were with him. They had found Scoby's horse and were looking for Scoby."

"Did they get him? Jeff asked quickly.

"He'd been noisy down in the cellar," Beth said huskily. "Screaming about gold and big dogs tearing at him. But he was quiet when they came. I stood on the porch while Ben Cantwell raved, too. He called Scoby a thief and said he'd hunt him down before morning. He wanted to know where Uncle Jim was." Beth swallowed hard. "I stood there, waiting for Scoby to scream out again. . . ."

"Was Bob Cantwell or his brother along?"

Beth shook her head. She was staying calm with an effort. "I halfway couldn't believe what Uncle Jim told me at the corral today, until Scoby came here. And then Ben Cantwell. . . ."

Jeff started to speak, and then held it and said: "I'd better have a look at Scoby. I've seen what those dogs looked like."

Beth lit a lantern for him and stood by the open trap door in the kitchen floor while Jeff descended the few steps. He had played down here as a boy; the storage shelves his father had built were at his elbow as he went to a knee beside Fat Sam Scoby, who lay on folded blankets. What was left of Sam Scoby. The big dogs had shredded Scoby's clothes and torn his body, his arms, his hands. A cheek had been laid open. Fangs had worried his throat, just missing his life. Beth had washed off much blood and bandaged where she could. But Fat Sam was still covered with dried blood and his mouth hung open in a kind of twisted, horrified grimace.

Jeff said: "Scoby." He put a hand to the man's shoulder. Then hastily he reached for Fat Sam's pulse. Moments later he caught the lantern off the damp earth and turned to the steps.

"How is he?" Beth asked tightly, in the kitchen.

"Dead," Jeff said, letting down the trap door. He heard Beth's breath catch and said: "You couldn't have helped him. He had

47

Cantwell's bullet inside somewhere. He was dying from the time it hit."

Beth walked into the front room and Jeff followed her. "Nothing you could have done," he repeated. "Did Scoby say anything else?"

Beth sat down and said with an effort: "He was out of his head. He talked about queer things like Mexican soldiers breaking up a horse drive and men scattering back and finding a horse, and a man called Long Steve who was dying, and who told them a man named Dongo had been murdered and gold was loaded in packs at the *hacienda*. It didn't make sense."

"Anything else?"

Beth said: "It sounded like the men came to Skeleton Creek and told Ben Cantwell. And when Scoby wouldn't talk, he was put out unarmed among the dogs. He screamed that the dogs were at his throat, were dragging him down and tearing him to pieces." Beth was on the edge of her chair. Jeff reached for her hand. Beth held tightly. "When he got here, he wanted you to know about Skeleton Cañon, but he didn't speak of it again . . . ever again."

"Still in love with Bob Cantwell?"

Beth pulled her hand away. "I wasn't in love. But I don't like to be told what I have to do."

"I'll remember that," Jeff promised, and stood up. "It'd help if I could warm some coffee. I missed grub in town."

"Why didn't you say so?" Beth protested.

He ate at the kitchen table, watching Beth move deftly about the room. *Pretty. Pretty.* He was lingering over a last cup of coffee when galloping horses stirred the night outside. Jeff blew out the table lamp.

"If it's the Cantwells again, stay close inside here."

Beth's voice in the darkness was tight again. "They'll kill you."

"I'm hard for a Cantwell to kill," Jeff said, and went out back to the black horse he'd moved behind the house.

Three riders took shape in the starlight. Horse Riley's voice hailed the house. "Jeff! Beth!"

"Here!" Jeff answered, riding out to them. "Ed Bellows with you?"

"He stayed with the sheriff," Riley said. "Here's his men . . . Chris Strong and Tex Porter."

"Howdy," Jeff greeted. He didn't know the two, but if they were with Bellows, they were good. But he was dubious about the sheriff. "Bellows isn't trying to use the sheriff, is he?"

Riley said dryly: "Sheriff Trotter is organizing deputies to collar bank robbers back in the mountains. Two thousand reward. Bank robbers can't vote. Trotter's a curly wolf out after that reward."

"It might work until Trotter finds he's up against the Cantwells," Jeff decided. "Then we'll be hanging alone on our long rope."

"What did Scoby tell you?" Riley demanded.

"He was dead."

Riley whistled softly. "So we're leading the sheriff after a reward which ain't there, and into something we don't know anything about. Might be there *isn't* anything."

"Fat Sam wouldn't lie about it after Cantwell's dogs got him."

"Well, the way Ed Bellows dressed it up, you and me located the outlaws," Riley disclosed. "I rode to Paradise for Bellows. We'll pick up the posse at Black Butte. I'll guide 'em in a long swing over the mountain and drop 'em down toward the head of Skeleton Cañon around daybreak. We'll see what we find."

"Might work," Jeff said. "I've got an idea that'll help."

"Ten minutes rest for coffee," Riley stated. "Then I'll be good for all night. Help me down, boys. Dern a no-'count cripple like me."

Beth served scalding black coffee in the kitchen, meat and biscuits and beans she'd warmed for Jeff. She was worried, silent as they went to the front door, Horse Riley thumping on his crutch. Jeff lingered as the others went out. "Afraid to stay with Scoby?"

Beth made a helpless gesture. "I'm afraid of what may happen to Uncle Jim."

Jeff grinned at her. "I'll bring him back safe."

Beth smiled. "Is that a promise?"

"Sure is. And if I get lost, here's a paper I wrote out while the men were eating."

Puzzled, Beth took the folded paper. Jeff grinned again. "I sold you the ranch here for a dollar and other considerations. I reckon it's legal enough."

"No," Beth refused instantly.

"There's no one else to get it, ma'am. Today, when I rode here, you looked like my mother stepping off the porch. You like her ranch. She'd want you to have it if I got lost."

Beth looked at him gravely. "You don't expect to come back."

"I'll sure try, just to see you get mad again," Jeff said. "You're pretty that way. Pretty this way, too. I didn't say what else went with the sale." Jeff kissed her quickly, lightly. "Collected," he said, and he went out with Beth's startled, half-laughing protest following him. "You didn't have to trade a ranch for that, Johnny Sullivan!"

Horse Riley called in the night, "Jeff! Ready?"

Jeff stepped on his horse and looked toward Beth's figure on the porch, against the lamplight.

"It's still a fair trade," he said under his breath.

Beth's reply had the sound of laughter and tears. "What will you have left to trade next time?"

"I never thought of that." Jeff chuckled, and he had to ride, sobering as he thought of her waiting above Fat Sam's body.

IV

The posse was in the *vega* below Black Butte, a sizable group of men, and Ed Bellows. Sheriff Trotter, a dimly seen, fleshy figure, wheezing a little, said as they moved on: "We got more men than we need."

Bellows answered with a hint of grim humor: "We might ride into a surprise."

Horse Riley, riding in the lead with Jeff, said under his breath: "I want to see Trotter's face when he learns what we're after."

They were heading up a small grassy valley and presently they swung up a shale-covered slope to ridges ascending into the pines, saddles creaking, horses blowing. Cliffs lifted, black against the sky, and clouds were drifting over the stars. A low-pitched rumble crawled across the clouds.

"Thunder," Riley said.

"Might help," Jeff concluded.

Coyotes were clamoring in the distance. Jeff rode in silence, thinking of Beth Riley and the irony of Fat Sam and his gold.

Long Steve Willard, on the white horse at Little Woman Pass, had known Fat Sam had knifed the man at the *hacienda,* and had known about the gold. When the horse drive had been scattered south of the pass, the Cantwell men had turned back and found Long Steve still alive, and had ridden to Ben Cantwell with Long Steve's story.

Jeff wondered how much Fat Sam had told Ben Cantwell, talking for his life. As little as possible, probably. But Long Steve's story had been enough. Jeff pulled a deep soft breath, thinking what would have happened if he'd ridden back to Skeleton Creek. Worse than Fat Sam had gotten. Ben Cantwell was like that. He'd been the same when he rode to the Sullivan Ranch, years ago.

Lightning glowed briefly in the far sky. Thunder echoes boomed softly along the high cliffs. Horse Riley led them up a steep trail. Rock lifted at their right stirrups. Black space dropped off on the left. The sheriff's wheezy doubt rang hollowly from the strung-out riders. "Ain't getting lost are you, Riley?"

"Short cut!" Riley called back.

Another man said: "I don't want no bad storm on a goat trail like this."

Dawn, Jeff guessed, was not far off. Horse Riley brought them over a knife-back shoulder. Lightning flamed, blue and raw, over lower country beyond. They angled down across rough mountain face in blackness that had the men cursing.

Horse Riley dropped back beside Jeff and spoke under his breath: "We're coming down on the head of Skeleton Cañon. A trail there, outta the cañon, cuts west to Apache Basin."

"Never heard there was a trail that way," Jeff admitted.

"It ain't much. Valley folks don't get back in here," Riley said. "They'd have to come up Skeleton Cañon mostly, over Cantwell land. How far down the cañon do we take this bunch?"

"All the way to Ben Cantwell's wolf dogs if we don't find anything. With Fat Sam dead, I'll play it out."

"Here we go," Riley said calmly. He turned in the saddle. "Quiet from here on, men!"

Thunder caught Riley's last words. A stormy feel was in the air, electric, stringing nerves tighter. Now the way was down, the trail still invisible save to Riley and the horses. But rising sides of the narrow cañon showed steep as light flickered beyond the peaks. The first pines showed, too, straight and dark, and water on the left raced over rocks. Dawn slowly bleached the darkness above the clouds.

Horse Riley eased back beside Jeff. "The sheriff'll be wanting his outlaws soon. Reckon we've made a fool's ride?"

"Fat Sam wouldn't have lied," Jeff said stubbornly. "I'll scout ahead."

The pines had taken on a blurred ghost look in the half night. Jeff galloped ahead with carbine across the saddle. Wind came at his back and moaned in the pine tops. Thunder trumpeted through the cañon.

One final crash brought the storm roaring overhead and rain in a veiling rush. And beyond a strong fence the cañon widened into a pine-dotted cañon *vega*. Hat pulled low, shoulders bowed before the storm, Jeff rode briskly through the open fence gate almost before he realized it was there. The darkening storm blotted vision again.

This would be the upper limit of Ben Cantwell's Cross-Bone range. The fact of the open gate struck hard. Jeff pulled up, peering back into the drive of rain. Men must have ridden through that gate, on up the cañon and along the little known Apache Basin trail. The gate hadn't been left open by accident, which meant the Cantwell men were returning. But why ride out that wild lonely trail and return? Jeff suddenly laughed. Now he knew. Cantwell men would be coming back any time after dawn. If the Paradise sheriff could be held here in the *vega*, he'd have his choice, bullets or votes—if the Cantwells gave him a choice.

The black horse went with the storm again, ears pricking nervously. Jeff cleared water from his streaming face and suddenly pulled the horse to a stop. It could have been wolves running toward him. But they were dogs, six of Ben Cantwell's man-mauling brutes. Jeff swore explosively and lined the carbine with savage purpose. His first shot missed a bounding yellow shape. He levered another shell furiously and knocked the dog rolling. The others came on, clamoring. The nervous feed-barn horse sidled away, fighting the bit.

The dogs were worse than wolves, for they weren't afraid of

men. The first one up leaped like a yellow bolt, fangs tearing into Jeff's leg. Other huge dogs came at the horse's hind legs. It screamed, lunged, kicked as Jeff's handgun slug blasted the brute off his leg. It was the same nightmare through which Fat Sam Scoby had run on foot. It bred a kind of primitive revulsion against tearing animal teeth. Jeff savaged the kicking horse around, twisted hard in the saddle, and shot a second leaping form that clawed, snarling up the horse's flank, trying to get at him.

On the other side fangs tore at his thigh. Wild now himself, Jeff shot the thing. It seemed like Ben Cantwell was at him, tearing, snarling. Then, abruptly, only two dogs were left. They broke away into the rain, barking at something upcañon. At the posse, Jeff guessed. His legs were bleeding. He was chilled with rage as he quieted the frightened horse and reloaded fast. He wondered if Ben Cantwell were following the dogs. Then he tightened, listening, and memory leaped back to Little Woman Pass, on the border.

Wind gusts whipping down the cañon brought a low, deep, drumming sound. Through it the more distant crackle of gunfire. Then out of the stormy half dawn a strung-out horse herd came stampeding behind two riders who quirted furiously. They funneled through the fence opening, ghost-like in the drive of wind and rain. Jeff held the carbine, aware suddenly that he didn't know the men in the posse, or they know him, after meeting and riding in darkness. The two quirting toward him might be friends or Cantwell men.

They saw him. One shouted to the other. They veered apart, to pass on either side of him. And suddenly they were Bob Cantwell and another man. Cantwell opened fire at full gallop. And then the other man added shots to the close scream of hot lead. Jeff missed his shot at Bob Cantwell. He thought of Fat

Sam Scoby as he levered the carbine. Now a Cantwell was killing again.

His horse leaped and staggered. They'd been aiming at the horse, and as it lost footing Jeff sighted fast and regretfully on Bob Cantwell's horse and fired. He had to throw himself convulsively from the saddle. He slipped and went down on the wet earth and his horse fell just beyond.

Lead spattered mud close by. When Jeff staggered up, the other Cantwell rider was racing past. The horse herd, pouring into the *vega* at full gallop, was fanning out. Bob Cantwell's horse was down. Bob Cantwell's long thin figure was also scrambling up, left afoot by the rider who quirted on. Add that to the dogs, and it meant the man was riding for help that must be near.

The scattering herd poured by as Jeff hauled on his hat and made sure the carbine barrel was free of mud. He slipped in fresh shells, and thunder shook the cold gray dawn as he started toward Bob Cantwell. Behind him one of the herd horses crashed down. He glimpsed Bob Cantwell afoot, shooting through the rain and blur of the racing animals. Jeff went on.

The last of the herd pounded by. Bob Cantwell fired and missed, and ran forward toward shelter of the nearest pine trunk. He had no saddle gun. It had been caught under his rolling horse. Jeff had a queer thought as he halted. He wondered if this was the first break in the long luck of the Cantwells. He sighted the carbine, and had no feeling at all as he squeezed the trigger. Bob Cantwell was almost behind the pine trunk. He spun on beyond it, legs tangling as he went down, gun flying from his hand. He'd rolled to his side, holding his middle, when Jeff reached him.

Bob Cantwell gasped: "I should 'a' killed you yesterday."

"Where's your brother?" Jeff demanded.

"Up the cañon, holding that damn' law posse you and Scoby led here."

"Fat Sam's dead. Did you Cantwells have to hold stolen horses up here until things got straightened out across the border?"

"Sent a man out to turn 'em this way," Bob gasped. "Hardy and his men'll have help quick now. They'll run your bunch out and get them horses away. The Old Man's handled worse'n this before. There won't be any proof, you double-crossing dog."

Jeff, down on a knee in the rain, said: "Take a look. The name is Johnny Sullivan."

"Scoby said so. The Old Man knows who crippled him now. He'll get you. Turn me over. My belly hurts. I'm all torn up inside."

Bob Cantwell groaned that request, but his glance looked past Jeff with lidded intensity. Jeff looked over his shoulder and whirled up fast, studying the lurching buggy and team coming up the *vega* at a lashing run.

Five riders sided the buggy, but it was the fierce, slashing run of the buggy horses that brought the savage feeling back to Jeff. Old Ben Cantwell was riding the horse-thief trail again—but helpless, unless on wheels, though still cunning, dangerous, implacable.

Jeff used the pine tree for cover and steadied his carbine against the rough bark. Once more he disliked what he had to do. The sharp bark of the gun seemed wasted for a moment. Then one of the buggy horses lunged violently over and fell. The lurching buggy overturned, hurling the crippled Cantwell out as Jeff fired again. He knocked a man out of the saddle with the second shot. The other riders were pulling up, looking at the wrecked buggy and the riderless horse. One pointed excitedly toward the pine tree where Jeff levered the carbine. Another pointed hurriedly up the cañon through the slackening rain.

Jeff shot that one reeling in the saddle, then looked up the *vega*. Four men riding recklessly had burst past the fence. Not sure who they were, Jeff turned back toward the Cantwell men, who had scattered among the pine trees.

Ben Cantwell was sitting up. His fist was shaking at his uncertain men. His rage was a thin, strident note in the dawn. Then Ben Cantwell waved wildly at the four men racing toward the wrecked buggy. The first one pulled up, rearing near the seated, raging figure and pointed back upcañon. Jeff's coolly aimed bullet knocked him off the horse. The other three men looked wildly around and spurred on. The scattered riders closed to meet them, and they all went on.

"Did you see it?" Jeff asked, turning.

Bob Cantwell lay holding his middle. His eyes had a sullen, whipped look. Other riders were following into the *vega* more cautiously. This time Jeff stepped out, knowing who they were. He recognized the spare erect figure of Horse Riley among them, and saw Ed Bellows spurring away from the others toward him. Riley followed. The others went on.

"Damnedest tangle I ever seen!" Ed Bellows exclaimed as he climbed stiffly down to examine a bullet tear in his leg. "Thunder, lightning, and them horses on us like the storm spit 'em out. The riders with 'em seen law badges and started shooting. It was Kelly hold the milk bucket and the cow kicking."

Horse Riley rode up and heard the last. The great scar welt on Riley's cheek was purple with excitement and he was smiling broadly. "I seen the sheriff's face when he found what he'd been led into. He hailed friendly and got his hat shot off. His jaw dropped to his belly. He bellered and clawed for his gun, and he ain't had time since to think about bank robbers and rewards." Horse Riley looked around. "Been busy too, ain't you?"

"I had to scratch fast," Jeff admitted. "Ben Cantwell's sitting there by his buggy."

Horse Riley's jaw dropped, too. "You ain't killed him yet?"

"He can't get away. The rest of his men are heading for home. My guess is they'll keep going. Ben Cantwell can explain how the Cantwells happened to be killing sheriff's men while bringing stolen horses down into this cañon hide-out."

"Hardy Cantwell's dead up the cañon," Horse Riley said. He peered at Bob Cantwell, on the wet ground, holding his middle. "Gut-shot, huh? And Old Ben's caught, cold."

"There'll be rewards," Ed Bellows said. "Something for all the men." He looked at Jeff. "And some gold waiting in El Paso. All yours now, ain't it?"

"I'd forgotten it," Jeff admitted.

"He'll have better than gold when the law handles Ben Cantwell," Horse Riley said with flat belief. "Johnny, you're home for good now, I reckon?"

"I don't know," Jeff said. "Have to deliver you back safe, like I promised Beth. Then I'll make up my mind."

A thought occurred to Jeff and he smiled with increasing relish as he thought of Beth's challenge. *What will you have left to trade next time, Johnny?* "Rope me one of those stolen horses," Jeff requested, grinning at the thought. "We'll get back home and talk it over. I've got gold to trade with now."

* * * * *

CANTRELL

* * * * *

I

There had been sixteen savage days of it, and nights, too—riding, fighting, watching, waiting for the next attack. On the Texas plains, Comanches had looted Tom Cantrell's trail herd. West of the Pecos, Apaches had stolen most of what was left. Four of the crew had been killed. Earlier, Jess Macey had been murdered in the Texas settlements. Now, smoke signals were lifting from the foothills to the south when Tom Cantrell rode forward to George Sell, at the point of the herd, and ordered: "Keep them bunched close ahead of the wagon."

George Sell, a quiet man with sweeping brown mustaches, a fierce man in a fight, said briefly: "Think we'll last through another ambush?"

Tom Cantrell, a long, muscular young man, scoured and leaned-out, smiled with a total lack of mirth as he turned on the sweaty saddle and eyed what was left. Two hundred and twenty-six gaunt steers and cows were hoarsely bawling as they scuffed dust westward toward Fort Ross and the Frío Plazas. They had been twelve hundred. Most of the remuda was gone. "We'll get through," Tom said slowly.

"Still think all this was planned against you?"

"Everything that's happened," Tom said, "points that way. If I could guess what Jess Macey tried to tell us. . . ."

"Jess," George Sell said, "tried to tell something."

They walked their horses side-by-side, both thinking of that far-off, dark alley in a little Texas settlement, where Jess Macey had sprawled inertly and muttered: "Hand. His ha-n-n. . . ."

Jess had been gathering legal documents from scattered ranches. Only the signed documents had been taken with him. No money. George Sell said tersely: "You guessed then we'd have trouble. We sure had it." George reined over to check the long-striding lead steers.

Tom dropped back, trying to judge where the attack today would come. Two miles to the south the first low foothills lifted, piling, climbing to the great, forested peaks that were the ramparts of the eastern Apaches. In the west, ahead, bold ridges ran down along the skyline to a stark pinnacle of rock. It would happen, Tom guessed, somewhere this side of that soaring pinnacle. He had no idea that a girl was standing by the pinnacle, gazing hopefully toward his herd. He would not have cared. Nerves and watchfulness tightened as the slow herd advanced. And it was Eagan, on the flank ahead, who suddenly stabbed an arm south and wheeled his horse back.

Riders, barely visible, were emerging from the first foothills. Swiftly Tom used his binoculars. His arm went up in reassurance as Eagan's running horse swung around to a walk beside him. "White men," Tom said. He gave the binoculars to Eagan, and added: "About thirty miles to the Frío Plazas. We'll make it now."

For the first time in days, Tom relaxed. This morning the little mirror on the wagon side by the water keg had reflected sandy hair hacked off with a knife, and his dark face gaunt and smoldering. His eyes had been bloodshot. They felt gritty under the lids and tired; he was tired all over, to the bone.

"They got that roan Box Six gelding with a white stocking on the right front leg!" Eagan exclaimed. "Remember that 'un?"

"Comanches got that roan," Tom said as he took the glasses. He looked through the binoculars, and the gaunt planes of his face hardened. "Since Jess Macey was killed, I've been looking for white men who might be trading with the Indians. Eagan, don't speak of the roan when they get here."

Eagan shrugged and rode out with Tom to meet the strangers: six men, well mounted, heavily armed, blanket rolls tied behind their saddles, grub sacks and canteens dangling, and out of Apache territory, with a horse that Comanches had stolen on the plains.

The white-ankled roan was reined alongside Tom's horse. It had the familiar Box 6 brand on the right flank. Now there was no doubt. The rider's greeting was genial: "I'm Matthew Fallon. This a Texas herd?"

"What's left of a Texas herd," Tom said. "I'm Thomas Cantrell."

Fallon sat the stolen roan gelding in jaunty confidence, right hand thrust carelessly in the coat pocket of his gray suit. His brown straw sombrero had a swagger of silver braid around the crown. He looked cocky, prosperous, prideful as he inquired: "Had trouble?"

"Too much trouble," Tom said. "I've lost men. Lost most of the herd. Smoke signals in the south this morning suggest more trouble today." Tom paused, and then suggested: "With you men helping, we'll do all right now."

"We're riding north in a hurry," Fallon said without interest.

"I had twelve hundred head," Tom said. "Nine men in the crew. You see what's left. Old Sam Butterworth, driving the wagon, has a bullet-crippled leg. We're low on ammunition. We need help."

Fallon said indifferently, "We can't help guard every strange herd that expects trouble. But I'll always trade for a profit. I'll buy your herd here for cash."

"How much?"

"Two dollars a head. Keep your wagon. You can reach Fort Ross or the Frío Plazas by tonight and be safe."

Eagan gave a jeering whistle. Fallon swung sharply in the saddle as if suspecting a signal. The startled roan snorted, jumped. Fallon blurted an oath as he went off balance. His right hand jerked out of the coat pocket, and Tom's stare narrowed and hardened. The hand was twisted and claw-like. From the dark alley far back in Texas, Jess Macey's mutter came again: *"His hand. Ha-n-n. . . ."* Here was a hand, on this stolen roan horse.

Puzzling bits of murder and disaster fell into place with this. Eagan's lobster-red face was startled, too, as Fallon almost viciously shoved the twisted hand back into the coat pocket.

"Ride to the wagon," Tom quickly ordered Eagan. "Tell Sam Butterworth we'll get no help from these men." Eagan's red face was showing belligerence. "Now!" Tom ordered sharply.

Reluctantly Eagan rode toward the wagon. Fallon glowered after him. "That man's known the Army."

"How far away is that wagon?" Tom asked.

Fallon's genial manner had vanished. The crippled hand, Tom guessed, was a chink in the man's cocky pride. He listened to Fallon's surly guess about the wagon: "Maybe a hundred and fifty yards away. Why?"

Eagan had reached the wagon. "Sam Butterworth," Tom said evenly, "is a tough old hickory knot. Sam went into Mexico in 'Forty-Six with General Wool's men. He used to trap beaver with Kit Carson. Sam can drop buffalo all day at better than a thousand yards with his Sharps rifle and rest sticks. At a hundred and fifty yards, Sam won't miss a man who leaves him with a bad leg for the Apaches."

"That," Fallon said, "sounds like a threat."

"It's advice," Tom said coldly. "Get off that roan horse that was stolen when the Comanches hit us."

★ ★ ★ ★ ★

At the great rock pinnacle miles to the west, the girl Tom Cantrell had never seen was making a hopeful guess to her companion. "Judge, it could be the Cantrell herd."

"Or, *ipso facto,* any other herd," was the judge's calm reply. He was a tall old man in white shirt sleeves, red suspenders, and a high, shabby stovepipe hat, tilted slightly on his sweeping gray hair. The rock pinnacle towered over them. The judge had strolled back from the stunted cottonwood where Virginia Bratton stood, and their two horses lazed with reins dragging. The tall stovepipe hat gave extraordinary length to the judge's shirt-sleeved figure as he drew slowly on a black cheroot and squinted intently into the west along their back trail.

Virginia Bratton was peering eastward where the green foothills reached into haze-hung distance. Far out there on the vast sweep of landscape, a tiny white object lay motionlessly upon the distant, shimmering land. When one looked long and intently, the white dot slowly sank into hidden folds of the earth and vanished. Finally, gradually it reappeared, canvas on a moving wagon. The barely visible black dots by it were cattle. Virginia said: "They'll not get this far today."

"Probably not," the judge agreed.

"If we ride to meet them, we can't get back to the Plazas until after dark." Virginia was rueful. "All this ride, without knowing whether it is the Cantrell herd."

The judge faced around. "Three Apaches," he said calmly, "rode out from behind that first ridge, cut our tracks, and went to cover in an arroyo out there. They're watching us."

One lived with this sort of thing and made the best of it. "You advised me not to ride so far, and I kept going," Virginia said contritely.

The judge said cheerfully: "Suppose we follow an old fogy's hunch and ride on and see if it is the Cantrell herd."

"So it's that bad?"

"*Expertus metuit*," the judge said wryly, "which is to say . . . 'having had experience, he fears.' "

The first fear touched Virginia. He was an old man, tall, benign, oddly and awkwardly and impressively dignified when he wished. And always he was shrewd, with depths of droll wisdom forever surprising her. The judge's squint now at her long linen riding skirt and flat-brimmed straw hat told exactly nothing, really. She remembered that the judge was a feared poker player.

The judge gave her a hand up to the side-saddle, mounted his own horse, and pulled the tall hat firmly onto his forehead. Long gray hair curled down against the back of his neck. He might be seventy. Virginia herself did not know. His shrewd, lined face had carried this pinkish, youthful glow back through her memory. Now the judge said cheerfully: "Go slowly until we're down the slope out of sight." His small smile considered her. "Then ride, Ginny, like the Old Snake was close."

Virginia adjusted her skirts and surveyed him dubiously. "It will be a hard ride for you."

Wrinkle by wrinkle his smile spread. "If we're followed, watch how young an old mossback can get." His squint tightened. "More of them may be infesting the landscape. No matter what happens, keep going until you reach that herd. Keep going, Ginny!"

Virginia tightened the chin cords of her straw hat. "I'm ready," she said.

At the trail herd, Matthew Fallon was flaring at Tom Cantrell: "This roan stolen from you?"

"I've a bill of sale, all marks on him written down," Tom said coldly.

Temper, chagrin darkened Fallon's heavy features. "My horse

broke down. I bought this roan from an Indian. If I have to pay again, I will. How much?"

Eagan was returning from the wagon at a swinging canter. On the jolting wagon seat, behind the long-six-horse team, old Sam Butterworth's long, heavy Sharps buffalo gun lay across his lap. Sam was watching them. "You knew the Box Six brand meant the roan had been stolen from some white man," Tom said curtly.

"How much for the horse, Cantrell?"

"We buried men after that raid on the herd, Fallon. Get off."

Eagan reined alongside as Tom watched Fallon's broad face go dull, muddy with malice. "Cantrell, you're being a fool."

Softly, coldly Tom said: "You offered two dollars a head. Is a two-dollar horse worth it?"

Their horses were walking. The hot sun struck between them on the long grass and baked earth. The question hung between them for tightening seconds. "No, not worth it," Fallon finally blurted under his breath.

"Then get off."

Fallon's head came around. His eyes had a dark shine. "You're the starry-eyed lieutenant who turned in his commission at Fort Union to try to start a big ranch, aren't you? You went partners with a land speculator named Rogers, who had land scrip he'd picked up cheap. You two used the land scrip and some cash to get title to most of the good water north of Fort Ross." Fallon yanked the roan to a halt. The claw of a right hand stayed concealed in the gray coat pocket as he dismounted. "Fools," Fallon said in a strangled voice, "usually get what they deserve." He called to his men who had pulled up: "One of you put my saddle on your horse!"

Eagan dropped his rope around the surrendered roan's neck, and kept silent until Matthew Fallon and his riders were heading on north through the thin dust drift behind the herd. One man rode awkwardly, straddled behind another. The extra saddle was balanced in front of a second rider. Eagan's boiled-looking face was redder when he finally asked explosively: "Did y'see his hand, Lieut'n't? Remember what Jess Macey said, back in Texas before he died? A hand. It didn't make much sense."

"It makes sense now," Tom said.

"You let him ride away."

"His crippled hand didn't prove anything." They were walking their horses toward the wagon, which had started on. Tom was sober and thoughtful. "It all fits, Eagan. We were watched from the time we reached the Texas settlements and started talking to ranchers who'd lost stock in Indian raids."

"Reckon Fallon and his bunch were in the settlements then?"

"No proof," Tom said. "But Fallon is here in New Mexico now. We'll meet him again. I took the roan from him to see if he'd talk while he was angry, and try him in a showdown."

Eagan's wide red face grinned. "You wet down his fire."

"He used his head, Eagan. He's dangerous. Never get careless about that man."

"You can handle him, Lieut'n't," Eagan said comfortably.

"Stop calling me lieutenant. We're out of the Army now," Tom said.

Eagan had been a sergeant, the pride of barracks and stables, and a sulphurous memory on officers' row. Tom Cantrell had been his line lieutenant. Now Eagan was indulgent: "I'm looking after you, Lieut'n't, until we're back in." Eagan virtuously believed it.

Eagan had never been cursed, Tom thought wryly, with the beckoning dreams that had driven into new, unsettled country— and sometimes destroyed—the younger men of the Cantrell generation. Eagan took the roan horse toward their scanty remuda and Tom rode to the jolting wagon.

Sam Butterworth said: "That was a cold-blooded bunch, not

helping us." A small, irascible splinter of a man with a wisp of iron-gray chin beard, wearing a disreputable leather shirt belted at the middle with rope, Sam hunched on the hard wagon seat with his feverish left leg at an awkward angle.

"Remember that man, Fallon," Tom told Sam. "He'll be waiting for us."

"Better shoot him first," Sam advised.

Tom grinned at the dour little man on the jolting wagon seat. Sam met trouble without scruples. "I might have to kill him," Tom said, and the hard, deep anger returned as he rode up alongside the herd. His partner, Steve Rogers, was waiting expectantly at the ranch. Cattle and horses were gone now. Men were dead. He and Steve had used most of their money.

Steve Rogers had trusted Tom Cantrell. Rebuilding what had been lost was a driving, personal thing now. And if Matthew Fallon was the man who had planned all this disaster, what lay ahead would be doubly dangerous. Tom rode thinking about it and watching the foothills closely. When he finally sighted movement, the swiftly focused binoculars brought the green scrub cedars and spiky amole clumps on the nearest hill crest leaping close . . . and Apaches.

One Apache, sitting a dun horse, had moccasined feet toed-in under the horse's belly. Red cloth circled the Apache's forehead. A red cloth streamer dangled from one brown arm. The gun held carelessly in one hand appeared to be an efficient Spencer repeating carbine.

On that distant hill the Apache had a greasy look as he spat and scratched his bare ribs. A moccasined heel kicked the dun horse lunging, sliding down the steep ridge slope, and Tom lowered the binoculars. His arm wave started Eagan back to the wagon. Tom rode there, too.

"Get under the canvas, Sam, ready to shoot when the wagon stops," Tom ordered. "Eagan will drive."

Sam halted the long six-horse team and grimaced as he swung his injured leg back over the board seat. Eagan stepped up on the wagon, and stood for a moment in front of the seat, watching the lone Apache, down off the ridge now, heading toward the herd at a leisurely trot.

"Just looking at him rises my gooseflesh," Eagan said. He looked into the west before he sat down. "Lieut'n't," Eagan blurted suddenly, "gimme them glasses. Quick." Eagan peered through the glasses a long moment. "A white girl and a old gent!" Eagan's cluck was approving. "She's a young one. Pretty! They're heading toward us on the whip. Three Apaches chasing 'em."

"You idiot," Tom said, and tersely he ordered: "Sam, get inside! Eagan, drive out from the cattle and stop when Sam tells you to." Tom slashed with the rein ends and rode ahead. His beckoning arm brought the three other men of the crew to him. "Hold the cattle here," Tom said. "George, come with me."

"What's shaping behind them hills where that Apache showed?" George Sell asked.

"We'll know," Tom said, and took George Sell in a furious ride out ahead into the west. The pale drift of dust out there was clearly visible in the shimmering distance. The girl took shape on a side-saddle, riding beside the man. The quirt on her wrist, Tom decided, could have lashed her horse into the lead, and she was holding back.

George Sell bent for the carbine in the scabbard under his leg. Tom did the same. The three Apaches were whipping furiously, trying to close. The girl's horse and the man's horse were ridden-out. Flaring nostrils and froth-spattered withers grew clear as the flung dust of their run swept close. Tom waved them on, and as the drumming rush went by, the girl's wan smile brushed his glance. Her companion held a long stovepipe hat in one hand. Gray hair streamed back. He rode bent forward, bobbing awkwardly. Yet, from some reserves of spirit behind the face gray with exhaustion, the old man brought the long hat toward his forehead in salute as he swept by.

II

Miles to the northeast, distant now from Tom Cantrell's herd, Matthew Fallon rode apart from his men in silent rage. He knew the five men were covertly, derisively thinking of the surrendered roan gelding. When he finally swerved his horse over to them, Fallon was cocky and a little arrogant, as usual. "Anyone see any sign of the boy around Cantrell's outfit?" he called.

Joe Sloan, a hard-faced, surly man, straddled awkwardly behind Red Kane and visibly resenting it, called back: "Why'n't you ask Cantrell while he was taking your horse?"

Fallon stared coldly. "Why didn't I ask Cantrell about several things, Joe?"

"Dunno."

The slow lope eased to a trot, then a walk, as the other men listened with interest. "I'll tell you why," Fallon said with sudden vicious malice. "That old goat on the wagon, Joe, could have cut you in two with his big buffalo Sharps. He would have at a word. What do you say to that?"

Joe Sloan licked his lips. "Ain't saying. Just bouncing on this horse's hard back."

The other men stared curiously, sensing obscure meaning in the clash of words. Fallon eyed them all disdainfully. "Most of you are alive now because I think for you. Cantrell and his men were ready to fight. Where's the profit in a gun battle over a worthless horse, which belonged to Cantrell anyway? The Apaches will handle Cantrell and his outfit."

Fallon pulled his horse to a stop and dismounted, keeping his right hand in the coat pocket. The other men stepped down, stretching, relaxing while their horses started to nip grass. There was no derision now.

"Joe, saddle another horse," Fallon said curtly. "You're riding to the Frío Plazas. If Cantrell gets there, I want to know what he does next."

"Want him shot?" Joe Sloan asked matter-of-factly.

"Cantrell is too much man for you," Fallon said coldly. "He'd shoot you, and know I'd sent you, and be on his guard. I'll take care of Cantrell."

Red Kane said: "Why bother about Cantrell?"

"He's starting the first big ranch in this part of the territory," Fallon said. "Others will follow. Men like you will be run out." He watched them, thinking about Cantrell narrowly now, and said: "Where's young Lee Bratton?"

Red Kane grinned. "After you left for Texas, Lee Bratton beat a horse buster at your Gallinas Ranch all bloody. 'Busting 'em too rough,' Lee said. 'A horse is better'n a man most times,' he yelled, and hit him."

"Lee Bratton is a wild young stallion himself," Fallon said with faint contempt. "His hot-headed ideas will get him shot. Where did he go?"

"Took most of his pay in a blood bay stallion that was the pick of the bunch they were breaking," Red Kane said with amusement. "Said he was heading for Las Vegas."

"Find Lee Bratton, Red," Fallon said, after a moment's thought. "Tell him some new horses are coming in from the trading camp over on the Tongue. There's a big yellow-gold horse with a white mane and tail that I picked for myself. I've never seen a finer one. Tell Lee he can have the horse, and his pay, too, if he'll hustle back."

"For a horse like that, he'd go anywhere," Red said. "Likely he's racing horses and swapping horses around Vegas or Santa Fe. I'll bring him back."

"Where will you be, Fallon," Joe Sloan asked, "if there's word about Cantrell?"

"Finding out how things have gone while I was in Texas," Fallon said. "Look for me at Largo Cañon or the Gallinas Ranch." He added: "Cantrell may not get past those Apaches today."

This hope stayed with Fallon when he rode on. Cantrell's men would be outnumbered today. They were short of ammunition. Any hour now, the last of Cantrell's outfit, and Cantrell, too, might be wiped out.

Virginia Bratton had noted the old judge's youthfully gallant salute when they passed the two riders. The worst of her tight fear had eased off. She had been afraid the judge would not last. He was too old for this kind of desperate riding. Their horses were blowing dangerously and weakening. Virginia slowed the wild run and wondered if one of the two strangers was Thomas Cantrell. Perhaps the younger man, clean-shaven, dark, angry-looking as he had waved them by. She hoped with lifting spirits that he was Cantrell. All she had heard, all she expected made the prospect pleasant.

The judge called: "That was close, Ginny!" It had a weary sound, but under his white shirt and red suspenders, the judge's lean old shoulders were visibly bracing with new energy. They both looked back as a gun slammed dully, then another. An Apache pony plunged sideways in a swirl of dust, its rider sprawling off and bouncing up.

"That should stop them!" Virginia called to the judge. Her interest reached ahead to the bunched, restless herd held by two riders. "Not enough cattle to be the Cantrell herd," she told the judge.

"Any herd is good enough now," he answered dryly.

Virginia had watched the canvas-topped wagon in the far,

shimmering distance. Now powder smoke bloomed lightly from the side of the wagon. Over near the foothills, a lone, breech-clouted rider leaped off his falling horse and ran back toward the hills. Other riders poured down the ridge front—seven—thirteen, Virginia counted. She thought they were coming on, but the running Indian swung up behind a man. They all rode back up on the ridge and vanished. "It doesn't look good," Virginia said.

The judge nodded. The wagon driver's wide red face held an understanding grin as they pulled up by him, and Virginia slipped from the side-saddle. Her knees were weak. Her horse drooped, its lathered sides heaving. The judge dismounted from his equally exhausted horse and said: "Young man, a pleasure to be with you."

"I bet."

Virginia pulled off her straw hat. Her hair was damp at the roots. She felt disheveled, shaky as she inquired: "What herd is this?"

"Cantrell's herd, ma'am. He's coming now."

The rider nearing the wagon was the younger man who had waved her on. The officers at Fort Ross had served with him at Fort Union. Their fond tales had made him sound rather fabulous—tall, laughing Tom Cantrell, joyful with a bottle or with ladies, cards or soldiering, to the surprising day he'd turned in his lieutenant's commission and left to start a new ranch in the wildest part of New Mexico Territory. The stories she had heard at the fort did not fit this lean man who swung off his blowing horse and called: "Sam, what d'you think?"

The answer came through the weathered wagon canvas: "They've counted us, Tom. They'll ambush us and stampede the horses and cattle."

"There's enough of them to try for the wagon, too," Cantrell said.

The judge had set his tall shabby hat back on his disarranged gray hair, and was shaking out the black coat, which had been tied behind his saddle. "Thomas Cantrell?" he inquired.

Cantrell had pulled off his black hat and was wiping a blue kerchief over his gaunt face. "Yes," he said.

"This is Miss Virginia Bratton," the judge said. "I'm Barnaby Polk, her lawyer, and guardian also in some matters."

Brown, indifferent eyes flicked over Virginia. "Miss Bratton," Cantrell said without interest. He was blunter to the judge: "You almost lost this young lady."

"I was to blame," Virginia said. "I kept riding, hoping we'd sight your herd." She smiled faintly, anticipating his surprise. "I'm your new partner."

"My partner is Steve Rogers," Cantrell said.

The judge explained: "Steven Rogers, your former partner, is dead."

Cantrell seemed to freeze. An edged hardness entered his demand: "What happened?"

"Rogers," said the judge regretfully, "was shot off his horse between the Frío Plazas and the ranch. No one seems to know what happened. Missus Rogers sold her inherited half of the ranch partnership to Miss Bratton, and returned to Maryland."

A look of tired, smoldering anger crossed Cantrell's gaunt face. "Steve, too," he said, and then, flatly: "I can't use a new partner."

Nettled, Virginia said: "You have a partner, nevertheless." She turned to her drooping horse.

"Steve and I agreed that if either of us died, the other would buy his share," Cantrell replied. "You don't fit my plans, Miss Bratton."

Virginia turned back to him, holding her straw hat by its leather ties. "I have plans of my own, Mister Cantrell."

"*My* plans, ma'am, are all I'm interested in."

Her black hair, caught back and pinned, barely reached his broad shoulders. She had to look up at his weather-scoured face. "We own a ranch together, Mister Cantrell. Judge Polk will tell you so."

"All this can be discussed later," the judge suggested.

"Where is the mixed herd of over a thousand head, which Missus Rogers said was being purchased in Texas?" Virginia persisted.

Cantrell's sober look considered her. "Two hundred and twenty-six left. Indians got the rest. I'll buy you out, Miss Bratton. Haven't the cash now, but my note will be good."

"I don't care to sell."

"I've had men killed in Texas," he said patiently. "The partner I counted heavily on is dead. There will be more trouble connected with this ranch. Bad trouble. A helpless girl simply won't do for a partner."

"I'm not helpless!"

For an instant she thought Cantrell's disturbed look was flecked with humor as he considered her. Then his hard somberness returned as the man inside the wagon called: "Tom! That Apache who rode out first is Senya, the kid says!"

"So that's him?" Cantrell said with interest. "He led the bunch that ambushed us four days ago."

"They had luck fust time . . . can't blame 'em for trying again," the voice said.

"This time we know they're around," Cantrell said. He turned to the judge. "Your horse is run-out. Get on the wagon seat with your carbine. The lady can ride inside."

"I'll ride my horse," Virginia said coolly. She turned to catch up the dragging reins, and unbelievably Cantrell's arms caught her up from behind. Outrage broke from her. "Put me down!"

Silently Cantrell carried her to the rear of the wagon. His closeness reeked of horses, tobacco, powder smoke, sweat. The arch of his deep chest was against her. She was breathless and helpless as he deposited her in hostile silence, like a sack, on bedrolls inside the wagon. "You've made enough trouble today," he said curtly, and was gone.

It was hot under the wagon canvas, and a sour voice chuckled: "Welcome, partner. I'm Sam Butterworth, and I oughta have better sense, too, than be here."

He sat on a bedroll near the middle of the wagon, a lean little man in a greasy leather shirt. His scant gray chin beard looked awry and bristling. A heavy Sharps rifle was propped on crossed, brass-bound rest sticks in front of him, its muzzle in a hole he had cut in the canvas. Virginia dropped her hat and stumbled to her hands and knees as the wagon started with a jerk and a rising screech of dry axles. She could see the judge's lanky figure on the wagon seat beside the driver. As she balanced unsteadily on the bedrolls, a thin, chocolate-brown figure sat up beyond Sam Butterworth.

"Who is *that*?" cried Virginia. At first sight, in the hot shadows, the figure looked Apache. Wild hair hung Indian-style below the ears and was hacked off across the forehead. The tails of an oversize gray shirt, belted with a piece of rope, hung almost to small, bony knees. Then Virginia saw that the wild hair was brown, and the blue eyes of a white boy stared impassively at her.

Sam Butterworth said, laconically: "Says his name is Eddy Morton. Comanches got him and his mother in Texas, and traded 'em to the Apaches. Cantrell almost shot him when the kid snuck up to the wagon last night."

"And the mother?" Virginia asked quickly, concerned.

"Says he run away to get help for her. That buck I put afoot was Senya, who had the kid for a son. If he guesses the kid is here, he'll get him."

Virginia looked at the small, sun-browned figure in the baggy shirt. "Eddy, how old are you?"

The boy gave her an impassive look, old beyond his possible years. Slowly, as if his tongue and mouth were stiff with the language, he said—"Eleven."—and looked away, ignoring her.

The six-horse team was trotting. The heavy wagon swayed and groaned. Canvas slapped on the wooden bows as Virginia made her way forward unsteadily over the bedrolls and picked up one of three carbines beside Sam Butterworth. "We buried the men who owned 'em," Sam said simply.

Silently he handed her a sheath knife. Virginia slashed an opening in the canvas and looked out. Apaches, Comanches, Navajos, and Utes had been in the background of her life. The three toy-like riders she could see over near the foothills were an accustomed part of this wild, lonely land. "Will the others ambush us?" she wondered aloud.

Sam Butterworth's shriveled face showed no visible concern. "Can't tell what an Apache'll do." He scratched a hip, and grumbled: "The kid must 'a' brung lice."

The lurching wagon came to a halt ahead of the bunched herd. Virginia looked out the back and saw a rider hazing the few remuda horses off to one side. Cantrell and two other men were moving the cattle slowly toward the first hills. They fired handguns. The cattle lumbered into a run. The three riders swerved out of the dust and turned back toward the wagon.

"The son-of-a-gun," Sam Butterworth muttered. "Giving 'em away."

"Part of them are mine," Virginia said.

"I'd tell my lawyer." Sam Butterworth scratched again, and looked reproachfully at the boy.

Cantrell rode to the back of the wagon. Virginia called indignantly to him: "Half of those cattle are mine, Mister Cantrell!"

His gaunt face regarded her without expression. "Get them if you like." He spoke past her to Sam Butterworth. "There's an arroyo ahead, Sam, which comes out of the hills. I think the rest of the rascals are in it, waiting for us. More, probably, than we've seen. A coyote ran out of the draw and looked back. I'm hoping the cattle will bait them away."

"They'd rather have the horses, Tom."

"We'll need the horses," Cantrell said. "Those three Apaches over by the hills are trying to hold our attention. If the others are in the arroyo ahead, I'll pull them into the open."

"They'll stay hid till the last minute, Tom."

"The arroyo swings northwest," Cantrell said. "We'll go closer to it, then turn north, as if we're missing it. There's no other cover close. If they want us, they'll have to come out in the open."

"They'll come, if they've got a chance," Sam Butterworth guessed. "And they'll fade back if they don't win quick."

"Keep the lady safe," Cantrell said, and reined away.

The groaning roll and lurch of the wagon continued on. The remuda was brought in close. Sam Butterworth gnawed a chew of tobacco from a dark twist and relaxed on the bedrolls. It was hot under the canvas. Virginia's mouth was dry as she thought bleakly of Cantrell: *What a man for a partner!*

Abruptly the wagon turned north. Sam sat up and adjusted the long, heavy rifle on its rest sticks. "If they come, don't git rattled," he advised Virginia.

She smiled wanly. Her hands felt hot, moist as she thrust the carbine barrel through the opening in the canvas and looked out. The drop-off into the arroyo was visible not two hundred yards to the west. Only grass, low cactus, and clumps of rabbit weed lay between. Cantrell, his riders, and the remuda were on the east side of the wagon.

"I've never shot a man," Virginia said aloud.

"Sight and shoot," Sam Butterworth said calmly. "Easy."

Virginia tightened as Cantrell's great-lunged shout lifted outside the wagon: "Pull up!"

Horses carrying painted, breechclouted riders with high moccasins were bursting up over the arroyo bank. Scattered out, they raced toward the wagon, and began to shoot. Sam Butterworth's big rifle bellowed. A rider toppled off his horse. The judge had left the wagon seat. Cantrell and his men had dismounted. The driver fired his carbine. The sights of Virginia's carbine wavered as she lined them on a naked chest painted in black and red, and squeezed the trigger, then quickly closed her eyes.

The dismounted men were shooting. Sam Butterworth's long rifle spoke again. Other Apache horses were swerving, running without riders. All of it was unreal, Virginia thought as she aimed again, fired, and again closed her eyes. When she looked a moment later, the attack was dissolving in dust and floundering flesh, and the surviving Apaches were galloping back toward the arroyo. Cantrell shouted: "Let's go!"

The six-horse team surged into a run so quickly the judge barely regained the seat. Virginia had fired twice and probably had not hit anything. Sam Butterworth pointed to three bullet holes that had not been in the canvas previously. "They shoot high," he said casually.

The Apaches had vanished into the arroyo, leaving riderless horses and bodies in the open. Presently Sam Butterworth scratched again, cast another reproachful look at the silent boy, and lay back on the bedrolls, closing his eyes. "That," he said, "baked their potatoes."

III

Traveling fast without the slow herd, the wagon crossed the big arroyo without incident. Tom Cantrell, riding watchful sweeps out ahead, pondered somberly the high, hopeful plans he and

Steve Rogers had made. The new herd was gone, and most of the remuda. Jess Macey had been murdered in Texas. Steve Rogers had been murdered near the ranch. Half the crew was lost. Money had run out. And back of it all loomed the man named Matthew Fallon. In the dangerous weeks ahead, there would be more of Fallon, Tom decided. He made plans as the long miles ran into a blazing sunset, and the massive Black Butte marked where the little valley of the Frío turned through the foothills to Fort Ross.

Eagan drove the wagon pitching, sliding down the sandy Frío bank. The jaded horses gulped at the shallow Frío current as Tom rode, splashing to the wagon. Virginia Bratton was sitting between the old lawyer and Eagan. She regarded Tom with hostility.

"Sam Butterworth will go to the post surgeon in the wagon," Tom said. "You two can ride your horses to the Frío Plazas with the crew."

Virginia Bratton said coldly: "Will you be at the Upper Plaza tomorrow to discuss business?"

"If I can buy you out with a note, ma'am, I'll make a point of being there."

"I'll not sell."

"The herd's gone. There's no other business to discuss," Tom said indifferently.

Her flush was visible. "We own a ranch together, Mister Cantrell. I'm a full half-partner in everything. Judge Polk will tell you my rights."

The old lawyer said calmly: "As administrator of this young lady's inheritance, and that of her younger brother, Lee Bratton, I advised the purchase of this half-interest in the ranch. It's all legal."

"Is a brother in this, too?" Tom demanded sharply.

"Miss Bratton used her own money." Barnaby Polk leaned

out from the wagon seat and offered a worn leather cigar case.

Tom bent from the saddle and took one of the villainous black cheroots. He guessed this tall old man knew every trick in the law books and a few more, and they'd be used for the Bratton girl's benefit. "I'll be at the Upper Plaza in the morning," Tom said, and put his horse up the opposite bank.

Eagan drove the wagon, lurching up to level ground. The girl and old man mounted their horses. Virginia Bratton reined over to Tom. "Mister Cantrell, what about the boy?"

"He's going to the fort with me."

"He needs a home. I'd like to take him."

Tom regarded her with faint malice. "He left a good home, Miss Bratton. An excellent Apache wickiup, where he was the adopted son of a sub-chief named Senya, petted, learning their ways, and rather liking them."

"No civilized boy could like living with bloodthirsty savages!"

"He was taken from a two-room soddy in Texas," Tom said calmly. "He'd had to help with the hard work and get his lickings, too many lickings, I gather. He's had more fun with the Apaches."

"He ran away."

"To get help for his mother, who is not the petted son of a sub-chief," Tom said deliberately. He called to the wagon: "Want to go with this lady, son?"

"No!" came back through the canvas.

Tom put the cheroot between his lips and watched Virginia Bratton bite her red lower lip and wheel her horse away. Eagan stayed with the wagon. Gray twilight condensed about them as the wagon wheels crunched on the narrow rough road up the Frío valley to Fort Ross. Night came blackly, and Eagan pulled up as a sentry's challenge cut the night ahead. Tom called out. The sentry shouted: "Corpr'l t' guard! Post number seven!"

"Flugelmeir!" Eagan yelled. "What's E troop doing at this

coyote post?"

"C and E troops came from Fort Union six weeks ago." Tom called, "Who's commanding?"

"Major Alcorn."

Eagan's—"Ah-h-h."—held covert, amused meaning.

A man's past, Tom reflected ruefully, was never surely behind him. Eagan knew that Isabel Alcorn was probably here at Fort Ross with her father.

A summons for the doctor went through the post gate ahead of them. Eagan halted the wagon beside the dark parade ground, in front of long, low adobe barracks. Tom said: "I'll see Major Alcorn, if he's available."

He rode across the dark parade. He heard brisk steps on a porch at the end of officers' row, hurrying toward the wagon— the doctor, no doubt. Then a dimly seen white dress moved off the adjoining porch into the starlight.

"Tom Cantrell?"

"Isabel?" Tom rode to meet her and swung down.

"Tom! How nice! I was visiting the Dourtes and heard them calling the doctor." Memory filled in the details of Isabel's oval features, blurred in the starlight. She was taller than most girls, amusing, with the assurance of the commanding officer's daughter. "We're the tag-end of the regiment now," Isabel said. "Ordered here to Fort Ross and forgotten. Tom, how did it go in Texas?"

"Lost half my men, most of the remuda, and all the herd."

"Tom, I'm sorry." Then, quickly, Isabel said: "You can come back into the regiment."

"Who has some clothes to fit an eleven-year-old boy?" Tom asked, evading her suggestion. He explained about the boy.

"I'll see to everything," Isabel said.

Minutes later, waiting alone in Major Alcorn's small parlor, Tom smiled wryly. Isabel liked to manage. She had decided, evidently, to manage Tom Cantrell back into the regiment. The peace of the major's shabby little parlor was soothing as Tom stood by the front window, hat in hand. The long days and nights in the saddle, the savage fighting, bone-weariness, and endless hammer of ill fortune faded a little inside these whitewashed adobe walls. The few pieces of battered furniture were proof that Major Alcorn, as usual, was not trying to fare better than his junior officers.

Alcorn's energetic voice was audible from a back room, directing the orderly: "These to the adjutant. Tell him that mail for Fort Union must be ready by breakfast call in the morning."

The orderly hurried out through the narrow center hall. Major Alcorn entered the parlor with a half-smoked cigar in his hand. His shock of dark blond hair and his neat blond mustache were still only lightly touched with gray. Restless energy radiated from the lean figure. "You look like short rations and hard riding, Tom. Cigars in that box on the table. Sit down and tell me about it." A shabby rocker creaked under Alcorn's solid weight. Even relaxed, with his blue blouse comfortably open at the neck, he showed alert vigor.

Tom selected a cigar and dropped into another creaking rocker, smiling faintly as he recalled the rawhidings Alcorn had given him. Every one deserved. Alcorn was the general's trouble-shooter, which probably explained this new command at Fort Ross. The enlisted men in the barracks and stables called him Indian Charley, because of his grinding patrols or bloody skirmishes. Alcorn harried raiding Indians fiercely. He could be a help in what lay ahead, Tom hoped as he said: "I can't brag, Major. I lost my Texas herd and five good men. One man was murdered in the settlements. Comanches hit us hard."

Alcorn paid keen attention, munching absently on the frayed end of his cigar. "Too bad," he said at the finish. "Going back after another herd?"

"No money left, sir."

"You have a new partner," Alcorn said. "She has visited the fort."

"I met Miss Bratton today," Tom said without enthusiasm. "Have you any information, Major, about Steve Rogers's death? Who killed him and why?"

"A patrol from the garrison we relieved found him, Tom. That's all that seems to be known."

"The boy we picked up," Tom said, "ran away to get help for his mother. He has a boy's faith that she'll get help."

Major Alcorn's face clouded. "I've been thinking about the woman. Not enough men in the garrison to go into the mountains after her in force, which would be necessary. The Apaches would kill her, or move her fast, if we did go in. She's another tragic case, Tom. Too many of them these days. The Indian agent at Santa Fe will return the boy to Texas. He'll get over it."

"What boy gets over his mother? I'll keep him at the ranch. Something may happen."

"Don't give the boy false hope," Alcorn said soberly. "Many women and children have been carried off in the same way. Few return."

"Texas knows it," Tom said. "The Comanche raids were never worse. Homes are looted and burned, settlers killed, captives taken, livestock by the thousands run off."

"It will be stopped before long."

"It's not being stopped," Tom said. "Herds of cattle and horses are run north by the Comanches and Kiowas, and sold for trinkets to traders, who bring the livestock into New Mexico Territory and sell it cheap." Memory of what he had lost himself put roughness into Tom's promise: "I'll stop some of that."

"That's quite a statement."

"New Mexico holds well over a hundred thousand head of

stolen Texas stock," Tom said. "I collected powers of attorney in Texas that cover scores of brands that have been raided. I'll stock my new ranch that way, Major."

"Been tried, Tom. Any stock you replevin will vanish before the law can do anything."

"I'll take stolen stock where I find it."

Outside in the night, the hour call floated from sentry to sentry, and Alcorn sat motionlessly. His gaze had narrowed. "That means guns, Tom."

"Guns took my herd," Tom said. "Guns killed my men, and murdered Steve Rogers. There's no civilian law in this part of the territory. I'll make my own law."

Major Alcorn got to his feet and moved to the front window. On his feet, also, Tom waited. "You'll be shot if you try it," Alcorn said over his shoulder. "Come back into the regiment, Tom, where you can do some good."

"Not what I want, sir."

"What do you want?" Alcorn inquired patiently.

"I wanted new land to tame, and build on, Major. That's why I turned in my commission. Now I want back all I've lost, and more." The roughness came back, smoldering: "It's personal now. I'll break every man I find in the dirty Indian trade. I'll take their stolen cattle and run them out of my part of the territory."

"Fort Ross," Alcorn said calmly, gazing out the window, "will tame this part of the territory. You have five men left, you say, and no money to hire more. Try such a reckless scheme, and you'll quickly be hunted down and shot."

"The Army could help me, Major. Settlers in Texas who have lost their stock deserve help."

"The Army is not meddling in civilian affairs."

"Then I'll manage, Major. Men are coming from Texas to help recover stolen stock. They'll work with me, from my ranch."

Alcorn swung around. "How many men are coming from Texas? When are they coming?"

"I don't know how many men, or exactly when they'll get here. But they're coming. We'll take stolen cattle where we find them."

"Not in my district," Alcorn said. They stared at each other. Alcorn's lean features were tightening. "This part of the territory is just opening up," he said in an even tone. "The Apaches, and even Comanches from the plains, are making enough trouble. My orders are to pacify and protect."

"Protect who, Major? Cattle thieves and buyers of stolen cattle?"

"Texas gunmen taking cattle unlawfully will infuriate settlers and Indians," Alcorn said slowly. "A hornets' nest will be opened. If it happens, I'll intervene."

"And meddle in civilian matters, after all," Tom said, holding his temper. "You'll decide, perhaps, who dies, Major?"

"If you'll have it that way," Alcorn said after a moment.

"I'll have it that way."

"You've been warned, Tom."

And it would be this way, Tom knew regretfully as he left Major Alcorn's quarters. The Army, too, would be against him. He paused beside his horse in the starlight, thinking about the violence that undoubtedly lay ahead. His thoughts turned to the girl who was his new partner. She had mentioned her own plans. She would have the advice of that tall, shrewd old lawyer. And she had a brother. The talk with her tomorrow would bring another clash, Tom suspected as he rode to find Sam Butterworth and the doctor. He had little relish for meeting the girl.

IV

The judge had brought a hickory-smoked Missouri ham from Santa Fe. Virginia was cooking thick ham slices for breakfast when grease popped out of the large iron skillet. *"Ouch!"* Virginia exclaimed. She stepped back from the hot kitchen stove, in which chunks of aromatic cedar wood crackled cheerfully. "It should be in his eye," Virginia said darkly, rubbing her wrist.

The judge, relishing his morning coffee at the pine table behind her, inquired with interest: "Whose eye?"

"That Cantrell man's eye." Enveloped in a nainsook apron, Virginia stood, fork in hand, resentfully thinking of Tom Cantrell.

The judge had slept on a cot in the little parlor of this three-room adobe Virginia had rented on the outskirts of the Upper Frío Plaza. A shaft of golden sunlight through the small kitchen window turned the judge's red suspenders into gay bands across his lean shoulders, brightened the long gray hair falling down the back of his neck, highlighted the amusement on his shrewd, wrinkled face. "Still want to spit and skewer the young man?"

"Why did he have to be like this?" Virginia said resentfully. "Refusing to have a partner. Losing the herd. And now most of my money is gone."

"Cantrell has no money left, either," the judge reminded her.

"He's a man!"

"With an angry young lady partner . . . heaven help him," said the judge blandly.

"This is serious," said Virginia. She turned the smoking ham slices with jabs of the long fork. "I hoped a ranch might help Lee settle down. And all I have now is empty land and an impossible partner."

"So Lee," said the judge, "is back of all this?"

"Lee and his fine horses and wild ways," said Virginia unhappily. "He rides all over the territory to race his precious horses. He fights and gambles. He's friendly with outlaws. And he's getting wilder."

"I hear reports," said the judge dryly.

"If you'd given Lee his inheritance when he was twenty-one, he might have settled down."

"Tosh!" The judge was almost testy. "When did easy money cool off a young hothead?" The judge put down his coffee cup. "I watched you two grow up in Santa Fe, Lee only a year younger. But who protected Lee? Who covered up Lee's mischief? Who told everyone that Lee was the finest brother a girl ever had?"

"He was," Virginia said in a smaller voice. "He is. But Lee needs responsibility. I wrote him to come and help me. And now what is there to help? I can't even have Lee around this man, Cantrell. They'd fight. I know they would. All I've done is waste my inheritance."

"Not necessarily," said the judge. "Cantrell and his partner got title to parcels of land that control all the good water for forty miles north of Fort Ross. The water controls all the free range in that area. Fort Ross will increasingly control the Apaches and Comanches. The foundations of a great ranch are there, Ginny. And you have clear title to half of it."

"And no cattle and no money."

"Cattle live and die," said the judge. "The water, the land is important. I control Lee's inheritance for three more years. With Lee's consent, secured legally, I might let you borrow some of Lee's money to buy cattle. . . ."

"Would you?" Hope brought Virginia around—and the fast pound of a running horse held her listening. Whooping exuberance split the morning sunlight outside. "It's Lee!" Virginia ran to the front door.

The plank door burst open as she reached it. Lee bolted in, whooping: "Not a steer or cow left!" His strong arms swept Virginia into a whirling turn. "Heard it in the plaza as I came through," Lee jeered. "The old man wouldn't hand me fifty dollars of my own money, but he pushed you into a sour cattle deal."

As Lee released her, she warned: "The judge is in the kitchen."

Half a head taller, lean-hipped, and supple in his denim pants and canvas jacket, Lee shoved his hat back on his rumpled black hair and said: "Now I can beg again for a little of my own money."

"Lee, please. . . ."

"He knows how I feel." Lee stepped to the low kitchen doorway and leaned a hard shoulder against the jamb. "How much crawling does it take this time?" he asked defiantly.

"Had breakfast?" the judge said mildly.

Virginia remembered the ham and hurried past Lee to turn the slices before they burned. When she faced around, Lee was sulkily taking the chair opposite the judge. "How much do I get today?" Lee demanded.

"In three more years," said the judge, unruffled, "you'll have all your inheritance. By then, I hope, you'll realize that owning the best horses in the territory, and playing bad poker, aren't the most important things in life."

"I've owned horses that were better than most men I know," Lee said hotly. "What's wrong with a horse?"

"Nothing," said the judge. "I like a fine horse myself . . . as a horse." The judge drank from his coffee cup and set it down slowly. "But I admire a responsible man more."

Virginia held her breath as Lee flushed angrily. Increasingly Lee's temper flared easily. Her thoughts went to Cantrell, angry and forceful, and now such a big part of their lives. What would happen if Lee and Cantrell clashed? "Breakfast," Virginia said unhappily, "is ready."

★ ★ ★ ★ ★

The sutler's building at Fort Ross was a long, low adobe, with the post barbershop at one end. This morning Tom Cantrell was the first customer. Clipped, shaved, scented, Tom stepped next into the sutler's cluttered store to buy supplies for the ranch.

Clean clothes felt luxurious. Breakfast this morning—he was a guest of the bachelor officers' mess—had been a merry meal. While Tom made purchases, a Ute scout watched stolidly, and across the store an enlisted man's wife shushed a fretful baby in her arms. And when the gusto of Eagan's voice lifted in the barbershop, Tom stepped to the doorway and paused, smiling.

Eagan and a half dozen tough troopers surrounded young Eddy Morton in the barber's chair. Only the boy's thin, small face, dark as an Apache's, and his long, ragged, brown hair were visible above the barber's white cloth.

Eagan was telling the barber: "E troop helped scrub him with scouring soap last night. We doused lamp oil in his hair to run the bugs out. Then he wanted bear grease to rub on hisself! 'Not even bacon grease on E troop,' we told him, and rolled him in a blanket by tattoo, smelling like the major's clean Sunday shirt."

"Eagan," Tom said through the doorway, "bring him into the store here when you're through."

"Yes'r."

And when Eagan brought the boy into the store, Tom saw that Isabel Alcorn had managed well, as usual. Shoes and long black cotton stockings, baggy knee-length knickers, and a white shirt were the patched, outgrown Sunday best of some officer's boy. "You look great," Tom said, smiling. He sniffed. "Smell good, too. Now we'll buy you some new duds for the ranch."

Blue eyes in the thin, dark face stared anxiously up at him. The boy drew a breath: "Are they . . . ?" He swallowed. "Will the soldiers . . . ?"

Tom said casually: "I told the major about your mother. But these things take time."

He watched the thin face turn worried and desperate, and a little later, as he walked to the quadrangle, he was still trying to put the boy out of his mind. The yeasty fragrance of new bread drifted from the post bake house. Outside the guardhouse a glum prisoner was trudging an endless circle with a log on his shoulder. And on the quadrangle, Tom smiled when he sighted Isabel Alcorn emerging from the adjutant's building ahead.

Isabel opened a pink sunshade and waited for him. She looked fresh and summery in a white cambric suit as they fell into a slow walk together. "Father is disturbed about you," Isabel said.

"I gathered as much last night," Tom said dryly.

The old black field hat in his hand had a darker pattern on the front, where the crossed-swords insignia had once shielded the felt from sun and weather. Isabel's finger indicated the darker pattern. "Still in your hat, Tom." Isabel's glance searched his face. "And still in you, too, isn't it?"

"Only the memories," Tom said. His oblique glance was mischievous. "Many memories. . . ."

Isabel colored. "You could come back into the regiment, Tom."

"With all the future ahead? All the excitement and great things to do?"

Isabel regarded his bantering with smiling exasperation. "Still starry-eyed, Tom, aren't you?"

"Yesterday," Tom remembered, "a man named Matthew Fallon called me exactly that . . . starry-eyed."

Isabel flushed. "Matthew Fallon?"

"Yes."

Isabel bit her lip, then admitted: "Mister Fallon heard me say it, I suppose. Your name had been mentioned. I said what I thought about your leaving the regiment."

"Who is this Fallon?"

"He has a ranch on the Gallinas, I believe," Isabel said. "He visited Fort Union, and has been here, too. Mister Fallon seems a gentleman. Everyone likes him."

"Evidently."

Isabel's color heightened as she thrust back, "Isn't a pretty black-haired ranch partner most of the exciting future ahead?"

Tom's grin turned annoyed at the thought. "A stubborn, interfering female partner underfoot is the last thing I want."

Isabel regarded him with smiling interest. "I believe you mean it."

"I do," Tom said. "And I'll have to get along, Isabel. Promised to meet the young lady and her lawyer in the Upper Plaza this morning."

"Will you be back today?"

"Can't say." Tom lifted his black hat casually as he left her.

Too casually, Isabel decided as she watched him head across the wide, sun-drenched parade with long, easy strides. Tom Cantrell had come back from Texas a changed man. The dark planes of his face had a hard, remote look in repose. *Only his plans matter now,* Isabel sensed, and her conviction crystallized: *Tom is a dangerous man now. Even to a woman.*

Yesterday Isabel Alcorn would sensibly have rejected such a man. Now her pulses beat faster as she stood motionlessly, looking after Tom Cantrell. Her breathing was shallower as she walked slowly on, absently revolving the pink sunshade.

Tom rode from the fort alone, leaving Eagan to follow with the loaded wagon and the boy. The rough road skirted the singing current of Frío Creek out of the foothills and turned west at the Black Butte. Northward, the empty country reached out to far, smoky horizons, and the Frío ran west through a widening valley to the two Frío Plazas. The Lower Frío Plaza had been settled first by native families from the distant Río Grande country. The Upper Plaza was the larger settlement, where stagecoaches and wagon trains came, and express and trade.

Steve Rogers had thought the Upper Plaza a friendly place, and he had been murdered in the lonely miles between the town and the ranch. Any stranger in the Upper Plaza could be the man who had killed Steve, and could be waiting now to kill Tom Cantrell. The wary thought went with Tom past the outlying corrals and weathered sheds to the big sun-flooded plaza.

Low, flat-roofed adobe structures filled the east and south sides of the plaza. The west side held a feed corral and wagon yard. The open, sloping bank of Frío Creek formed the north side of the plaza, and a patrol returning to the fort had dismounted there. In the center of the plaza, teamsters were hitching long spans of mules to loaded freight wagons. Men, women, and children of the town were out in the open, watching the activity. Tom rode toward the dusty, unshaved troopers, watering horses and pack mules down the Frío bank. A dust-floured lieutenant standing on the Frío bank showed fatigue in every sagging line. Tom pulled up behind the lieutenant's weary back and said: "Fitz, your cot was mighty comfortable last night."

Second Lieutenant Horace Horatio Fitzpatrick wheeled around, bloodshot eyes squinting. "Blast us! The new Battle king!" Smiling, Fitz came to the stirrup and thrust up a hand. "We're out eighteen days," Fitz said. "South, then west into the Jornado. Hot and dry." Fitz squinted up. "How about an easy job on your new ranch?"

Tom sighted George Sell, ducking under a hitch rack on the south side of the plaza. He lifted the reins and grinned down at Fitz. "Your job's waiting, Fitz. Never hot, never dry, sleep all you want. . . ."

"Look for me!" Fitz called after him.

Smiling wryly, Tom skirted the freight wagons. Fitz, he knew, would never do it. Like Major Alcorn, like Isabel, Fitz would follow the guidon to the end. Tom met George Sell and stepped down from the horse, asking: "How is it?"

George had on his clean denim pants and wore a new gray shirt under his open vest. His hair and brown mustaches were freshly trimmed. George resembled a sober deacon with a gun on his hip. Faint disapproval tinged his report: "Buck Ellis and Pete Yancey celebrated last night. They're over at the feed corral holding their heads."

"They've earned a headache," Tom said tolerantly, then regretfully added: "I left Sam Butterworth at the fort. He may lose the leg."

"It'll finish Sam," George said. "Shy a leg, Sam'll give up. Any help from the Army in what's ahead?"

"Worse," Tom said. "Troops will intervene if Texans help us take stolen Texas cattle."

"So?" George was thoughtful as he rolled a smoke. "That finish your plans?"

"No."

George twisted the brown paper at one end. "Five of us left. Every man in a hundred miles who owns Comanche-stolen cattle, or who's stolen cattle, will be at us first move we make."

"Want to pull out?"

George considered deliberately. Mule teams at the nearby freight wagons were trampling dust. Trace chains were jingling, teamsters cursing loudly as George struck a match on the heavy buckle of his gun belt and lit the cigarette. "I'll stay," George said. "One of the hardcases who was with that Comanche-trader, Fallon, rode in last night."

"Which man?"

"The one who gave Fallon his horse yesterday. Name's Joe

Sloan. He was in the saloon last night. Handy with a gun, I hear."

"All Fallon's men are probably handy with a gun." Tom's eyes were sweeping the plaza. "Fallon is making a move quicker than I thought he would."

"About an hour ago, Fallon's man was in the saloon buying a drink for your lady partner's brother," George said.

"Her brother's here?" Tom frowned at the news. "What's he like?"

Surprisingly George Sell's serious features relaxed. "He's a young tomcat," said George, tolerantly. "Big young fellow. Good-looking. Busts horses for ranches all over the territory. Swaps horses, too, and races horses for bets. Crazy about fine horses, the man at the feed corral says. Likes his gambling, too." A smile touched George Sell's stern mouth. "The world's his oyster, from what I hear. Young Bratton goes after it a-whooping."

Tom had to smile himself. "He doesn't sound too bad."

Almost sheepishly, George admitted: "Makes a man hanker to get young and have a fling again. But don't take young Bratton careless. He's a hot-headed wildcat, quick to jump if he's crossed." George grew speculative. "I wonder why Fallon's man was siding him so close this morning? Young Bratton didn't look too happy."

"Trouble for us," Tom guessed, frowning.

George remembered something else. "Your new partner is buying supplies for a ranch crew."

"I bought supplies at the sutler's," Tom said quickly. "Eagan is bringing them in the wagon."

"She's buying barrel flour, sack beans, lard, sowbelly slabs, and plenty more," George said. "Who's she aiming to feed at the ranch?"

"I'll ask her," Tom said angrily. "Which store is she in?"

V

Virginia Bratton stepped out on the shady portal of the Frío Mercantile with her lightweight purchases stacked in her arms. Humming under her breath, she reached her buckboard at the hitch rack, and Tom Cantrell was standing in front of her, tall and unsmiling. She remembered his strong arms lifting her into the back of his wagon, and remarked coolly: "Judge Polk will be here in a few minutes."

Cantrell lifted her packages and put them in the buckboard. "Is the man really a judge?"

"Barnaby Polk was a judge admired by everyone," Virginia said with pride. "But he would rather practice law in Santa Fe. He's here to see me settled on the ranch."

Cantrell impassively regarded her blue dress with its gay red coral buttons. His remark was calmly business-like: "I'd still like to buy Steve Rogers's half of the ranch."

"With a note?"

"Best I can do at this time."

"I'll not sell, even for cash," Virginia said. "I've arranged to buy my own cattle for my half of the ranch."

The dark angles of Cantrell's face hardened a little. "Who will handle your cattle?"

"I'm hiring my own crew."

"It won't work," he said. "Two crews in one bunkhouse won't work. Two cooks in one kitchen won't work. Two owners in one ranch house won't do."

"Rogers and his wife occupied half the ranch house," Virginia reminded him tartly. "I've hired a Mexican woman to live with me. My brother will be my foreman. We'll use our legal half of everything. Do as you wish with the other half."

Cantrell's dark face tightened. "Your brother will boss things?"

"Lee will boss our crew."

A smolder grew in Cantrell's eyes. "Steve Rogers was murdered, Miss Bratton. You've bought into a dead man's shoes. It can happen to your brother."

"We have nothing to do with that."

Cantrell was deliberate. "I left the Army to start a ranch, which evidently isn't wanted in this unsettled part of the territory. I've lost my partner, and men and money. From now on I'll call the trouble. This ranch will be bigger than Steve and I ever planned. And I'll break every man who tries to stop me."

"If you're alive," Virginia said coldly.

The corners of Cantrell's mouth quirked in a faint smile. For an instant he was likeable, even when his sarcasm followed: "That's something to look forward to."

"I never wish misfortune for anyone."

"I don't believe you do," Cantrell said, studying her, "but serious trouble is ahead. You don't belong in it."

"I want no part of it, Mister Cantrell."

"You've bought into it, Miss Bratton. You should sell and get clear of it. Make no mistake, it will happen!"

Virginia was familiar with Lee's bursts of temper that blazed quickly and were as quickly forgotten in Lee's reckless zest for life. This Tom Cantrell was different. His hard purpose was ominous as he watched her. Suddenly she was a little afraid of him.

"I don't frighten easily," Virginia said steadily. "The judge will tell you my legal rights."

"You've been warned," Cantrell said.

Virginia looked past his tall figure and saw Lee riding to them. Cantrell turned. He stood motionlessly, watching Lee and Lee's horse. Virginia had seen other men transfixed as Cantrell was now, when Lee appeared on one of his prized horses. This horse was a magnificent bay gelding, almost black, with a snowy face blaze and a pink lower lip. The horse's eyes were wide-set, alert, withers broad, haunches lean, powerful. Every silky hair had been lovingly groomed until the sun glinted from the burnished coat. Mincing sideward to them on long tapering legs and small, light-stepping hoofs, the horse had a proud look of tremendous speed and endurance.

"What a pair," Cantrell said under his breath, and Virginia wondered if she would ever completely dislike the man after his involuntary tribute to Lee.

The saddle and horsehair bridle were plain. There was no dandyish affectation about Lee. None was needed, Virginia thought with a catch of pride. Lee was superb, even in his plain denim pants and canvas jacket. Sitting straight up, molded to horse and saddle, Lee was completely confident of himself in a wild young way.

Lee swung a leg easily over the horse's neck and slid lithely off, dropping the looped reins over the saddle horn. He landed lightly, his right hand steadying his holstered gun, and pushed his hat back on his tousled black hair as he stepped up to them. The horse stood still, ears pricking after Lee. Lee's expression made Virginia apprehensive. She had hoped these two men— Lee with his reckless temper and Cantrell with his hard strength—would not meet today. Reluctantly she said: "Mister Cantrell, my brother, Lee Bratton."

"So this," Lee said, "is the partner?" He did not offer his hand.

"I'm the partner," Cantrell said calmly. The hand he had meant to offer relaxed at his side. "You have a fine horse."

Lee's instinctive grin faded. "You're the man who lost Ginny's half of the Texas herd." Lee pushed his hat farther back and looked Cantrell up and down.

They were about the same size, yet Cantrell's maturity gave the illusion that he was slightly taller and heavier. The thoughtful gravity in Cantrell's reply made Lee seem young and recklessly brash. "I'm that man," Cantrell agreed.

"I hear Indians maybe didn't get all your trail herd. A slick trick was worked on a girl you thought was helpless."

Disciplined control kept Cantrell silent, watching Lee. "That hardcase who Matthew Fallon sent after us put the idea into your head, didn't he?" he asked slowly.

"Matthew Fallon?" said Virginia. "Lee, isn't he the man you broke horses for?"

Cantrell regarded Lee more intently. "So," he said, "you've worked for Fallon?"

"Who I've worked for is my business," Lee said. "I get around, I hear things."

"A man fool enough to listen can hear anything. If he jumps when a man like Fallon pulls strings," Cantrell said, "he can find trouble fast."

Virginia had the helpless feeling of being trapped between these two big men, each so important in her life. Quickly she begged: "Lee, will you get the judge?"

Lee's shoulders had pulled back stiffly. "Never mind the judge. I'm here now."

"I'll talk to the lawyer," Cantrell said. "Tell him, Miss Bratton, I'll be at the feed corral."

Lee moved closer. "Talk to me. My money's buying the cattle for Virginia's half of the ranch. I'm hiring the crew. I'll boss 'em. I'm not a helpless girl. Or an old man who'll be back in Santa Fe."

"Don't play Matthew Fallon's game," Cantrell advised quietly. "You've been fed lies to start trouble. And I don't want trouble with you."

"We'll talk about the herd. Ginny's half of the herd."

"I'll talk with your sister. I'll discuss it with your lawyer," Cantrell said curtly. "But not you, buster."

Lee hit him. Virginia gasped as Lee's hard fist smashed

Cantrell's mouth, driving Cantrell reeling. But suddenly she had a strange feeling of triumph. She was not alone. Now Cantrell knew it. Then she remembered that they wore guns. She reached Lee's side and caught his arm. "Stop it, Lee!"

Lee shook her off, and a hand caught her shoulder from behind. The judge's grim voice said: "Keep out of this, Ginny." He drew her back to the buckboard.

"They'll kill. . . ."

"Cantrell," the judge said, "is not a killer."

"But Lee. . . ."

"Lee is not a killer . . . yet," the judge said. "Fools who dance must pay the fiddler. Lee must learn before some gunman kills him. Go into the store. Don't watch this."

"No," Virginia said. She was watching Tom Cantrell and she was desperately afraid.

Tom Cantrell was not afraid. Through dizzy shock Tom was thinking: *Fallon planned this, too!* The warning of Major Alcorn followed: *Someone will kill you!* This could be it; this young hothead egged into rage by the lies of Fallon's man, and Fallon himself once more out of sight, in the background, planning and maneuvering. Tom threw a dizzy look around for Fallon's gunman, or strangers who might be backing Lee Bratton. Only the sister and the tall old lawyer stood beside the buckboard. Men were running toward the fight. Tom spat blood. He ducked Lee's next overeager swing and jumped back, circling while his head cleared.

Lee ran at him. Lee's slashing fist skidded off Tom's cheek bone, spinning him off balance again. Lee Bratton was big, strong, and fast, with the bursting tide of youthful stamina and reckless confidence. The Army tamed young roosters like this with sweat, drill, and discipline, and they made the world's finest. But here was one who had never met discipline. The sister had made this cocky, reckless young hothead a vital part of Tom

101

Cantrell's whole future. Lee missed another furious swing and crowded close, strong and confident. He was dangerous. His bursting youth could wear down an older man. He could win this useless brawl, and, if Lee did win, all the future would fall apart. Tom realized how it would be. Lee Bratton's swaggering malice would dominate the ranch. The tale would spread far, giving confidence to dangerous men Tom Cantrell had to meet. Fallon's long-reaching enmity had made this unexpected hazard, which had to be quickly, ruthlessly beaten down. The opening Tom wanted was suddenly there. His long, looping blow struck tremendously, shockingly on Lee's nose.

In the crowd, someone yipped shrilly as Lee's head snapped back. Tom could feel the nose flatten under his slashing knuckles. Lee's big frame shuddered. But a bloody nose did little damage—only to pride, to temper. Tom belted a left viciously into Lee's middle. A gasp escaped Lee. Tom drove his right fist again to the broken, bleeding nose. He slid away as Lee yelled thickly in pain and rage.

Lee swiped his hand over his nose. He glared at the red smear that came away, and charged in wild temper. A flailing fist struck Tom's chest. It was like being clubbed. Lee was breathing through his mouth. Whistling breaths sprayed red droplets from his streaming nose. Tom dodged another rush and stepped close as Lee swung around. His clubbing blow struck Lee off balance. Tom followed with sledging blows that beat Lee to his hands and knees in the churned dust.

Tom waited as Lee bounced up with another yell. Then his right fist smashed Lee's blood-smeared cheek. His left fist sent Lee's head bobbing. With brutal blows, Tom beat Lee, staggering back against the close-packed spectators. Great breaths shuddered from Lee's open mouth. The hands of strangers pushed him upright. All the high, reckless youth and temper had quickly been beaten into desperation.

A bearded teamster holding his coiled bullwhip called in heavy sarcasm to Lee: "Ye started hit! Whup 'im!"

Lee staggered forward.

Tom was drained and gasping, too, but his explosive—"Don't do it!"—came as Lee reached desperately under his canvas jacket for the gun holster there. Already Tom was lunging and grabbing to hamper Lee's gun wrist, and his right hand was pulling his own revolver. Lee was dazed, slow. Tom whipped his gun up in a fast arc. The steel barrel struck Lee reeling. He fell hard, sprawling, scattering dust, rolling to his side.

Tom stood unsteadily over him, gun in hand. And in a swirl of her blue skirt, Virginia Bratton went to her knees in the dirt beside Lee. Tom heard her croon of pity over the smeared, beaten face. Then her aversion and fear came in a choking blaze as she looked up: "Have you killed him?"

"He'll live," Tom gasped from burning lungs. "Keep him away from me."

Sweat rolled down his face as he swung away from her, gun in hand. During the fight he had caught a blurred glimpse of the man named Joe Sloan, back in the crowd, expectantly grinning. Sweating, trying to get his breath, Tom looked for Fallon's man, who had started all this. The close-crowding spectators stared back. Fallon's man was not among them now. Barnaby Polk, the tall old lawyer, stood beside the buckboard, remote and thoughtful, and a little sad. The old man seemed to be musing on what would follow this. And over the heads of the crowd, Tom saw Lieutenant Fitzpatrick watching him from the saddle. Fitz had brought his departing patrol close to the fight and halted. Now Fitz grinned at Tom's sweaty, panting figure.

"One of your easy, pleasant jobs?" Fitz called as his arm went up. Fitz's order to march rolled back along the column.

They passed on by twos, sun-blackened troopers grinning as they went by. Tom Cantrell still was one of them, obviously, and they considered that the Army had won this skirmish against a civilian.

The crowd gave way silently as Tom shouldered through into the open. His glance swept the plaza. Fallon's man was not in sight. Tom started for the saloon on this side of the plaza, gun in hand.

He was breathing more easily when he reached the open doorway of the saloon and looked in. The place was deserted, emptied by the fight.

George Sell's call reached Tom: "You want that one leaving the feed corral?"

The quick pounding of a spurred horse's hoofs sounded from the west side of the plaza as Tom ran to the edge of the saloon portal. Fallon's man had ridden his horse out of the adobe-walled corral, and had seen Tom or heard George Sell. He spurred recklessly down into the trough of the Frío channel and up the opposite side, riding north. Tom holstered his gun with a shove and walked out to meet George Sell.

"He's heading back to Fallon," Tom said. "George, he started it by telling young Bratton we hid out most of the girl's cattle, instead of losing them."

George Sell, quiet and formidable when aroused, said: "Want me to go after him?"

"It's done now." Tom drew a sleeve over his wet face. "She's going to run her own cattle on the ranch. Have her own crew. Her brother will be her foreman."

George Sell looked startled. He lifted a hand to his sweeping brown mustaches, and, after frowning a moment, said quietly: "Not good."

They walked toward the feed corral, both of them reflective. "There'll be more of Fallon," Tom said. And when George nodded agreement, Tom said briefly: "We'll go to the ranch and get ready."

VI

New Mexico Territory was an immense, sun-drenched, empty land, yet news could race across the far horizons. The man named Joe Sloan rode north, pushing his long-striding gray gelding. Lieutenant Fitzpatrick's patrol carried word of the furious fight to the Fort Ross garrison. And a buckboard carrying the mails rolled south, its driver mulling over the fight he had witnessed. Far south, the deep-dug well of the Lobo Flat relay station held the only sweet water in parched miles of mesquite and cactus. Sunset laced the western sky with scarlet streamers as six rangy Texans on tired horses, and leading two pack horses, reached the Lobo station from the south. Night was falling when a dusty stage from the south swung into the walled yard of the station. Minutes later the mail buckboard rattled in from the north.

The six Texans had the feral look of dangerous brush cats as they took seats at the station's long, plank supper table and ate wolfishly, ignoring others. But the mail driver's account of the fight in the Frío Plaza was abruptly interrupted by the Texan opposite him.

"The name, suh, was Cantrell?" the Texan drawled over the thick antelope steak he had been demolishing.

"Tom Cantrell."

"Back from Texas with a herd?"

"Back with nary a nubby steer," said the mail driver. "Lost his herd and half his crew."

Knife in one hand, fork in the other, the Texan chewed reflectively. His shirt was buckskin without fringing. A brace of long-barreled revolvers, and a long bone-handled knife in a leather sheath well back on his left hip, seemed a casual part of him. The driver had noticed such things when this Texan had washed his face and hands outside, and used his broken half of a comb on his yellow mustache and long yellow hair. Thereafter this man had drawn apart, rangy and silent, with restless eyes watching every movement in the walled yard.

Thoughtfully the Texan's polite drawl persisted: "This Cantrell's got a ranch?"

"Call it a ranch," the driver said humorously. "All he needs is cattle on it." The driver waited expectantly for more questions, which did not come as the Texan silently attacked his food again.

In this same sunset the man named Joe Sloan, far north of the Frío Plazas, spurred his exhausted gray gelding up a shallow cañon of the Secundos, to an isolated adobe hut with a small corral alongside that held three horses. A Mexican hurried out of the hut and helped switch the saddle to a fresh horse. A silent, dark-faced woman brought wheat tortillas and a tin plate of meat chunks laced with fiery red chili. Sloan ate ravenously, hardly speaking. He rolled a smoke, swung onto the fresh horse, and the inky night swallowed him as he rode on. When he met the blaze of the next morning's sunrise, Sloan was through the Secundos, heading east through a tremendous country of long ridges, colorful buttes, and hidden, cañon-like valleys.

Hours later Sloan followed a faint trail through black brush, and down red rock steeps into a valley running sinuously southeast between red and yellow rock sides. A glint of water wandered through the middle of the valley between silvery-gray *chamiso* thickets. After a time grazing cattle appeared. Finally tall cottonwoods lifted ahead and the temporary Largo Cañon camp was there.

A weathered wagon with a chuck box built in the back stood by the cottonwoods. A sooty coffee pot rested on smoking embers. Bedrolls were scattered on the ground. Ropes stretched between the cottonwoods where the horses were corraled. Matthew Fallon, standing beside the wagon with several men, recognized the approaching rider and walked out to meet him.

Fallon had not been under a roof since he had first encountered Tom Cantrell. His expanding interests kept him moving over all this vast, unclaimed wild country, where only the strong dominated. The war had spun him off, bitter and unwanted, his health gone and his right hand forever useless. He had built this new life with only superior intelligence and ruthlessness. The claw of a right hand, which he regarded every day with revulsion, had driven him like an excoriating demon. Without a gun hand, he had found health, profit, and power—and the power meant most. He got an immense feeling of satisfaction when men with two perfect hands jumped to his bidding. Matthew Fallon's name was important, even among savage tribes that looted and slaughtered most whites. Now Tom Cantrell threatened everything that Matthew Fallon valued.

"Is Cantrell dead?" he called out. He realized it sounded too eager for a man who tried to present a jaunty confidence to all men.

The rider did not notice. He was too tired. "I took a chance you'd still be at the camp here. That Cantrell beat the hell out of Lee Bratton in the Upper Frío Plaza yesterday."

"Young Bratton at the Frío?"

"Got there yesterday morning." Sloan dismounted stiffly and stood a moment, working his cramped shoulders. He grinned wearily. "I got in my talk before Lee seen Cantrell."

"What talk?"

Fallon listened intently as Sloan told him. Part of Fallon's mind jumped back, as it did constantly these days, to Cantrell's arrival in the country. A man sent surreptitiously to Cantrell with an offer of cheap cattle and horses for the new ranch had been rebuffed by Cantrell with cold temper. No stock, nor any man connected with the Comanche trade, would be on the new ranch or near it Cantrell had warned. It had been threat and challenge, even though Matthew Fallon's name had not been mentioned to Cantrell.

Joe Sloan was saying: "No young hellion like Lee Bratton'll forget a beating like Cantrell give him yesterday. Next time Lee won't try fists."

Fallon's thoughts went back to the first try he'd made against Cantrell. Dropping everything, he had followed Cantrell to Texas, to block the man before Cantrell dug in near the Frío with his first trail herd. And in Texas he had discovered Cantrell was using his crew to gather legal claims to stolen stock.

Joe Sloan said: "Cantrell don't want Lee Bratton's sister for a new partner. They've had words. Lee has throwed in with his sister."

Fallon drew a slow breath. Cantrell's herd was gone. Cantrell's first partner was dead. But Cantrell himself loomed astride the Frío country, more threatening than ever.

"Lee Bratton said he was heading north to Las Vegas. He'll hire a crew, and buy cattle and horses for their half of the ranch."

"A crew of his own?" said Fallon. "On the ranch with Cantrell? After Cantrell beat him bloody?" He stood thinking about it. "Did you tell Lee about that yellow-gold horse with a white mane and tail?"

"Made his eyes shine. He'll come by the ranch on his way to Las Vegas."

"You've earned an extra hundred dollars," Fallon said impulsively. "Get some rest, and follow me to Gallinas Ranch."

Fallon knew cynically that men like Joe Sloan stayed at heel only while money came easily. But Sloan had earned this gift. Lee Bratton could be handled. For Cantrell this was the beginning of the end.

VII

Far south toward the Frío, it was Eagan's warning shout that rang through the wide ranch yard: "She's bringing gunmen with her!"

Tom Cantrell stood motionlessly in the small adobe saddle shed, remembering the gun Lee Bratton had tried to draw. Reluctantly Tom checked his own revolver before he stepped outside.

South, where the rough ruts from the Frío Plazas lifted out of a wide, grassy draw, three wagons and a number of riders were in sight. The boy had been examining Eagan's big revolver. Eagan was reaching for the weapon. George Sell was coming purposefully from the corral. Pete Yancey shouldered out of the bunkhouse, cocking a carbine.

"No guns!" Tom called.

Bareheaded, the sleeves of his old blue military blouse rolled back, Tom walked forward and watched the groaning four-horse wagons approach. Virginia Bratton and the old lawyer were riding ahead. Lee Bratton was not in sight.

Wind stirred the Bratton girl's long straw-colored skirt as she sat the side-saddle lightly. Her small red hat looked gay in the sunlight. She hardly reached his shoulder, Tom remembered. Her blue eyes and fair skin were unusual with such black hair. When she had kneeled in the plaza dirt beside her brother, her anger and aversion had been a choking blaze. She seemed calm now as she wheeled her horse back. Tom heard her call: "First wagons to the back of the house! Last wagon to the front!" She knew he was standing there and she rode toward the front of the house, ignoring him.

The old lawyer rode up to Tom. "Young man, I find no basis in the suggestion that Indians did not take your trail herd." Under his breath, the old man added: *Experientia docet stultos.*

Tom put the words into dry English: "Experience teaches

fools." He added more dryly: "Who gets the experience? Are those gunmen the teachers?"

Barnaby Polk looked surprised, then detached and unconcerned as he turned his horse toward the corral. "They joined us a few miles back," he said as he moved away. "They have asked questions and been told nothing."

Tom gazed toward the armed strangers with new interest, and walked to meet them. One rider advanced. "Yo' name Cantrell?" a polite drawl inquired.

The man had long yellow hair and a yellow mustache. He was not much past thirty, Tom decided. The plain leather shirt and two long revolvers were on a rangy, sinewy frame. "I'm Cantrell," Tom said. "How's Texas?"

The reply was a cool drawl: "Bleeding from Comanche raids. Damnyankees all over the place, reconstructing folks. I'm Ashley Hampton." He stepped down with cat-like litheness. His reserved glance estimated Tom.

"Passing through?" Tom inquired.

"All depends," the polite drawl said. "Yo' the man who was gathering power-of-attorney papers in Texas?"

"What papers?" Tom said with his own reserve.

Ashley Hampton drawled: "Folks spoke well of you in Texas. Old Will Seabright, near Five Springs, said he gave you power of attorney covering his JV brand, that Comanches had raided bad. There was talk you'd welcome help."

"I need help," Tom said, "but only from men interested in recovering stolen Texas cattle. Not from Texans fired-up to raid damnyankees. Or wild ones who won't take orders."

"I gave orders in the war," Ashley Hampton said coolly. "I can take orders from the right man."

"Who are your friends?"

"All of us from the same county. Rode the war together. Been down in Chihuahua and didn't like it. Riding north, we heard yo' name mentioned and stopped by."

If the other five strangers were like this one, they were not a breed to be working for Matthew Fallon, Tom decided. He made a tentative decision: "There's the bunkhouse. Make yourselves at home. We'll talk it over." His glance went to the loaded wagons. "This ranch has two owners. My men and I are the only ones here interested in stolen Texas stock."

The Texan regarded the loaded wagons gravely. He knew, undoubtedly, about the fight with Lee Bratton. He might be aware of the clashing emotions involved in the Bratton girl's taking over her half of the ranch. No hint of it was in the Texan's comment: "A man can't be too cautious when fighting is ahead."

Something like a glint of humor came into the Texan's gray eyes as he turned to his horse. His remark could have had several meanings. Tom's own humor warmed his reserve as he watched the Texan beckon to his companions and lead his horse toward the bunkhouse.

But when George Sell walked over, Tom said: "They're Texas men. See if they ring sound, George, before I make any decisions."

As he walked to the house, Tom thought soberly of Major Alcorn's warning. Texas men, helping Tom Cantrell recover stolen Texas stock, would bring Alcorn and his troops into any trouble. Alcorn was a man of his word. Yet without help from Texas, Tom's future on this empty new ranch was hopeless. When Tom thought about it, his anger came again. He put decisions aside now, and watched what was happening to his home.

Wiry Mexican men from the Lower Frío Plaza had driven the wagons. Virginia Bratton had brought furniture and personal effects. She was moving in with her treasures, calmly making her own nest, no matter who she crowded out.

In the kitchen, Tom had to step aside as two Mexicans staggered in with a heavy leather trunk. A moment later the old lawyer stepped in, removed his high hat, and glanced around with interest. Then he had to move quickly aside himself as two more Mexicans lurched in with a large feather mattress. Feathers! Not even Steve Rogers's bride had brought feathers.

Shrewd lines deepened at the corners of Barnaby Polk's blue eyes as he noted Tom's darkening look. "After the storm, the sunshine, young man," the old lawyer said, smiling a little.

Tom looked at him without humor. "When will Lee Bratton be here?"

The old lawyer frowned. "I've ordered Lee to stay away for a long time," Barnaby Polk said. He placed his tall hat on the kitchen table. "You seem to have built well here."

"My partner and I had plans." It was difficult to resent this benign, tall old man. "I'll show you the house," Tom offered.

He and Steve Rogers had been proud of this massive, adobe headquarters, which was not yet finished. They had built a side wing for each of them, with a huge living room between. Peeled logs held up the low ceilings. Dirt twenty inches deep covered the flat roof. Floors were of hard-dried, puddled adobe mud, until lumber would be easier to get. They had run back high side walls enclosing a spacious patio. Across the back they had put kitchen, eating room, storeroom, cook's room. Against possible siege, a second well had been dug in the patio. The house was a fort, with small windows and heavy shutters. And now this Virginia Bratton owned half.

They met her small, busy figure. Her preoccupied smile flashed for the old lawyer and ignored Tom. A plump Mexican woman—*Doña* Sarina, Tom heard the Bratton girl call her— bustled about vigorously in an enveloping apron of a violent-hued floral pattern, scolding the native men in bursts of liquid Spanish.

Life had filled this house when Steve and his bride had been in it. The thick-walled rooms had held laughter, gaiety, love, and enthusiasm. Tom had returned from Texas to the lonely aftermath of grief, from which Steve's wife had fled back to her tidewater Maryland. Now life filled the house again, brisk and purposeful.

They returned to the kitchen. Barnaby Polk offered his black leather cigar case. Tom accepted one of the villainous cheroots.

Thoughtfully Barnaby Polk said: "You have an establishment. Ginny Bratton was fortunate in her purchase." The lines at his shrewd blue eyes deepened again as his glance considered Tom. "It should be possible to endure this partnership without friction."

They both had to move quickly out of the way as four Mexican men staggered in with a walnut organ. Tom watched this ultimate in feminine domesticity vanish toward the front of the house.

"It should be possible," Tom conceded, but there was no conviction in his voice as he thought of the stubborn girl and her hot-headed brother, here in the house, squarely in the midst of his own life and plans.

At Fort Ross, Major Alcorn sat at his desk in the small headquarters building, and chewed the frayed end of his cigar while Adjutant Blount waited silently.

A trooper, posted for desertion, had been found back in the hills, his head sliced off like a turnip top and wedged in the crook of his stiffened arm, as if the unlucky man were desperately retaining his separated part. These Apaches had a foul sense of humor! Alcorn could think of worse they'd done, and would do. He took the cigar from his mouth. "There's some doubt the fellow did desert. We'll bury him properly and straighten out his record."

"Yes, sir."

Before Adjutant Blount could leave, Alcorn added thoughtfully: "Any more news about Tom Cantrell?"

"Not since Cantrell's fight with the girl's brother, sir."

"Very well."

Alone, Alcorn ran his fingers through his shock of graying blond hair. Under his breath he muttered a heartfelt cavalryman's oath. At Fort Union, for a time, there had seemed some slight possibility that Tom Cantrell might end up in the family. Alcorn doubted it now as he looked at his daughter's framed photograph on top of the desk. Isabel's assured smile told him exactly nothing. But Tom Cantrell's gaunt, angry face the other night had held promise of what was going to happen soon.

Cantrell was the man to do it. He would take armed Texans through the country like a destructive scythe. Make a shambles of peace and order. Worse, Cantrell would be right, and the man at this desk would have to stop it, no matter how he felt. Alcorn felt gloomy and annoyed as his thoughts jumped to the boy that Cantrell had picked up, and to the boy's mother, held by the same sort of Apaches who had caught the deserter and no doubt thoroughly enjoyed his frantic screams before tiring of the sport.

Nothing practical could be done at this time about the boy's mother. Alcorn caught himself glancing at Isabel's picture and wondering—almost guiltily—what he'd do if Isabel were held by the same Apaches. He suspected what he'd do, and swore again under his breath as he bent to the reports on his desk. That small boy and mother would stay on his mind, Alcorn knew.

Isabel Alcorn was thinking about Tom Cantrell when she met Adjutant Blount near the post hospital. Archie Blount was a young man of energy who fancied himself; he caught off his garrison cap and might have been aware of her thoughts.

"I wonder," Adjutant Blount said expansively, and knowingly, "if Tom Cantrell would be interested in a report about his former partner that the sergeant-major ran across in the files?"

"Why ask me?" Isabel said calmly.

Adjutant Blount half closed a knowing eye, decided not to pursue the matter, and said: "A patrol from the garrison we relieved found the body of Cantrell's partner. The sheriff's office being over a hundred miles away, the lieutenant put all the facts he could find into his report."

A quick thought speeded Isabel's pulses. She had wanted some reasonable excuse to visit Tom Cantrell at his new ranch. Her smiling request made Archie Blount a co-conspirator in a way. "Can I have a copy of the report, Archie?"

Adjutant Blount beamed. "Have it for you tomorrow."

Isabel walked on to the hospital building, already planning the visit. It put her thoughts again on the Bratton girl, at the ranch every day now with Tom. Isabel frowned and tried not to think about it.

VIII

It was evening when Virginia Bratton relaxed in her bedroom, cross-legged in a wooden tub of water, her hair caught up in a towel. The gourd dipper in *Doña* Sarina's brown hand cascaded cold water over her bare neck and shoulders.

"C-c-o-o-ld!" Virginia gasped. "The towel, Sarina!"

Wrapped in the towel, Virginia sat and looked contentedly about the lamplit room. Her own walnut spool bed, fetched all the way from Santa Fe. Her walnut bureau with French-plate oval mirror. Her walnut lowboy, with Lee's smiling photograph on top. Bright chintz curtains over the window and closed shutters, through which seeped the yapping clamor of coyotes in the near night.

Virginia drew a satisfied breath. "Home, Sarina."

Doña Sarina spoke in Spanish. "This house of strange men.

And only we two women. Who," said *Doña* Sarina darkly, "knows what?"

Someone knocked on the heavy plank door. *Doña* Sarina made the sign of the cross over her ample bosom. Virginia chuckled, and called out: "Yes?"

The judge's genial voice spoke through the door. "Too tired, Ginny, to play the organ for us this evening?"

"For those men?"

"It would be nice."

Virginia sat in frowning, stubborn silence. The judge's mild voice coaxed: "For me then, Ginny? Your first night in a new home should be a happy one."

"Of course, if you want me to," Virginia said.

He was a wise old man. His purpose was plain. Warmth under this roof—even if friendliness were impossible—might be best for her and Lee. Especially Lee. Virginia stood beside the tub, toweling herself. "I think the black challis skirt and the pink basque," she said in reflective Spanish. "And my red-and-yellow gold earrings."

"For *Tejanos*," *Doña* Sarina muttered.

Virginia laughed as she stepped to the thick rag rug on the hard mud floor. Her life had been encompassed by such rough men. She understood their great strengths and violent weaknesses, from which most of them rallied sheepishly. She got dressed, and then, with the small glass lamp glowing beside the mirror, she lightly used chamois skin backed with flannel and filled with face powder. A twirl before the mirror flipped the long red-and-yellow gold earrings against her neck. She opened the door and walked into the living room. She heard *Doña* Sarina take a watchful position in the open doorway behind her.

Bracket lamps glowed on the lime-washed walls of the long living room. Firelight from blazing cedar chunks in the big stone fireplace danced over the men who stared silently at her.

They seemed to fill the room—big men, booted and spurred, wearing cartridge belts and guns. The judge, tall and dignified in his black suit, beamed at her like a pleased conspirator. Tom Cantrell stood tall, gaunt, and unsmiling, at the far end of the fireplace. In his own half of the living room, Virginia noted.

The judge said: "Ginny, this is a great favor to us all."

"The fire," Virginia said, smiling, "looks so cheerful." The small boy stood there, solemnly regarding her. Virginia went to him and put her hand lightly on his shoulder. He moved away.

Smiling, the judge indicated the wide Axminster carpet on the dried-mud floor. "Even carpet."

"Missus Rogers brought this carpet from Maryland, for her new home," Virginia said. She kneeled down and ran her palm lightly over the bright colors. "A little of her far-away Maryland underfoot, in this wild country which seemed empty and dangerous to her." Virginia straightened soberly. "And it did take her man and her happiness."

Cantrell spoke coolly from his end of the fireplace. "Evidently you have no such fears."

"I was reared in New Mexico Territory," Virginia said quite as coolly. "I find it friendly . . . mostly."

The walnut organ was at her end of the long room. The judge brought a wall lamp as Virginia adjusted the stool. The silent Texans, she was thinking, were as formidable a group as she had ever seen. What were they doing here? Casually, without looking around, she said: "Eddy, don't you want to stand by me while I play?" When she sat down, the small silent boy sidled close.

"What shall I try first?" Virginia asked over her shoulder.

A lean Texan impulsively said: "You know 'Dixie', ma'am?"

Quiet fell as Virginia started to play. Then the rich baritone of the Texan named Ashley Hampton caught up the words. Others joined in. As the singing gained volume, Virginia noticed that all the Texans were unobtrusively shifting position behind her. They were gathering around Ashley Hampton, at her right. Standing together, the massed ardor of their voices lifted, wild and a little frightening. At the end, a fierce, challenging Rebel yell rang through the room.

Virginia looked up uncertainly at the red, grim face of Cantrell's man, Eagan, at the left side of the organ. Eagan had started to sing the great, moving marching song of the North: "The Battle Hymn of the Republic".

This should be amusing, Virginia thought uneasily as she caught it up with the organ. But the deep passions of the late war lurked in all these men. Eagan's singing grew in force. Cantrell's voice, back of her, joined in—and his men. There was little enthusiasm from the Texans now.

Virginia let them have their second verse—"I have seen Him in the watch fires of a hundred circling camps . . ."—and then she struck a discordant chord, and softly began to play and sing: "Should auld acquaintance be forgot. . . ."

With relief, she heard Cantrell join her. Did he sound a little amused? All the men sang, some of them sounding slightly sheepish, and passion drained from the room. At the end a Texan said pensively: "My mother used to sing 'Rock of Ages' to us kids."

Virginia saw the small boy at her elbow dip his head and close his eyes. "How about 'De Camptown Races'?" she said quickly, and started the merry tune. But the damage was done.

The boy was silently moving back behind the men. When Virginia looked around, he was slipping out into the dark patio. Small and alone. Her impulse was to follow. Then Virginia saw the stolid Eagan following the boy into the patio. She turned to the organ, feeling better.

Finally she swung around, smiling up at the half circle of rough men. They grinned back at her. Only Cantrell's dark face was unmoved.

"We're leaving in the morning," Cantrell said. "There are several things you and I should discuss, Miss Bratton."

"We can step outside. I'll get a shawl," Virginia said.

In her bedroom, from a drawer of the lowboy, she took her prized India shawl of filmy black cashmere, with exotic designs in silver and gold thread. Her glance stopped on Lee's photograph on top of the lowboy. All of Lee's bursting, youthful confidence grinned at her. Who would have thought, when this picture was made in Santa Fe, that she would go to her knees in a remote plaza of the territory, frantically wiping blood from Lee's ferociously beaten face? Or that Lee, lurching on weak legs in the kitchen of her rented house, washing caked blood from his features, would be so deathly quiet? Even the judge, watching from a chair, had seemed deeply troubled. They had never seen fury so tightly coiled, so silent in Lee.

Sober, troubled, Virginia was still thinking of Lee when the front door closed behind her and Cantrell. They walked out into the velvety starlight. Cantrell loomed beside her in his faded blue military blouse, open at the neck. His slow steps crunched; his spurs chinked softly. He sounded grudging when he spoke.

"I can't take the boy along. Will you keep him?"

"Of course."

The vastness of the empty country had closed about them. Coyotes clamored to the massed stars. Cantrell's voice sounded uncompromising. "Is your brother still planning to bring cattle and a crew on this ranch?"

Thinking again of his savage handling of Lee, Virginia said coldly: "What business is it of yours, Mister Cantrell? Have I asked what these Texans are doing here? Or where you are riding tomorrow?"

"No," Cantrell admitted.

"Half this ranch. . . ."

"Half is yours," he cut in dryly. "But I've had a sample of your brother. I don't want any more trouble with him."

"I don't want trouble," Virginia said.

They had strolled beyond the house, and now turned back and stopped. The stars, almost brilliant enough to read by, struck glints from the gold and silver threads in her shawl. Westward, the great bulk of the Lizard Butte lifted darkly. The thick walls of the house seemed to dominate the infinity of distance about them.

All this is mine, quickened in Virginia's thoughts. *My land! My home . . . half of it, anyway!* She could visualize it, wild, empty, lonely, with fierce Apaches lurking in the dark mountains to the south. That unfortunate bride from Maryland had feared all that stretched out, lonely and empty, in this night, and she had been wrong!

The rich promising future, as the judge had wisely said, was rooted in this immense new ranch. Every vibrant inch came alive as Virginia stood beside Cantrell's tall figure and thought about it. Cantrell's arms had been hard, ruthless when they had lifted her into the back of his wagon. She resented him. But he was strong enough, ruthless enough, to take this wild land and make it his own. She sensed it now.

"This new ranch is not wanted here," Cantrell's even voice said. "I believe I was followed to Texas. My men were killed, my herd was taken, my partner was murdered while I was gone. The Apaches can't be trusted. Being a woman won't make you safe."

"I will not sell or leave," Virginia said quietly.

Laughing voices lifted at the back of the house—men heading toward the bunkhouse. "I'm beginning to believe you," Cantrell said. He sounded bitter.

In silence they returned to the house. Firelight still danced across the long, empty living room. *Doña* Sarina waited watchfully in the bedroom doorway. They stopped in front of the fireplace. Cantrell's sober gaze touched her black hair, gay pink basque, and black skirt. The light wavered across his dark, big-boned face as he looked back into the fireplace. Reverie held him.

"Good night," he said abruptly. His spurs chinked across the carpet. His own bedroom door closed behind him.

A housewifely thought quirked humor on Virginia's mouth. He had forgotten that lamps must be put out. Man-like, he had left it to the woman. "Sarina," Virginia said, "we'll put out the lamps."

In the morning, horses were outside her window, trampling, bucking as they unkinked in the first run from the corral. Virginia sat up in bed, pushing back her hair, listening.

Cantrell and his men were leaving. The massed drumming of hoofs swept by her open window and pounded into distance. She wondered again where they were going. Cantrell had no cattle, no money, yet he was riding away with bold, dangerous men.

IX

At Matthew Fallon's ranch on the Gallinas, a note of wild defiance screamed in the bugling challenge of the golden horse as Lee Bratton walked to the corral bars. Matthew Fallon's crippled hand tightened in his coat pocket as sullen moroseness vanished from Lee's bruised face. Challenge leaped visibly in Lee.

"Arabian in him," Lee said. A smiling, dreamy look caught him as the powerful, fleet-looking horse wheeled into a run that half circled the big corral, and faced them again. Sunlight gleamed on the burnished golden coat and the snowy mane and tail. Another defiant bugle challenged them.

Casually Fallon asked: "Ever see a finer horse?"

"Comanche-stole, out of Texas," Lee guessed, without taking his eyes off the horse.

"No brand on him," Fallon said indifferently.

"He was stole," said Lee, faintly contemptuous. "Like that horse Cantrell took from you."

Fallon's smile whitened at the corners. "I bought that roan gelding in good faith. When Cantrell claimed him, I didn't argue."

"That's not the way Cantrell's men told it in the Upper Frío Plaza." A jeer came into Lee's tone. "They were laughing over how Cantrell made the fellow with the crooked hand hop on another horse and get going."

The anger that tore Fallon in a great tide made him a little sick. His twisted, useless hand mocked before saloon drunks, and by this swaggering young hothead, who stood two inches taller than Matthew Fallon, both his hands strong and whole. All the rest of him was wild and irresponsible as the big golden brute in the corral, but how Cantrell had mauled Lee's face.

Breathing softly, Fallon looked vindictively at the mashed-looking nose, the dark bruises still puffy on Lee's cheek bones. But his warning was casual: "Two men who tried to ride this horse were half killed."

Lee took the bait. "They didn't know their business. I can ride any horse."

"You're not over the beating Cantrell gave you," Fallon said maliciously.

Lee's glower showed memory of the fight still clawing, white-hot and deep. *He's powder, ready to blow,* Fallon decided with satisfaction. "Make the ride," he suggested, "and we'll trade. You're heading to Las Vegas to hire a crew and buy cattle and horses. Why go there? Everything you need is here."

"Comanche-stole out of Texas. Gun jumpers on the dodge."

Lee was contemptuous.

"The Comanches have traded cattle and horses in New Mexico for fifty years," Fallon said. "All I've done is put the trade on a business-like basis."

"Wish I had a dollar for every Mexican Comanche trader you've crowded out, had shot, or frightened off," Lee said. "You think the Mexicans don't talk behind their hands about you? Anybody gets in your way, you take care of him."

"I can't stop talk," Fallon said, shrugging. "I'm a trader, making money for myself and the men who trade with me. I'll sell you more cattle and horses for your money than you'll get anywhere else. And you can hire a crew here cheaper."

Lee's gaze was still on the horse in the corral. A slow grin of anticipation spread on his bruised face. "He's a beauty," he said, drawing a breath. "I'll get my saddle."

Lee had the brash look of youth, lean-hipped and confident as he carried saddle, bridle, and rope into the corral. The big yellow horse watched him. *Two wild ones!* Matthew Fallon thought.

Extra men Fallon had brought in to this home ranch on the Gallinas were drifting to the corral. They watched silently as Lee shook out his rope and moved forward. The big yellow-gold horse stood with head high, immovable, even when the loop snaked over his neck. It struck Fallon that the horse had a humanly intelligent look of waiting. Intently he watched Lee swiftly bridle and saddle the horse without using blindfold, foot rope, or snubbing post.

Lee removed the rope. His sinewy body flipped into the saddle. Suddenly without warning, the horse tried to kill. A snake-like lunge whipped Lee's body violently before his feet were set in the stirrups. A bugling, defiant scream filled the corral as the big horse flung up and back on hind legs, intending plainly to hurtle over backward and crash down on the rider.

Fallon's crippled hand strained in his coat pocket as the great golden horse went straight up on its hind legs, its mouth open, its nostrils red and wide, its snowy mane and tail streaming in the sunlight.

Lee had mounted without a quirt. Instead of trying to twist off to safety, Lee yelled with joyous exuberance. Riding the almost perpendicular horse, in the instant before hurtling over backward, Lee struck his clenched fist tremendously behind the horse's ears—and struck again, almost too fast to follow.

Later, the men around Fallon argued that the horse must have changed his mind. No man could strike that hard with a bare fist. But the horse went forward again, leaping, twisting in the air before landing on stiff legs with a bone-snapping jar. Instantly it was in the air again in another violent whirl. Lee swayed dangerously and barely stayed on. The horse lunged across the corral in bone-jarring pitches, ending in another whirl. Then a tremendous pitch, a dizzying swapping of ends as he soared up again.

Lee had stopped smiling. His lithe body whipped and snapped. Blood started from his nose. His hat dropped off. His black hair fell over his eyes. A grim, fierce exaltation filled him.

Lee had left the corral gate open. He yelled suddenly and spurred for the first time. The horse bucked toward the gate and bolted out of the corral, across the ranch yard toward open range.

An eighth of a mile out the wild, skimming run whirled off another spasm of bucking. Then the run took up again, toward the nearest low hills, and vanished from sight.

"Somebody better ride after him," a man near Fallon warned. "That devil won't stop till the saddle's empty. He'll scrape Bratton off in the brush, or throw him."

"Two of you go," Fallon ordered. He wished now he hadn't allowed this. Only a sound, strong Lee Bratton, hating Cantrell, was of use to him.

Two men spurred off toward the hills and disappeared. Fallon left the corrals and entered his square-built stone house. It was a small house, indifferently furnished. He was usually away, moving over the vast, empty land.

Alone, Fallon tossed his brown straw sombrero on a hide chair and drew the claw-like right hand from his coat pocket. He wore suits, always, so a coat pocket could conceal this derisive affliction. But in the Upper Frío Plaza Cantrell's men had laughed about this hand. Lee Bratton had laughed, too. Fallon lit a cigar and paced the floor, thinking about it in shame and fury.

He was standing in the back doorway of the house almost an hour later, irritably smoking a second cigar, when one of the men shouted from the bunkhouse steps and pointed. Lee Bratton had vanished among the low hills to the south. He was returning from the west. The big yellow horse was still running, its white mane and tail streaming.

The horse's golden coat was flecked with gray foam. Its nostrils flared widely. Lee ran the horse through the open gate of the corral, pulled up, and swung down. And staggered.

"Help him!" Fallon ordered sharply.

Lee's harsh, strained voice came back: "Keep away!"

Lee jerked the latigos free, hauled off the saddle and bridle, and turned to the gate with lurching steps. Like a man half dead, Fallon thought. Lee had bled from the nose and mouth, and smeared the blood with the back of a hand. He stumbled through the open gate on stiff, numb-looking legs, and turned and looked at the horse. Lee's drawn, smeared face was grinning when Fallon joined him.

"Come to the house and have a drink," Fallon said.

The look Lee turned on him was hot and exultant. "I'll ride Cantrell like this!" he said fiercely.

When the two of them were alone in the house, Fallon watched the blazing emotion drive Lee in jerky strides over the wide, rough-sawed planks of the parlor floor. Lee held a second drink of whiskey, forgotten for the moment. Standing by the table, Fallon held his own untasted whiskey and spoke casually.

"You can have the horse cheap. But what about cattle and other horses you'll need? And a crew?"

"Comanche-stole cattle."

Calmly logical, Fallon said: "You're hot to buy a Comanche-traded horse. What's the difference in buying cattle, too?"

Lee swung around at the end of the room. Blood, started by the furious ride, was oozing again from his smashed nose. He yanked a blue bandana from his hip pocket, patted his nose, and malignantly regarded the cloth.

Coolly Fallon prodded; "You'll need good men when you get home, or you'll jump to Cantrell's orders. He'll be at you again."

"When I go on that ranch with my herd and a crew," Lee said in a low voice, "Cantrell will jump."

"You'd better have a crew that Cantrell can't bluff. Men like I've got outside," Fallon said. He watched Lee as Lee considered the proposition. Idly he suggested: "If something should happen to Cantrell, you'd end up with all that big ranch."

Lee nodded. "Old Barnaby Polk is lawyer enough to see to that."

"You can have the horse. I'll sell you a mixed herd at five dollars a head. You'll never buy that cheap again."

Lee's grin came thin and jeering. "After Cantrell made you hop off a horse, you'd lose money to get your own gunmen on Cantrell's ranch, inside his guard."

"I'm a businessman," Fallon said. "More cattle are coming in from the plains than I can use right now. I need cash money. You've got cash, I suppose?"

"I've got authority to draft against my own money in Santa

Fe, which Barnaby Polk holds in trust."

"That's more than good. How many men would you need?"

Lee calculated for a moment. "Cantrell lost half his men coming from Texas. He has four men left. No money, no cattle. He'll probably fire one or two of the men he has. With five or six men, I can run him off the ranch."

"I'll give you bills of sale for range delivery," Fallon said. "You can take men from here and meet the cattle coming in from the plains. Cull them as close as you like. After that, you're on your own . . . if you think you can handle Cantrell."

"Handle him? I'll. . . ." Lee drew a breath and drained his whiskey glass. "I guess there's no difference between the horse and your cattle," he conceded. "Might as well get all I can for my money."

"Other men have," Fallon said.

X

The small cañon in the Horse Hills where Tom Cantrell stood sipping hot coffee from a tin cup was a hundred and twenty-five miles north of the Frío. His men and the Texans had scattered out when they left the ranch. On a front more than a hundred miles wide they had moved north. Rendezvous was in this isolated cañon where a shallow little stream roiled out of the high hills, and the white limestone cliffs were topped by pines and rugged cedars that seemed to brush the blue sky. Half an hour ago the last of the Texans had ridden in. All the Texans, Tom noted, were more sober than when they had left the ranch.

"We'll decide here," Tom said deliberately.

His saddle and his leather saddlebags were on the ground near the small campfire. He left the tin cup by the saddle and returned with two small leather-bound tally books and two tin cylinders with waterproof caps.

The Texans were watching him closely. Tom ran a look over

them. "I've waited, because I can't use any man who'll get faint-hearted and back out. Once this starts, the country will be boiling. Strangers can run. I have a ranch to hold. Only men who'll take orders and stay to the end will do."

Ashley Hampton, the tall Texan with yellow hair and mustache, drawled quietly: "Are you man enough to do what you think you can do?"

Tom eyed the rangy figure in leather shirt, with long, holstered revolvers. Hampton evidently had been an officer in the war, although he had not said. By tacit consent, Hampton seemed to speak for the other five Texans. Tom said: "I'm man enough to keep going until I'm stopped. I wanted you men to see what's in the country. When everyone compares tallies of cattle and brands sighted, we'll all have an idea what's between here and Fort Ross."

"I've seen enough," said Hampton.

"These tin cases," Tom told them all, "hold powers of attorney I gathered in Texas. These tally books have brands and earmarks of stock run off by the Comanches. And the number of cattle and horses that different ranches have lost. Also dates of loss, and other sworn information. I'm not a lawyer, but in Texas I spoke with lawyers. I'm told that the right to recover these brands will stand in Texas or territorial courts."

Ashley Hampton was rolling a smoke. His silent nod approved.

"But any man," Tom said, "who tries to replevin stolen stock in this territory will find politics and hostility. Law will tie him up hopelessly. There's only one quick, certain way . . . take the stolen cattle where found on free range, and let so-called owners try to prove legal purchase from the rightful owners."

"Might I see one of those tally books?" Hampton inquired.

Tom handed him one. An ember popped in the small fire as Hampton scanned the pages of the tally book. "Many of these brands I know. And the losses in cattle and blood their owners have suffered." He looked up at Tom. "What do we get out of it?"

"What I offered men in Texas . . . half of all you help recover. Settle with the Texas owners yourselves. Men in Texas who can't come will accept a third of anything recovered, remitted when possible."

"Lucky to get it," Hampton murmured.

"Do you know of any other men on the way from Texas?"

"No, suh."

"We're not many," Tom said. "When we take the first cattle, men will rise against us. They'll know that if they stop us, they'll be able to stop other tries at their illegal stock. This is the time to wait for more help, or back out. If we start, we can't stop."

Ashley Hampton handed back the leather-bound book. "Might be a good idea to tally up now and see what the country holds."

The men drew small tally books from their pockets and began to call off brands of cattle and horses they had sighted in the wide sweep north. Tom checked against the brands he had brought from Texas, giving attention to ear-marks.

Now and then a man would exclaim, "I know that 'un!" Other remarks burst out: "Him an' his oldest boy was kilt!" "Them folks got burnt out!" "I rode to their place nex' day. They was a bloody mess, womenfolks still a-cryin' " Once—quietly, fiercely—a Texan exclaimed: "Them cattle is mine! They got my cousin, damn' 'em! 'Most twenty Comanches jumped the place!"

Ashley Hampton spoke for them soberly. "We will ride with you." He looked around at the other Texans, was satisfied, and drawled: "All the way."

They camped in the cañon that night, and rode at dawn, each man leading an extra horse he had brought. And as they emerged from the mouth of the cañon, the new sun burst up in the east. Southwest, the distant Secundos lifted under their placid white cloud caps.

Hampton, riding beside Tom, looked long and silently. Finally he spoke in a somber drawl: "Too fair a land to fatten on the blood of Texas."

And the next day, before noon, the sudden screaming of a bullet made Tom duck in the saddle. The hidden gun was to his right, in brush along the crest of this long, broken slope, which dropped into a wide, grassy draw.

Tom had just turned three lanky steers down the slope toward a small bunch of cattle that one of the Texans was holding. The steers bolted as the slapping gun report echoed. Tom slashed his horse with the rein ends, and raked his spurs. He saw the Texan grabbing for the carbine under his leg.

Tom put his plunging horse straight across the broken slope. Another bullet whipped by his neck. Too close! Only this spurred, furious race across the open slope held any safety. The Texan was riding full gallop down the draw. Now they were hunted men! Tom rode for a rain-gouged gully in the slope ahead. He put his horse recklessly over the gully bank, plunging down over eroded, yielding earth into the rough gully bottom. He spurred and slashed up the steep gully over rocks and wind-blown tumbleweeds. He wondered how many guns were waiting in the brush above.

Carbine in hand, leaning low in the saddle, Tom rode a furi-ous weaving charge through green junipers and branched cholla cactus along the crest of the wide, grassy draw. In the brush ahead an indistinct figure move convulsively on the ground. Tom reined in hard and tossed the reins to the ground as he jumped off.

He landed running, whipping up the carbine to shoot, and a shrill, warning whistle froze his finger on the trigger. Eagan's red face came up from the ground, yelling: "Don't shoot, Lieut'n't!"

Eagan was glowering at a stranger in leather chaps and brown vest who sprawled face down on the ground, arms stretched out. A carbine and revolver had been kicked away. Empty brass shells marked where the man had been shooting down into the draw.

"Eagan," Tom said, breathing hard, "you pop up in the damnedest places. You're supposed to be miles away."

"I was scouting around. When this fellow started shooting, he forgot to look back."

"You were riding flank on me, ready for trouble," Tom said. He ordered the stranger: "Sit up!"

The man pushed himself up and scowled malevolently. Eagan regarded him with hostility. "He grabbed for his holster. I had to bust him with my gun barrel."

The stranger wiped blood off his mouth with the back of his hand. The Texan's horse burst through the brush to them.

Tom called: "His horse is over there, tied to a juniper! Have a look at it." And to the prisoner: "What's your story?"

The man mumbled: "I ride for Ben Poole. Orders is to shoot rustlers."

"How many men ride for Poole?"

"Three."

The Texan shouted: "He's riding Cross D brand, vented!"

"Stand up," Tom said to the prisoner. On the short side, the man stood warily. Tom studied him. "This Ben Poole lives in that cañon some miles east of here, doesn't he?"

"Uhn-huh."

"Get going. Walking."

The man caught up his black hat and started. He looked back once, apprehensively. His steps lengthened out along the crest of the draw and he vanished in the brush. The lanky Texan rode back, leading a saddled horse.

"Take that horse," Tom said, "and shove the gather we made on to the main bunch. Tell Ashley Hampton that Eagan and I are taking the man's guns and saddle to his boss."

"Ain't that asking to get shot?" the Texan drawled.

"We'll risk it."

The Texan shrugged, and moments later departed with the horse. Eagan balanced the extra saddle and bridle before him on his horse. Tom took the man's carbine and revolver. They rode east, quartering knife ridges and gashed arroyos. Eagan had fallen into a morose mood. Finally he said: "All this don't look like you mean to go back in the Army."

"Did I ever say I would?"

"I figured you would."

"Why don't you pull out now for Fort Ross and enlist again?" Tom suggested.

Eagan considered it. "I'll stay around for the trouble," he muttered finally.

Tom's faint smile was understanding. Army had been home and family. Eagan was lonely for the reassuring routine, reveille to taps, and all the hours between fenced in with orders and custom. There were no bold, beckoning dreams in Eagan. But Eagan would stay. He was stubborn.

Miles to the east, they struck the wide, shallow cañon and rode along the brink of the immense trough. Glistening water in the cañon bottom wandered through white sands and gravels of the flood channel. Willows and *chamiso* thickets grew along the water.

"Good winter shelter down there," Tom commented.

Eagan was looking ahead, where two corrals were taking shape in the sun-flooded cañon. The ranch house, still invisible, would be among the tall cottonwoods that lifted between the corrals and the small stream. "This is risky," said Eagan dubiously.

"All of this is risky," Tom reminded him. "If we ever run from them, we'll never have a chance. I want to see if this Ben Poole bought his cattle and horses from Fallon."

Eagan kept silent as they followed the steep pitch of a crude wagon trail down the side of the cañon. The wheel ruts led them through bunch grass and low yucca clumps to the corrals. "Cheap-jack outfit!" Eagan said with distaste.

"Trying for a quick profit with cheap Comanche-raided cattle," Tom guessed, looking about.

The two sagging corrals, holding seven horses, had been carelessly constructed of cedar and juniper stobs thrust into trenches, dirt tramped around the bottoms, green cowhide strips sloppily woven among the tops. Three open-front sheds were as carelessly built of unplastered adobe bricks. A long, low adobe shack squatted under the first towering cottonwoods. The back door was a soiled bull hide, nailed at the top. Tin cans and trash had been tossed out and left scattered on the ground. The man who shouldered out past the bull hide was solid and untidy.

"Howdy?" Tom called and got no reply. The flat cheeks and broad nose of the staring man were lined with purple veins. Under his dark mustache he slowly munched tobacco as Tom rode to him.

"I'm looking for Ben Poole," Tom said.

"You got him."

"I'm Cantrell, from the Frío country."

Poole spat a thin jet to one side. "Heerd of you," he said with more interest. "Startin' a big ranch, ain't you?" He eyed the saddle balanced in front of Eagan. "Lost a hoss?"

Tom placed his hands on the saddle horn, by the extra carbine hanging there from a leather thong. "The saddle belongs to one of your men. Give it to him, Eagan."

Poole looked surprised as he swung the saddle to the ground. "What happened?"

"Your man was riding a vented Cross D horse, Mister Poole. Where did you get the horse?"

Poole's flat thumb hooked under a fraying suspender strap. "That's my business. What's it to you?"

"You're aware, I suppose, that the horse's owner was John Kent, in Texas."

"Mebbe."

"Kent never sold any horses. He lost stock twice in Comanche raids."

"That ain't my business."

"It's my business, Mister Poole. I hold Kent's power of attorney to recover any stock he's lost. You have your saddle and bridle. These guns belong to your man. He's walking in. I've taken the horse."

Poole's mouth had loosened under the tobacco-stained mustache. His temper flared. "What the hell is this? Comin' on a man's land, snatchin' his hoss!"

"You're using open range," Tom reminded him.

"My brand's on that hoss!"

"Where's your bill of sale from John Kent in Texas?"

"Damn the bill of sale! I ain't no hoss thief!"

"A horse thief," Tom said coolly, "risks a bullet. You let Indians steal for you. Going to tell where you bought that horse?"

Poole's callused thumb had clamped hard on his suspender strap. His eyes were hating. "I ain't tellin' nothin'. I'm through talkin'!"

Tom gave him a dark look. "I'm not through. Take your man's guns!" Poole came forward and caught the carbine and revolver Tom handed down. Tom ran the reins through his hand and gave the man another dark look. "Poole, you were jobbed by the man who sold you horses and cattle."

"Nev' mind."

"It's your worry. I'm taking about two hundred head of your cattle, too. They were raided out of Texas."

"Tryin' to take my cattle, too?" burst from Poole. It had a strangled sound.

"I've taken them," Tom said coldly. "After this, be careful what you buy."

Half sobbing his rage, Poole jumped back. "No slicker with a long rope runs a whizzer on me!" His thick yell lifted: "Stop 'em boys! Only two here!" Poole was jacking the carbine action and jerking up the muzzle.

Tom spun his horse as Poole pulled the trigger. The carbine did not fire. The plunging horse smashed into carbine and man. Poole was slammed into the bull hide, and helplessly past it into the interior. The spin of Tom's horse brushed the doorway. His left stirrup struck the rotten adobe bricks beside the door frame and dragged off loose bits as the horse lunged along the house wall. As Tom reined around the end of the long shack, his quick look noted no window at this end, where guns could reach after them from shelter.

Eagan was close behind as they raced into dappled shade under the great cottonwoods, ducking low branches. The spiteful report of a carbine reached after them. More guns opened up. A storm-toppled cottonwood loomed across Tom's path. Massed roots bulked at one end; the tangle of dead branches started a few feet away. Tom rode at the short space of clear trunk. He yelled and lifted his horse over.

Eagan's hoarse yell was audible behind. The booming strike of a hoof on the tree made Tom look back. Eagan's horse was coming down in a half stumble on the sandy soil. Eagan hauled its head up and the horse recovered stride.

The dangle of dead cottonwood top was a screen of sorts

behind them as they raced out of the trees into glaring sunlight. Half a mile down the cañon, Tom pulled up and looked back. He was regretful when Eagan halted by him. "I hate to run horses like this."

Eagan's broad face was a deep, sweating red. "Them horses in the corrals were sure sign more men were in the house," Eagan said. "We almost got kilt there."

Tom grinned. "The other end of the house had no window, Eagan. Ben Poole was blocking the doorway. I had an idea that when he heard about his cattle, he'd not stop to see whether the shells had been taken out of the guns I handed him."

"We could have throwed revolvers on him when the talking started," Eagan grumbled.

"And had the men inside slipping around the ends of the house, boxing us," Tom said dryly. "I had my talk with Poole. Let's get out of this cañon."

They found a difficult way up the eroded steeps of the cañon and, from the rim, looked back. Horses had hurriedly been saddled at Poole's place. Men were riding out of the cañon on the opposite side.

"After help," Eagan guessed. "They'll have the country boiling."

"We expected it," Tom reminded him. "It will be days before enough men get together to trouble us."

"And then what?" Eagan said under his breath.

Tom watched the distant riders climbing the opposite side of the cañon. Some of the deep, persisting smolder returned to his face. He said slowly: "Then you'll wish you were back in the Army, Eagan. And every man who owns stolen Texas stock will begin to know I'm in the Frío country to stay."

XI

Virginia Bratton was sewing buttons on a blouse when Barnaby Polk came to the open door of her bedroom. Virginia looked up from her rocking chair, smiling at his tall, shirt-sleeved figure with jaunty red suspenders across the lanky shoulders.

"Visitors are approaching," the judge said.

"Is it Lee?" Virginia asked quickly.

"A young lady is coming, escorted by three soldiers," said the judge. His glance grew quizzical. "Still worrying about Lee?"

"How can I help it?" Virginia dropped the blouse and thimble into the sewing basket beside her chair. She stood up, voicing the small fear that never quite left her these days: "Suppose Lee meets Cantrell and his men?"

"Lee went to Las Vegas to buy cattle," the judge said. "And where is Tom Cantrell? He's been gone over a week now, with all those armed men. Why not let Cantrell manage his half of the ranch as he pleases? You ordered him to, emphatically. Remember?"

With shrewd logic, the judge usually could deflate her, Virginia thought ruefully as she walked outside, in front of the house. With pleasure she saw that a corporal and two troopers from Fort Ross were escorting Isabel Alcorn, the major's daughter. She had met Isabel at the fort, and called a warm greeting. Isabel's reply was gay.

A trooper swung off and held Isabel's horse. The corporal jumped to give Isabel a hand down. Tall, smiling, Isabel stripped off her leather riding gloves and surveyed the massive adobe house. Her hat was white felt, her jacket soft doeskin; she was booted, with a riding crop tucked under her arm.

"The house is larger than I thought," Isabel said, approving. "Where is Tom Cantrell?"

"Gone over a week now, with his men," Virginia said, and she saw disappointment appear visibly on Isabel's face.

"Where did Tom go?"

"He didn't say," Virginia said. "Tea water is hot. And if you haven't eaten. . . ."

"Tea will be nice," Isabel said politely.

Barnaby Polk was in the long living room, wearing his digni-fied black coat now. His blue, shrewd eyes twinkled at Isabel. "An old man hardly deserves two such delightful young ladies all to himself," said the judge gallantly. "You will be with us some time, I hope, Miss Alcorn?"

"Only until tomorrow," Isabel said. She was thoroughly curi-ous as she glanced about the big room.

Doña Sarina, plump and beaming in a gaudily flowered apron, brought tea and little spiced cookies called *biscochitos* on a tray covered with bright, hand-hammered tin. The judge glanced at the teacups with a droll lack of enthusiasm. He murmured an excuse and unfolded from his chair.

Isabel's thoughtful glance followed his tall, gray-haired figure through the patio doorway. "Does Mister Polk live here, too?"

"I wish he did," Virginia said, pouring tea. "His old friend, Judge Augustus Andrews, is holding court in Mesilla, and will join him here for a few days, before they go to Santa Fe together." She handed a cup and saucer to Isabel and urged: "Can't you stay longer?"

Isabel shook her head. "I'll use Tom's room tonight, and start back to the fort in the morning."

Remembering Cantrell's Spartan room she had viewed through his open doorway, Virginia said without thinking: "His bunk is hard and uncomfortable. I have a feather mattress."

Isabel's quick glance probed such intimate knowledge of Tom Cantrell's room. "Tom's bunk will do," she said coolly.

You should see how the man acts! Virginia thought angrily. And during the afternoon, with mixed feelings, she watched Isabel

Alcorn calmly and coolly assume command of Cantrell's part of the house.

The judge's dry tones penetrated Virginia's thoughts. "For the third time, Ginny, the sunset is colorful."

"Isn't it?" said Virginia hastily. She looked west at the blaze of crimson above the bold Lizard Butte. "I was thinking what it would be like if Cantrell brought her here as his wife," Virginia confessed.

"The possibility," said the judge, "had not occurred to me." His—"*Hm-m-m.*"— had a judicial sound. "Two women in the same house. Each owning half," the judge mused. Reflective humor grew in his eyes.

"Isabel Alcorn," said Virginia, frowning, "is very nice, I'm sure. But it's plain already she'll always have her own way."

"A court of law," said the judge gravely, "would have difficulty with such a case. There was a man named Solomon. . . ." The judge cleared his throat. "For my client, Ginny, I would plead, *exitus acta probat*, the outcome justifies the deeds."

"It is not amusing," Virginia said. "This is my home. Everything I have is here now. You don't understand."

"An unregenerate old sinner," said the judge, "could muse upon the possibilities. Especially upon our friend Cantrell, caught in the crossfire."

"The man is a business partner, not a friend."

"An unfortunate figure of speech," said the judge. His veined hand dropped to her shoulder. "Ginny," he said quietly, "old sinners were young once. They do understand, even if they seem calloused."

"You were never calloused, and never a sinner, old or young," said Virginia. She covered his gnarled hand with her hand.

"Some of that could be debated," said the judge. "However, Ginny, I want you to be happy in this home I advised you to

139

buy. Suppose, before worrying, we wait for the worst to happen?"

"In other words, be sensible," Virginia said. She remembered Cantrell's warning: *Dead man's shoes on her feet.* She hadn't been afraid. Now, smiling, she looked up and nodded. The judge's twinkling blue eyes looked back with approval.

And the next morning, with detached composure, Virginia was able to watch Isabel Alcorn impatiently lingering for some sign of Tom Cantrell's return. Finally, in the long living room, Isabel held out a brown sealed envelope.

"Will you give this to Tom when he returns?"

"Of course." Virginia took the envelope, thinking of the letter this disappointed girl must have penned in Cantrell's silent room last night.

"It is a copy of an Army report, with information about the death of Tom's former partner," Isabel said.

"Oh!" Suddenly the brown envelope was important. Virginia moistened her lips, remembering her flashes of uneasiness that Lee might be a target for the same guns that had murdered Steven Rogers. *Dead man's shoes on her feet. On Lee's feet, too.* She asked: "Does the Army know who killed Rogers?"

"The Army isn't interested," Isabel said, drawing on her riding gloves. "But this report may give Tom some ideas." Isabel tapped the riding crop on her long skirt. "This place is not safe. Certainly not for you. And Tom, I believe, is in danger. He'll come back into the Army, eventually, of course. It's in his blood. He doesn't. . . ." Isabel's glance ran over Virginia. "Tom doesn't belong with cattle."

"I wouldn't know," Virginia said evenly, and she thought: *Do you really know him? I wonder.*

She stood silently out back with the judge, watching Isabel and her escort canter off. She knew now Isabel's reluctance to leave another woman in this house to greet Cantrell's return.

Isabel so obviously disapproved of the way Cantrell was forced to share his home.

Barnaby Polk gazed placidly after the riders. "She will be at Fort Ross," the judge mused. "You will be here. *Facia non verba.*"

"What is that?" Virginia asked absently.

"Deeds, not words," said the judge reflectively.

During an afternoon after Lee Bratton had departed from the Gallinas Ranch with a tough new crew, to meet and select his herd, Matthew Fallon indulged in some hours of complacent drinking. It was a thing he seldom allowed himself to do. Whiskey stripped away intelligence and bared weaknesses to the world. He gave brusque orders first to the three men left on the ranch. He was not to be disturbed until the next morning. Then he locked the front and back doors of the stone house.

Sitting alone in the quiet parlor, in his undershirt, Fallon sipped whiskey from a water glass. Now and then he lit a fresh cigar. His complacency grew. Heady satisfaction mounted when he thought of Lee Bratton's arrival at Cantrell's ranch, backed with that hard, armed crew.

Late in the afternoon, Fallon lifted the twisted claw of a hand from his lap and regarded it solemnly. His sudden giggle came from whiskey, he knew, and did not mind. He wanted to feel like this. There was nothing, he knew disdainfully, that Matthew Fallon could not do with cool planning. Even Cantrell, in the distant Frío country, was not really a threat, merely a bumbling young ex-cavalry officer, recklessly bent on being a cowman in the wildest part of the territory. After Cantrell was swept aside, Matthew Fallon would stand astride all this vast, wild country, without opposition. Fallon lit a fresh cigar and fell to musing about the small boy who had run away from the Apaches.

The roan horse that Cantrell had claimed had come from a sub-chief named Senya, who had been hunting the boy. The

Apache had produced the roan readily, asking only that Fallon and his men watch for the boy, and return him if possible. Finding and returning the boy to the Apaches would have been an immense stroke of luck. Senya, with every fighting buck under him, would have been in Matthew Fallon's debt. Senya had been filled with shame that his adopted son, cherished proudly, had run away.

Fallon reached to the table at his elbow and filled the glass again, slopping whiskey over the side. Indians were simple savages. They risked their useless lives raiding cattle and horses, and then traded the loot for trinkets. They murdered and tortured like the heartless brutes they were. Then, child-like, they adopted a white boy and heaped great heart and pride on him. An intelligent man could use them as he wished. If the boy had been found and returned, Senya and his bucks would be available now to use against Cantrell, and no one in the territory would suspect Matthew Fallon's part in a bloody Apache raid on Cantrell's ranch.

Fallon giggled again at the thought and gulped from the glass. His spasm of coughing spilled whiskey over his undershirt. The claw of a right hand absently rubbed the wet cloth as Fallon sat musing on how he would handle the Bratton girl and her brother after Cantrell was out of the way. When he reached again for the whiskey bottle, he realized groggily that the room was dark.

He got to his feet with an effort, and staggered and fell to the floor, losing the glass. Some small intelligent part of his brain mocked that he was gutter drunk. A gentleman got to his bed, if possible. Carefully, slowly, with tremendous concentration, Fallon stood up. Holding to the glimmer of reason, he groped and staggered across the dark room, and into his bedroom. When he came against the edge of the iron bed, he fell heavily on it, face down, satisfied.

In the morning, a fist, hammering on the back door, made him painfully open his eyes. The first gray cheerless dawn hung outside the bedroom window. The urgent hammering on the back door continued. Matthew Fallon's name was loudly called. Mumbling, Fallon stiffly got off the bed. He groaned with the first lurching step. Pain stabbed his skull. A foul taste was in his mouth. His nerves were raw as he made his way to the locked back door and demanded: "What's wrong?"

The voice outside was furious. "I'm Ben Poole! Rode since yesterday to get here! A damned thief named Cantrell, from the Frío country, run off my cattle! Said they was stole in Texas an' ain't mine! You sold 'em, Fallon! What about it?"

"Wait until I get dressed."

Swearing under his breath, Fallon walked unsteadily into the parlor. The bottle beside the table lamp still held some whiskey. He drank from the bottle. It helped a little. He'd slept in shoes and pants, but he never appeared before other men without a coat pocket where his right hand could stay, out of sight. Fully awake, nerves jumpy, Fallon stepped into the bedroom and pulled on a shirt and coat.

The dawn was brighter when he emerged from the back door, his hand in the coat pocket. Ben Poole's solid, untidy figure stood by a sagging, half-dead horse. Poole was vehemently talking to the three men from the bunkhouse. In sullen rage at the thought of Cantrell, Fallon walked to the group.

"What happened?" he brusquely asked Ben Poole.

Purple veins on Poole's flat cheeks and large nose looked swollen. He was a furious, almost incoherent man despite the punishing ride he had made. Presently Fallon cut rudely into the torrent of words.

"Three other men in your house? And Cantrell rode up with only one man? And told you he was taking cattle and horses from you, and rode away safely?"

"The damn' gun wouldn't fire! Might 'a' been twenty more men waitin' out of sight," Poole said resentfully.

"You don't even know how many men Cantrell had," Fallon said disgustedly.

"He had enough to feel damn' certain of hisself! An' you ain't out of it, Fallon. He knowed who them cattle belonged to in Texas. Kept tryin' to find out where I bought 'em."

"Did you tell him?"

"Told him nothin'. But if he keeps pickin' up Texas cattle, he'll gut a strip of the range from my place to the Frío. Ain't there no way to get the law on him?"

"What law?" Fallon asked in surly scorn.

Ben Poole's heavy cheek muscles were bunching under dark stubble as he chewed tobacco hard. He spat forcibly. "Small folks like me ain't got the men to fight when we're stole out of pocket. We bought from you. Do we get help?"

Raw resentment jumped with the pain in Fallon's head. He hated this flat-faced Ben Poole for the dawn commotion he had made, and hated Cantrell worse. Cantrell was on the loose now, undoubtedly making a sweep back to his ranch. South toward the Frío country from Poole's place, Cantrell would probably cross Largo Cañon, where some of Fallon's own cattle were held.

"Cantrell lost his Texas herd, so he's stealing from honest men," Fallon managed to say coolly. "If he gets by with this, he'll be back again. Nothing to do but smash him quick. Drive him back to his new ranch, and run him off it and out of the country."

"It'll be a sweet day," Ben Poole growled.

"Cantrell only had four men and himself the other day," Fallon recalled.

"Four?" Poole repeated unbelievingly.

"He may have picked up another man or two. I have three

men at Largo Cañon. We might head him off there. We'll scatter out," Fallon decided, "and gather up help on the way to Largo Cañon. Where are your men?"

"Went for help."

"Go back by your place and see what help is there. We'll eat and get ready."

One of Fallon's men said: "What about the crew that went with young Bratton?"

"They'll be busy."

He had been thinking about Lee Bratton. As he walked back to the house, Fallon decided to let that affair stand. It was plain now what would happen if young Bratton got back to the ranch with the cattle he had bought, and Cantrell managed to get back there safely about the same time. Fallon even managed to find a thin smile. One way or another, Cantrell's time was running fast out.

XII

The deep-toned report of the sunset gun had rolled majestically across the earth-built structures that were Fort Ross. The high, streaming flag had been run down from the white pole on the sun-baked parade ground. Guard mount and bugle-laced retreat had ended the orderly activities of another day when Isabel Alcorn and her escort returned from Tom Cantrell's ranch.

Major Alcorn had paused at the front door of his quarters to wipe the sweatband of his gilt-corded black hat. His final, critical glance about the quadrangle sighted Isabel on her side-saddle. With warming anticipation, Alcorn walked slowly out to the hitch rack and watched Isabel, followed by the corporal, put her horse into a final canter across the deserted parade.

As he waited, Alcorn smiled fondly and wryly. Isabel had been so certain that she had maneuvered a slightly reluctant father into permission to visit Cantrell's ranch. Alcorn was fully aware, indulgently at times, irritably at other times, of Isabel's talent for having her own way. In this matter, Isabel's insistence had been a help. She had known nothing of Tom Cantrell's scheme of taking Texas cattle by force. Her visit to Cantrell's ranch would undoubtedly draw out the latest details now of Cantrell's intentions. There was even a small chance Isabel might yet toll Cantrell back into the regiment.

Isabel reached him and tossed her reins to the corporal. Alcorn gave her a hand down and dismissed the corporal. Smiling, he said: "You didn't stay long."

Isabel looked tired as she removed her white felt hat. "Tom wasn't there," she said, not hiding her disappointment.

The corporal had ridden out of earshot, leading Isabel's horse. Casually Alcorn inquired: "Where is Cantrell?"

"That girl at the ranch, Miss Bratton, didn't know." Isabel was removing her gloves with impatient jerks. "Tom has been gone over a week."

"I see," Alcorn said thoughtfully. "Take anyone with him?"

"That boy who ran away from the Apaches was there," Isabel said. "He told the corporal that Tom had taken all his men, and left with six strange Texans who had arrived at the ranch the day before."

"Tom needs cattle," Alcorn said noncommittally.

"I suppose so." Forgetting her disappointment, Isabel said: "The boy asked the corporal if Tom had gone to get his mother. He wanted to know if the soldiers were going to help. Dad, can't something be done for that woman?"

"I'm sorry," Alcorn said regretfully. "Not at this time."

"I keep thinking of her."

"It can't help the woman, or you," Alcorn said, and changed the subject. "You'll find Tom next time," he suggested, smiling. "Get some rest before dinner. I'll be in shortly."

He had been anticipating dinner. Now, when the house door

closed behind Isabel, Alcorn lit a cigar and walked slowly along the row, thinking. The smell of heat and dust from the hot day blended with the fragrance of piñon and cedar smoke from kitchen ranges. The blue-gray of first twilight was moving in, overshot by the brighter blue of the upper sky, where the vanished sun still reached. At the end of the row where Alcorn waited, slowly chewing his cigar, he presently sighted the man he wanted coming from the stables.

"Mister Fitzpatrick!" Alcorn called.

"Yes, sir!"

In blues and gilt buttons, black kerchief at his neck, 2nd Lieutenant Fitzpatrick reminded Alcorn of Tom Cantrell, at Cantrell's best. "Walk out on the parade with me," Alcorn said pleasantly.

"Pleasure, sir."

They strolled out on the deserted parade. Fitzpatrick, obviously, was curious. Undoubtedly he was canvassing his shortcomings, wondering what the Old Man was up to. Alcorn took the cigar from his mouth. "You and Tom Cantrell were close friends at Fort Union, I remember."

"We were, Major."

"You'll not relish the orders I'm placing you under now," Alcorn said without emotion. "You'll not discuss them with anyone." Alcorn inspected the frayed end of his cigar. "I'll have to explain. Tom Cantrell lost his Texas herd and needs cattle. He has a reckless scheme to take forcibly livestock that have allegedly been stolen in Texas by the Comanches."

Fitzpatrick's soft whistle was followed by a faint grin of admiration. "Wouldn't Tom Cantrell come up with something like that."

"He would." Alcorn made it stinging. Fitzpatrick reddened and silently waited. "To make it worse," Alcorn said, calmly again, "Cantrell arranged to have Texans join him. I have reason to believe he's out now, with his ranch crew and a party of Texans. You can guess what will happen."

Fitzpatrick's comment was a cautious understatement. "Tom won't find much of a welcome."

"Texas gunmen loose in the territory, taking livestock forcibly, will mean shooting and killing," Alcorn said tersely. "Much of it will draw in Apaches, Comanches, and perhaps even Kiowas."

"Does Tom have any sort of legal basis for such actions?" Fitzpatrick inquired carefully.

"Legality," said Alcorn brusquely, "is for courts and lawyers. There is no law in this district. Fort Ross has orders to pacify and protect. In the morning you will take out a patrol and discover what may be happening."

"Shall I patrol to Cantrell's ranch, Major?"

"Tom Cantrell won't be taking cattle off his own ranch," Alcorn said caustically. "Scout to roughly a hundred miles north of his ranch. You might cover the Upper Frío Plaza for any loose talk about Cantrell's intentions. Separate your men as you please. Ostensibly, and actually also, you will be looking for hostile Apaches and Comanches."

Cool now, Fitzpatrick inquired: "If I run into trouble involving Tom Cantrell, shall I take a hand?"

"Don't even go near Cantrell. Inform me by courier of any trouble involving Cantrell."

"Yes, sir."

The hoarse bawling of the advancing cattle was continuous. The scuffing hoofs struck the dry earth into fine dust that lifted and swirled, settled and clung. Tom Cantrell could taste the dust as he rode to the point of the growing herd.

Ashley Hampton, the rangy Texan, was riding watchfully out ahead of the herd. He smiled as Tom pulled the dusty kerchief off his face.

"Justice," the Texan said, "plagues this land and the inhabitants thereof!" He pointed to the east where a small bunch of cattle was breaking over a brush-studded rise, hazed along by three riders with carbines ready across their thighs. A sternness came on the Texan's tired, unshaven face. "Every hoof," he added with a bite, "stole in Texas, in tears and blood."

"And we'll see more blood when enough men get together behind us," Tom said soberly.

The Texan nodded. Tom rode, thinking of threats that had been hurled at them, and flurries of gunfire, usually at a distance, as they made this fast sweep south toward the Frío country. The men were ranging out for miles, sweeping cattle and horses back to the growing herd. Like General Sherman's foraging bummers gutting a strip through Georgia, Ashley Hampton had commented grimly. Only this was more pleasure to think about. West, the dark cañons and sheer escarpments of the Secundos were bold against the blue sky. Ashley Hampton gauged them and scanned the country ahead. "We're 'most to that big cañon-like valley I was telling you about."

"It must be Largo Cañon," Tom, guessed. "Water in it, you said?"

"And cattle for us," the Texan said grimly. "We can move down the cañon, gather the cattle, and bed along the water."

"Not in a cañon. We'd be targets from the rim. I'll take men and push the cattle in the cañon up to where we're crossing," Tom decided. "We'll bed to the south tonight." He was watching one of the three approaching riders running his horse out ahead to join them. "That's George Sell. Something's happened," Tom said.

George Sell had shoved his carbine into the saddle scabbard. The same tired, fierce look furrowed George's face behind his brown mustaches when he neared them. They had all been riding from dawn until dark, with only brief snatches of sleep at night.

George spoke tersely as he pulled his horse to a walk beside them. "Three men won't be enough out that way again. We run into five strangers who had an idea they'd cut us off."

"They didn't, looks like," Ashley Hampton drawled.

"Hot for a time," George said. "Buck Ellis took a bullet through his hat. We run 'em two, three miles. Hit one in the arm. It discouraged 'em. But they'll be back with more." George wiped his face with the end of his blue kerchief. "That ain't all. I saw a trooper watching the fun from a ridge over east of us."

Tom asked sharply: "Are you certain he was a trooper?"

"Wasn't half a mile away, plain against the sky, watching through glasses."

"Just one?"

"All we seen."

"One trooper means more," Tom said. "Could be a routine patrol that heard the shooting." He had not told these men of Major Alcorn's threat to intervene, and did not now. "I'll take three men ahead, and come back up the cañon. With luck, we'll find you watering in the cañon. Hold the rest of the men in close."

Tom chose Eagan, Pete Yancey, and one of Hampton's Texans. They cut off southeast, saving their horses, riding watchfully. The furious gun battle inevitably shaping would not come today, Tom opined. But beyond the horizons enraged men were gathering.

The cañon that gashed across the landscape opened suddenly before them, a half mile wide, with walls of red and yellow rock, and cattle grazing in the bottom. Tom used his binoculars.

"Texas brands down there," he said after some study.

They followed the rim, looking for a way down. Beyond a wide bend, a clump of green cottonwoods lifted beside the glinting band of water threading the cañon floor.

Eagan shaded his eyes with a palm. "Ain't that a wagon by them trees?"

Tom used the glasses again. "Have a look, Eagan."

The odd note in Tom's voice drew a questioning glance from Eagan as he reached for the binoculars. Amazement appeared on Eagan's red, bristle-covered face as he peered intently. "Old Sam Butterworth, sitting by the fire!" Eagan blurted.

"Sam," Tom said, "should be in a hospital cot at Fort Ross. That wounded leg of his can't be well."

Eagan returned the glasses, shaking his head wordlessly. Some distance on they found where the wagon had descended into the cañon. The rocky trail was difficult, even for horses. A barricade of brush at the bottom blocked the trail to cattle in the cañon.

Two saddle horses were staked out near the wagon. A blackened coffee pot rested on a smoldering fire. Two rough-looking men with carbines held ready waited silently by the fire as Tom rode up.

Sam Butterworth sat with his back against the rear wheel of the wagon, wearing the same old greasy leather shirt belted at the middle with rope. Sam's sparse, iron-gray beard and wrinkled features looked as irascible as ever as he gnawed meat off a strip of jerky. Sam's big buffalo Sharps lay on the ground beside him. Chewing slowly on the jerky, Sam ignored them.

The muzzles of two carbines covered them.

Tom studied the silent, challenging men a moment before saying: "I'm Tom Cantrell. Whose cattle are these?"

It brought quick, narrowing interest. "You the Cantrell who whipped Lee Bratton?" the taller one asked. He was a heavy man with a tangle of brown beard and hair matting the backs of big hands that held the carbine.

"I'm the man."

"Out buying cattle?"

"I'm looking for cattle. These yours?"

"Might be."

"I'm taking them."

"What's that?"

"They were stolen by Comanches in Texas." It was an old story now; Tom was brief. "I'm recovering them for their own-ers."

"Jake!" the man said, not taking his gaze off Tom. "Taking 'em, he says!"

"You can try with that gun," Tom said evenly, "or drop it. Make your choice."

Still chewing the jerky, Sam Butterworth picked up his long, heavy rifle. "He'll drop it," Sam said.

The two men froze, not risking a look back while four armed men faced them.

"Sam, do they own these cattle?" Tom inquired.

"Ain't said. They's one more man down the cañon."

The larger man swore in his tangled beard. "Jake, I told you we oughta run the old buzzard off. He sneaked in last night just for this!"

"It'd been an idea," Sam said. "You shoot now, and I'll shoot."

The carbines thudded to the ground. Eagan and the others had their revolvers out an instant later.

Tom dismounted and walked to the wagon, grinning. "How's the leg, Sam?"

Sam had put his rifle on the ground. He gnawed off another bite of jerky. "Still got it," he said. "Wrop enough fer four legs. That major's gal come back from your ranch with word Texans was out with you. I knowed what that meant. The doc throwed a fit when I hired me a hoss and saddle from the sutler and come on. I knowed you'd be out this way, somewheres. Wasn't much welcome here, but I laid up a day to rest."

"We'll push the cattle up the cañon a few miles, where our herd is crossing," Tom said. "Can you ride with us?"

"Tie these two up. I'll watch 'em while you clean the cañon," Sam said placidly. "Then see me ride."

At the end of this same day, when purple shadows filled the cañon bottom, Matthew Fallon let his shock and rage rake the three men who faced him by the wagon fire. "Cantrell came into the cañon with only three men? And took all the cattle you were hired to watch?"

The surly retort from the man with the matted brown beard was no help to Fallon. "Cantrell an' his men was in front of us. That old buzzard was back of us with his rifle. What would you have done?"

"Used my head. Not let a stranger loaf around all night and day." Fallon stood with his twisted right hand clenched in the coat pocket. "Did the old man have a Sharps rifle? And a scraggly beard?"

"That's him."

"Pour me coffee!"

Fallon moved away from the fire with the tin cup of coffee. He had been in a savage humor over Cantrell since Ben Poole had wakened him at dawn yesterday. Temper, Fallon knew, was not the answer. Cantrell was moving south fast to the Frío country. Fallon surveyed the eight men standing around the fire, glumly drinking coffee. He had met two of them this afternoon, discouraged from a brush with Cantrell's men. Thinking hard, Fallon moved back to the fire.

"In two or three days," he said with cool confidence, "we'll have enough men. Ben Poole is collecting them at his ranch. I've sent my men out to spread the word about Cantrell. On the way here, I started everyone I met riding for help."

They eyed him in dull silence, waiting obviously for him to

think for them. He despised them, while he talked coolly, confidently to them.

"Cantrell watered his cattle and pushed out of the cañon late this afternoon. He can't be far away. If we can stampede his herd tonight, he'll be held up a day or two. By then men will be gathering here at the cañon to stop him."

Their interest was visibly sharpening. "No moon tonight," Fallon said. "Cantrell can't have many men. Some of them will be asleep. Once his herd stampedes, he's in trouble. Anyone have a better idea?" And when he heard none, Fallon decided: "We'll hit Cantrell tonight, then."

XIII

A hand touched Tom Cantrell's shoulder, and he was instantly awake catching for the holstered gun in the blanket.

"After midnight, Lieut'n't," Eagan's voice said.

Tom stood up, buckling on his gun belt and yawning. "Everything all right?"

"Quiet," said Eagan. "Like nights when we were patrolling in hostile country."

Tom yawned again. "Eagan, you're going to have to reënlist. I can see that."

"No hurry," Eagan muttered.

But it was working in Eagan, Tom thought regretfully as he tied his rolled blanket behind the saddle of his waiting horse. The Army was home and family to Eagan. The big sergeant was lonely and lost in civilian life.

In the wan starlight, sleeping figures lay on the ground, a saddled horse ready on a short picket by each man. Eagan was spreading his blanket on the earth as Tom led his horse away from the sleeping men and stepped stiffly into the saddle.

Small restless sounds came from the bedded herd as Tom walked his horse through the starlight. Low hills half a mile east were visible. The Secundos towered black and indistinct in the west. Far westward the booming howl of a wolf floated to the stars, and a shadowy rider loomed ahead, holding a long rifle across his lap.

"Sam, you should be asleep, resting that leg," Tom said as they fell in together.

"Young fellers need the sleep," said Sam placidly. "They ain't no good reading the night anyway."

Tom chuckled. "You've been riding this country long enough to outguess it, Sam."

"Seen it forty year ago," Sam said. "Stretching out like it had fer a million years, no good to anyone."

"I've thought of it that way, too," Tom admitted.

"Seen towns on it, and cattle everywhere, didn't you?"

"Something like that," Tom said, smiling. "It made me turn in my commission, and get out to help put the towns and cattle here."

"Forty year ago," Sam mused, "Mexico owned it. But the Indians knowed who really bossed it. I seen it too soon. But I usta figure babies was being born who'd do something about it."

Tom had the queer feeling he was hearing a voice out of the past, regretting dreams that had been bold and too soon. He listened intently to Sam's words.

"When you quit the Army, I seen it in you and come along to help." Sam sounded slightly embarrassed. "Kinda like old Sam had growed six feet tall in you, boy. All young and brash again, and a chance to get roots down. Maybe a pretty wife and kids who'd want a man around when he got old."

Tom smiled in the dark. "I'm not interested in a pretty wife." He regarded the hunched, shadowy figure of this often vitriolic little man, who had seen so much and done so much and who still held the hungers of youth. "Sam, you'll see it happen now.

And you'll be wanted. There's a home for you on the ranch to the end, part of everything."

"You got a big heart," Sam said. In the starlight his hunched shoulders started to shake. "I knowed that'd get you soft as mush," Sam chortled. "Soft heart, soft head, Tom. You won't build nothing in this country if you git soft."

Tom had to grin ruefully. "I'm not soft, Sam. I'm mad, and I stay mad. They won't stop me now."

"You ain't homesick for the Army?"

"No."

"That major's gal come to the fort hospital. She seemed to figure you was still Army inside."

"Isabel is wrong."

"A managing gal," Sam said. After a moment he added: "That little black-haired partner you throwed in the wagon at me is kind of spunky. She shot at them Apaches real cool."

"Stubborn," Tom said shortly. "She'll cause trouble yet."

"I heard about your fight with her brother. That one'll make the trouble."

"They're a pair," Tom said. He rode, thinking of her small figure beside him in front of the house they owned together. She had hardly reached to his shoulder. The starlight had glinted off her pink basque and exotic shawl, and made every curve of her small face deceptively soft. And she had not budged an inch.

They met one of the Texans riding his slow circle, exchanged brief words, and walked their horses on. Sam Butterworth was silent, until he suddenly said: "Them coyotes in the ridges over east have shut up. Five minutes ago coyotes quit to the north."

Tom halted his horse, testing the night. "Trouble, Sam?"

"They ain't sleepy."

Tom made an immediate decision. "Tell the wrangler to push

the horse herd a mile or so south. I'll get the men in their saddles."

Minutes later Tom wakened the snoring Ashley Hampton. The Texan came instantly out of his blanket, bringing up one of his long-barreled revolvers. He lowered it when Tom spoke.

"Could be a false alarm," Tom said of the coyotes. "But if not, we'd better be ready."

Hampton was already folding his blanket, laying it behind his saddle. "Time for our luck to run out," he drawled. "I'd pick a night like this if I was them, and nigh eight hundred head bedded and ready to scatter."

"If the cattle run, try to hold them south," Tom urged.

He was reaching for his stirrup when Sam's big buffalo gun, out east of the bedded cattle, slammed through the quiet night. Ashley Hampton waked the other sleeping men with a wild Rebel yell as Tom went fast into the saddle.

Other guns smashed the night north and east of the herd, the nearest some hundreds of yards away. Sam's keen senses had jumped the attack before it was ready Tom guessed as his horse bolted into a run. Behind him, Ashley Hampton was shouting: "Nev' mind blankets! Keep south! South!"

The last was barely audible as hundreds of snorting, alarmed cattle lunged up on the bed ground. If they broke in the wrong direction, not much could be done. North a few miles, a stampede could pour blindly over the cañon drop. East and west were broken ridges. This bed ground had been selected because the country opened south for miles.

Tom spurred to the north side of the bed ground, firing his revolver, shouting. Wild at best, the herd broke in panic toward the south, where there were no guns and shouting men. The aimless tumult changed into the deep, dreadful roll of a stampede gathering momentum. Thousands of heavy hoofs hammered the earth in unison, faster and faster. Dust began to swirl up as Tom reloaded his revolver on the run and veered east.

No time to wonder about Sam Butterworth or the horse herd. Barely audible gunfire on the west side of the running herd showed that Hampton had men in place there.

The cattle were running faster, massing closer. Revolver in hand, Tom spurred up the east flank of the bolting mass. Two riders were cutting in ahead of him, yelling, firing revolvers directly at the herd. The shadowy mass of a running steer stumbled, plunged down, and rolled. Tom bore out toward the indistinct riders, throwing shots at them. One man veered away, the other followed, and they dropped back out of sight as the rumbling thunder of the stampede swept south.

It could be worse, Tom thought. An inky night, a storm with thunder, lightning, and sheeting rain, could have scattered the cattle beyond recovery for days. No other strangers rode in from this side. After a time Tom began to worry about Sam Butterworth.

Two hours later the cattle were still running south, but more slowly, less wildly. They had dropped to an uneasy trot when the sky lighted faintly in the east. By full dawn the pace had dropped to a shuffling walk. All the men but Sam Butterworth were with the herd. Tom rode to the front, where Ashley Hampton and three men were riding with carbines across their thighs, closely watching all nearby cover. Some eighty horses they had gathered with the cattle were out ahead, still together.

The Texan drawled: "Wasn't so many jumped us, evidently."

"Enough, if Sam Butterworth hadn't been watching last night," Tom said. "We'll push straight for the ranch now. With luck we can get there tomorrow night, before enough men gather behind us to make a real fight."

"That's best, probably," Hampton agreed. He brushed at his yellow mustache. His eyes were red-rimmed. He was frosted with dust, like all of them. "We'll fight 'em better without a herd to watch. Your house will make a good fort."

"I was thinking of that, too." Tom smiled faintly, then sobered again. "I'm going to take Eagan and look for Sam Butterworth."

"Your place is here, running this, Cantrell," Hampton said quickly. "Best let me go."

"Sam is one of my men," Tom said as he turned his horse back.

Eagan was concerned as they rode back along the churned path of the stampede. "Reckon old Sam got throwed and tramped?"

"Sam was in the clear when it started, I think," Tom recalled. "He may have been shot, or his horse downed."

"If they get their hands on Sam, he's a goner."

"So are we," Tom reminded him dryly. "Don't get careless."

It was Eagan, almost an hour later, who jerked up his carbine, then blurted: "Look at that!"

Sam Butterworth was riding out from behind scrub cedars not a hundred yards away. Long rifle balanced across his saddle, hat pulled low, Sam looked hunched, gnome-like in his old leather shirt as he walked his horse toward them and leisurely gnawed on a chunk of meat.

"You two lost?" Sam called.

"All this ride, and him loafing around, eating," Eagan said acidly as Sam joined them.

"I ain't stampeding all night with a wropped leg," Sam said calmly. "I rode over in the nearest brush and come on easy. Shot me a rabbit at daylight and cooked a bite, like any man with sense. Bet you ain't et."

"No time, hunting you." Eagan wet his lips and enviously eyed the well-browned haunch of jack rabbit in Sam's gnarled hand.

Tom was smiling with relief. "We're pushing straight through to the ranch now, Sam."

"If you get there," said Sam. "After the dust died down, I heerd one of them yell for a man named Fallon. And get his answer."

"Fallon?" Tom said.

Sam nodded. He gnawed off a bite of meat, saw Eagan staring ravenously, and held the rabbit haunch out to Eagan. "Two bites!" Sam said. "Your drooling takes a man's appetite."

Sam chewed his meat, swallowed it, and said to Tom: "Fallon yelled for the men to get back to the cañon. Told them there'd be enough help in a day or so to do the job right." Sam leaned over and took his rabbit meat firmly back from Eagan's fist. Sam's blue, splintery glance turned to Tom. "Fallon sounded like he was sure of enough men," he said. "You better get set, Tom, for a showdown fight."

XIV

The next morning they sighted the bold yellow mass of the Lizard Butte, and pointed the weary herd at it. The men were haggard, red-eyed. Two were wounded, not seriously. But not a man showed any wish to leave. Hampton and his Texans had proved themselves. Their fierce purpose was visible as they rode, watching the distance behind, ready for the guns gathering behind them.

Near midday, through his binoculars, Tom saw the ranch house clearly. He returned the glasses to the leather case at his saddle pommel and spoke to Ashley Hampton, riding beside him. "We'll bed the herd in that big draw south of the house. The grass is good. There's enough water from springs at the foot of the butte, and the house will be close."

Hampton's teeth gleamed under the yellow mustache. "That house will make them think. It's a fort."

"We built for something like this, and Apache raids," Tom

said. "May save the ranch now." He rode for some minutes, thinking of what was ahead. "They could jump us tonight," he said. "I'm going to send Eagan to the top of the Lizard Butte with my binoculars. He can watch more country from up there than we can. Even an hour's warning will help. Eagan can take a mirror and flash a warning from the top of the butte if there's sun."

"Suppose they've taken over the house before we get there?" Hampton drawled.

Tom frowned at the possibility. "Fallon would be the man to think of it. I'll go with Eagan." He smiled wryly. "If I don't come back, you'll know we have guests."

Tom rode from the bawling herd with Eagan, and, as they loped over familiar miles of his own land, Tom put the binoculars now and then on the house. When their horses trotted into the wide yard behind the house, and they dismounted at the corral, Tom stood a moment surveying the bunkhouse and outbuildings, and the house itself. Everything here gave him a renewed sense of accomplishment. Here the future would be solidly rooted, after it had been savagely fought for in the hours ahead.

Tom started to the house, and noticed the small, tanned figure of the boy moving uncertainly from the saddle shed toward the corral. Tom heard Eagan's gruff, offhand greeting to the boy: "Hi ya, kid? Been doing all right?"

If the boy replied, Tom did not hear him. Barnaby Polk, the tall old lawyer, had emerged from the back door of the house. "Welcome home, young man."

Tom smiled. "Glad to see you're still here, sir."

"It has been a pleasant visit," the old lawyer said. "Ending too soon, I fear."

"Are you leaving?" Tom asked courteously.

"Tomorrow or next day," said Barnaby Polk. "My old friend,

Judge Augustus Andrews, should arrive from Mesilla, where he has been holding court. We will go to Santa Fe together." He regarded Tom's haggard, dusty figure. "A hard trip, evidently."

"Not easy. We're bedding a herd near the house tonight. I rode in for a talk with Miss Bratton. Is she here?"

"In her room, I believe. Sarina is in the kitchen, and will tell Ginny."

The old lawyer was curious, Tom sensed as he walked on into the house. A smell of fresh-baked bread filled the kitchen. Sarina, the buxom Mexican woman, enveloped in an apron of bright flower print, beamed at him. Her hand indicated a cup of black coffee and a plate of cookies on the kitchen table.

"For me?" Tom asked in surprise.

"*Sí,*"

Tom grinned at her. "Like home. Will you tell Miss Bratton I'd like to speak with her?"

"I tell." She hurried toward the front part of the house.

Tom could feel the long strain and bone-weariness relaxing as he picked up the coffee cup and two cookies. The home-like feeling of this kitchen was soothing after the grueling days and nights. It gave a brief false sense of peace, of security against the trouble ahead. He carried the coffee and cookies into the spacious patio in the center of the big house and looked around critically.

The well he and Steve had dug in the center of this patio would be needed if the house were besieged. The thick, high adobe walls of the patio would not easily be breached. He inspected every shutter and loophole, through which they'd probably soon be holding off furious men and guns.

The Mexican woman returned through the patio, smiling. "She come."

Moments later Virginia Bratton stepped into the warm sunshine that filled the front half of the patio. "You wanted me,

Mister Cantrell?"

Her voice was pleasant and neutral. Her fine black hair, rolled back and pinned high, caught the sunlight in tiny gleams. She looked even smaller, more slender in the crisp white blouse and plain black skirt, and earrings of tiny, intricate Mexican silver wirework. A massive silver bracelet on her slender left wrist caught the sun as she advanced.

Still held by the sense of home-like peace, Tom smiled and indicated the cookies and coffee he held. "Nice to find this waiting after a hard ride."

"Sarina likes to please the men."

"She could do worse," said Tom amiably. He gestured with the coffee cup to the log well curbing. "A seat, ma'am?" And as she sat down, Tom glanced again around the patio. "Someday I'll have chairs here, and roofed walks along the sides, and rooms built outside. Flowers, too . . . hollyhocks, all colors."

Virginia looked around the patio. "Roses on trellises would do well. Yellow and white and red roses."

"I like roses," Tom said absently. He was studying the way a silver earring laid against her slender neck as she sat on the well curbing, head bent slightly, eyes half closed. She was smiling faintly as she visualized the walks and flowers. She looked up into his gaze, and sat motionlessly. Slowly her eyes opened wide, deep-blue eyes against fair skin and the blackest hair, Tom noted. She was probably judging his haggard, unshaved face, his dirty trail clothes, and sagging gun belt. The thought reminded him of the boiling trouble that was coming. And what had to be done.

"Right now," he said thoughtfully, "you'll have to move back to the Frío Plazas, I'm afraid. I rode in to tell you."

She closed her eyes. "You did say move, didn't you, Mister Cantrell?"

"You should get out today," Tom said. "There's going to be

trouble here. The place won't be safe for women. Use my wagon, if you like."

"Move out today?" Her voice had a stricken sound. "You are suggesting that I move out of this house which is half mine? Out of my own home?"

"I'm telling you to move," Tom said. "We're bringing a herd in close to the house. There's going to be trouble."

She stood up. "A herd? You've done well, Mister Cantrell, for a man who lost his cattle and my cattle, and said he had no money to buy more." She drew a breath. "Could this be the Texas herd you claimed to have lost?"

"Now you're talking like your brother," Tom said, cooling. He drank the last of the coffee and placed the empty cup on top of the windlass post of the well. "I took this herd from men who had bought it illegally from the Comanche traders."

"You *took* a herd?"

"Where we found them. Now we've got to fight to hold them. Anything may happen here." Tom regarded her unsmilingly. "I saw this coming, and didn't want a girl for a partner. Now I'll not have a dead woman on my conscience. I'll have to order you to move out before the trouble hits."

"*You* order *me?*"

"I'm trying to help you. Trying to be reasonable."

"When were you ever reasonable?" She was breathing faster as she took two steps to the right and turned back. "What right have you to put this ranch in danger? This ranch and this house, which are half mine."

"We can settle that later. Right now you'll have to get out."

"Oh, will I?" She moved away again, and turned back, flushed. "How could you bring danger and trouble on the home I'm trying to make for myself and my brother? Everything we have is here."

"Your brother seems to be able to take care of himself," Tom said, unimpressed. "Today I'll have to take care of you."

"You were never more mistaken, Mister Cantrell."

Her agitated steps were moving away again. Tom followed her, remembering old Sam Butterworth's tart advice: *Soft heart, soft head.* "Will I have to put you in the wagon, Miss Bratton?"

She whirled back. "Again in that wagon? *Never*, Mister Cantrell. You humiliated me once." She pushed the heavy silver bracelet up her arm and pulled it down. Her agitated steps went past him, and came back. "What kind of a woman do you think I am? To be bullied simply because you've stolen cattle."

"I took them on open range!" Tom said coldly. "Their owners. . . ."

"You *do* admit stealing them, then? And now you use stolen cattle for an excuse to put me out of my home." Her tapping steps were more agitated as she threw words at him. "I was born in this territory. I've known men like you. Bullies, brave against women."

"I'm not. . . ."

"You are! You've been scheming to take my ranch and home like you've stolen your cattle."

This, Tom knew in growing temper, was ridiculous. He remembered once passing a bird's nest, and bringing the small, enraged female swooping, twittering at him. Just like this. He grinned ruefully.

Virginia Bratton's agitated steps whirled beside him. "Is it so amusing, Mister Cantrell? You and your Texas gunmen trying to put me out of my home?"

"Please, will you get it through your head, Miss. . . ."

"Do you think I'm helpless, Mister Cantrell? When I grew up among better men than you will ever be." Tom never did see her hand move. Suddenly his gun holster was light. She was backing away, cocking his big revolver.

"Wait!" Tom shouted. He saw her finger contract on the trig-

ger and leaped instinctively aside as the crashing gun report
shattered the patio quiet. Hot powder particles flicked his hand.
The blast walloped his ears.

He barely heard her furious challenge as she backed away.
"I've a revolver of my own! Try putting me out of my home,
Mister Cantrell!" She threw the gun, skittering on the earth,
toward his feet. Head high, she turned and walked into the long
living room. Her bedroom door slammed behind her.

Tom had thought his nerves were sound. He was shaken now,
although the bullet had miraculously missed him. Heavy steps
pounded through the kitchen as Tom bent and picked up the
revolver. Eagan burst into the patio, holding his own revolver.
Eagan halted. Amazement showed on his red, bristle-covered
face as he saw Tom Cantrell, standing alone in this quiet patio,
gun in hand.

Eagan gulped. "I thought. . . ."

"Don't," Tom said curtly.

Barnaby Polk hurried in after Eagan. The old lawyer's evident
concern subsided as he looked around. He gazed at Tom, and
stepped over and picked a tin cup off the ground.

Tom glanced at the windlass post of the well, where he had
placed his empty tin cup. It was gone. The tall old lawyer was
regarding holes that a bullet had torn through the cup. "Shooting in the house at tin cups, young man?"

She had not meant to hit him. She had shot that cup off the
windlass post with lethal aim, to warn him. Tom swallowed.
"The impulse," he said, "comes at times." He holstered his gun.
"Eagan," he ordered, grimly, "ride up on the butte. I'll get back
to the herd."

XV

Virginia was furiously resentful the next morning as she stood
beside her bed and belted on her blue robe. Last night the

friendly coyote yapping had retreated. Restless cattle had been audible not far away. Heavy steps, rattling spurs had moved through the house, passing in and out of Cantrell's bedroom. Curt voices had been heard. She had dropped off into a troubled sleep.

Doña Sarina knocked, and entered with a breakfast tray. Virginia regarded the food with a lack of appetite. Sarina looked at her and chuckled. "Yesterday, in the patio, he bit a chili that heated him."

Virginia said in Spanish: "They are going to fight here with guns. You must go home to the Lower Plaza Frío today."

"*Aie!* Always the men fight," said *Doña* Sarina, shrugging. "I fear only Apaches and *Tejanos*." From the neck of her gaudy apron, Sarina drew a crude wooden cross on a length of cord. "The woman's tongue will do against men," said Sarina comfortably. "And I carry the knife little mother gave me. And the cross."

"A *knife*, Sarina?"

"Oh, *sí*. When I was nine, almost a woman," said Sarina cheerfully, "little mother gave the knife, and said . . . 'When the woman's tongue will not stop them, speak with the little blade. They will understand. And always the blessed cross on the heart.' "

Virginia was smiling when Sarina departed. She sobered again as she brushed out her hair and reflected on this undoubtedly dangerous day. Even Barnaby Polk had been troubled when he had heard the facts.

"It might be best to leave for a few days," he had suggested. But he had not insisted when Virginia had refused.

Her hair pinned up, Virginia gave a final critical look into the mirror, adjusting the collar of another crisp white blouse she was wearing with the black skirt of yesterday. From the top drawer of the lowboy, she took the brown envelope Isabel Alcorn had left, and carried it and the tray to the kitchen.

Doña Sarina looked at the uneaten food. "What man takes the chicken with the hungry bones?" Sarina scolded.

Absently Virginia said in Spanish: "The girl from the fort left this letter for him. He will take her, bones and all, and jump to her rope."

"You carry the writing for her? What woman is so foolish for another? Let the stove read her thoughts."

"Sarina!"

"Two women," said Sarina logically, "cannot have one man in the same house. You are here first."

"If Tom Cantrell were the last man on earth. . . ."

Sarina's—"God forbid."—followed Virginia out into the warm morning sunshine.

Barnaby Polk was not in sight. Saddled horses stood tied to the corral poles, ready for instant riding. Armed men lounged in the yard. Tom Cantrell and Hampton had leaned their carbines against the well curbing in the yard and were talking. Cantrell saw her coming and seemed to stiffen. He had washed, shaved, and changed into a clean blue blouse and trousers left from his cavalry days. His dark face still had a tired look as he watched her approach. Both men removed their hats.

Coolly Virginia said: "Miss Alcorn left this copy of an Army report for you, Mister Cantrell. It has information about the death of Steven Rogers, your former partner. I should like to hear what it says."

"If you wish," Cantrell said indifferently.

He opened the envelope and scanned the two sheets it contained. He frowned. Turning, he called: "I want all you men to hear this! You, too, Eagan!"

The men in the yard, six of them, converged on the well. Cantrell tapped the papers in his hand. His voice had hardened.

"This is an Army report, turned in by the lieutenant whose

patrol found Steve Rogers's body. Three unknown men had dismounted at the spot. Two had heel plates on their boots. One set of plates had a clover-leaf design cut out of the centers. The other set had an open, four-pointed star design, with the right heel plate worn or broken, leaving a three-point star mark in the dirt."

One of the Texans whistled softly. "Signing every step, wasn't he?"

"By now he may have new plates or new boots," Cantrell said.

Ashley Hampton drawled: "A man riding steady won't wear heel plates much."

"We can hope," Cantrell said. He shoved the brown envelope into his hip pocket. "Steve was killed between here and the Frío Plazas. The three men who murdered him probably go there often. That lop-sided star mark may be around the Upper Frío Plaza today."

"Today," Ashley Hampton said, "we're occupied."

Cantrell nodded. His hand slowly rubbed his black gun holster. "I'll take every man to town at the first chance. We'll look for this three-star heel mark."

Cantrell, in his anger, had forgotten her. Feeling unwanted, resented, Virginia walked to the corral, thinking about Lee. Suppose Lee returned while these dangerous men were fighting for their lives? Lee would probably join any men fighting Cantrell.

Her gelding nuzzled through the corral poles. While she petted him, the red-faced man named Eagan boosted the boy on one of the saddled horses and mounted another horse. They rode toward the Lizard Butte, Eagan carrying a mirror framed in wood. The boy looked small and important on the horse. He had been no trouble, sleeping with his small boy's dogged insistence in the bunkhouse.

Cantrell had told the judge of the night when the boy, a furtive shadow, had drifted to Cantrell's trail wagon through tall, wind-stirred grass. A frightened—"Don't shoot, mister!"—had halted Cantrell's finger on the hair-trigger of his carbine.

When Cantrell had seen what he had almost killed, he had been shaken. The boy, wearing only a breechclout and moccasins, carrying a knife and an old Dragoon revolver with one chamber loaded, had been almost stupidly exhausted. He had come fast and far off the great forested heights to the south, running, walking, skulking, hiding, trying to find the Army fort that Apaches had mentioned in his hearing.

Twice this last week, Virginia had seen the boy gazing south toward the mountains where his mother was held captive. Virginia had known helplessly what was in his mind. But he had not shared his silent, withdrawn little life of waiting. Something in the gruff, red-faced Eagan seemed to have reached the boy. A man might understand, Virginia thought as she left the corral and walked to the front of the house. Cantrell had told her she could never think like a boy.

With irritation, Virginia realized that her thoughts always came back to Cantrell. He seemed to dominate this house and all in it. She put Cantrell out of her mind. The judge was sitting in a chair in front of the house, in the warm sunshine, leisurely smoking a cheroot. He looked up, smiling, when Virginia joined him.

"Have you reconsidered about leaving?" the judge inquired.

"I won't leave."

The judge eyed the blue smoke curling from his cheroot. "Women do not belong in some things," he said slowly.

"This is my home."

"And Cantrell's home," the judge reminded her. "He is a somewhat different young man than I had suspected, Ginny."

"I'm not afraid of the man."

"The man would not harm you, Ginny. I made inquiries

about him before I allowed you to buy into this ranch."

"He harmed Lee. He's waiting to fight the owners of cattle he's stolen."

The judge sounded regretful. "Cantrell has started something evidently which can end only in bloodshed, I'm afraid," said the judge thoughtfully. "Cantrell is more like your brother Lee than I suspected."

"Never as good as Lee," said Virginia.

"As reckless in his way as Lee can be," said the judge. "Cantrell has risked his ranch, his future, and probably his life, on a desperate gamble. He can't stop now." The judge drew reflectively on his cheroot. His voice took the detached tone Virginia had heard him use on the bench, sentencing a man to death. "Cantrell will probably be killed before this is over."

"He has no right to do it to himself, or to us."

"He has done it," said the judge, gazing into the haze-hung distance. "And involved you, which I cannot quite forgive. I would advise, Ginny, going into town. If Mesilla court ended on schedule, Judge Andrews should reach the Frío Plazas tomorrow. Perhaps even today. We can meet him, and explain why his short visit to the ranch here should be delayed, or made another time."

"Lee might return. I want to be here when he does." Virginia put her hand on the judge's shoulder. "You go. Sarina insists on staying if I do."

"It has not been my habit to run and leave the women," said the judge.

XVI

Virginia felt stubbornly unreasonable as she walked into the house. She paused in front of the fireplace, remembering how the men had filled this long room with stirring song. And how Cantrell had stood briefly beside her, watching the fire in stern reverie, before he stalked to his room and closed the door. His door was closed now, as solid and forbidding as the man himself. Restlessly Virginia walked into her room, made the bed, and dusted. Still restless, she went back to the kitchen where *Doña* Sarina bustled and gossiped in bursts of cheerful Spanish.

Through the back door, men could be seen occasionally riding from the yard toward the herd. Other men returned and took up a watchful vigil in the yard. Dangerous, formidable men, grimly waiting. Shortly before noon Cantrell rode toward the herd.

Virginia ate a little meat and fiery chili. This waiting for gunfire to erupt made her taut. Cantrell and his grim men made her feel more unwanted and resented. Finally she went to her room and changed into a linen riding skirt and soft boots. From the lowboy she took a rolled cartridge belt and revolver and buckled the belt under her jacket. With her straw hat hanging on her shoulders by its leather ties, she went out back. She was in the corral, her rope loop on her gelding's neck, when Ashley Hampton spoke behind her.

"I will do that, ma'am." He took the rope. His suggestion was courteous: "Might not be best, ma'am, to ride out today."

"I will do as I please!"

He drawled: "North and South, ma'am, ladies seem to be alike."

He led her horse out of the corral, expertly tied on her side-saddle, and gave her a hand up. He took his carbine that was leaning against the corral bars and swung onto one of the waiting horses.

"I will accompany you, ma'am," he said politely and firmly.

She made the best of it, riding north, away from where Cantrell had gone. North, perversely, where danger was expected. The Texan followed silently.

Alone with her thoughts, Virginia thought of Cantrell again, of the Tom Cantrell she had heard about at Fort Ross, the laughing, wenching, drinking, gambling young lieutenant. Yesterday, in the patio, that Tom Cantrell had seemed to stand beside her for a moment, tin cup in hand, grinning down at her as they talked of hollyhocks and roses, and the home they owned together. Then abruptly he had reverted to the gaunt, smoldering man who was her hostile partner. His drive toward selfish goals brushed aside anything in his way. And he would probably be shot soon, as Barnaby Polk expected.

Low hills and ridges were ahead. The Texan drew up with her and said politely: "We'd best turn back." Their horses nibbled grass as he scanned the sun-drenched distance. "A fair land," he said quietly.

"I've thought so," Virginia said.

"Now you do not, ma'am?"

"I don't know," Virginia said after a moment. She reined back toward the ranch house.

They had not gone far when Virginia blinked and bent her face away from the flashing sun. A bright flick of light caught them. The Texan's exclamation was sharp: "Eagan's sighted something from the butte!"

Virginia recalled the mirror Eagan had carried toward the butte. Through binoculars, Hampton could see him plainly. He was signaling with the mirror.

"Horse coming off the butte," Hampton said. "Likely the boy."

A tiny ribbon of dust was lengthening down the steep north slope of the butte. One could visualize that reckless, dangerous rush of horse and small boy down the slopes.

"I'll meet him," said the Texan. "Get back to the house, ma'am."

He spurred his horse into a run. The mirror had stopped

flashing. A second streamer of dust followed the first. A single rider was leaving the ranch yard and heading for the butte.

Slowly Virginia rode toward the house, watching the small boy come off the butte in a reckless rush. The Texan was riding to intercept the boy, and did for a moment. The boy went on and the Texan waited.

All of it was distant and toy-like on the sweep of amber grassland ending at the yellow cliffs of the Lizard Butte. Cantrell must be the one riding fast from the house. He met the boy, and rode on toward the waiting Texan and Eagan, who was off the butte now.

The boy reached the ranch yard. A second man came fast after Cantrell. The Texan, Eagan, and Cantrell rode north toward the pinched-off ridges and low sugar-loaf hills, straggling out from the butte. Virginia turned her horse to intercept the fourth man. He saw her intent and swerved to meet her. He was one of the lean Texans hung with guns; he grinned as he pulled up his blowing horse.

"Only yo' brother, ma'am, bringing in some cattle," he said reassuringly. He touched his hat and went on.

Her horse worried the reins as Virginia sat motionlessly. Lee coming with armed men and cattle, and Cantrell meeting him. Virginia whirled her horse into a run after Cantrell and his men.

Beyond the first low ridge another brushy ridge lifted. Virginia whipped her gelding in a reckless, weaving run through the shin oak and cedar. Branches clawed at her. She had missed the tracks of Cantrell and his men. The low ridges and hills were confusing. She crossed two more ridges before she heard the distant, muted bawling of steers, and found the twisting, grassy draw that Lee's herd was traversing.

The smell of dust still hung in the air. A quarter mile to the left, the drags of the herd were moving away from her. When she caught up with them, Cantrell and his three men were in the midst of the herd.

Cantrell looked at her without expression. Ashley Hampton lifted a hand in surprised, disapproving courtesy. The red-faced Eagan stared grimly. She counted six men in Lee's crew. At the head of the herd, Lee was riding a powerful, beautiful horse of golden coat and white mane and tail. How like Lee to return on a new fine horse.

Lee was gazing back at Cantrell with visible anger. He called to her above the bawling, noisy advance of the herd: "Look at that! Meddling in my business soon as I get on the ranch!"

"Been lonesome without you, Lee!" Virginia said loudly, and tried to make it light and cheerful.

Lee was unshaven and trail dirty. His dusty hat rode back on his rumpled black hair. The marks of Cantrell's beating had healed. All of Lee's confidence was back, Virginia saw as her sweating gelding dropped to the trail walk at Lee's left side.

"What's Cantrell think he's doing?" Lee asked with suppressed temper.

"I don't know," Virginia said, looking back. "Here he comes."

Cantrell and his men had worked out of the herd and were riding forward at a slow trot. Lee's crew began to close forward. Lee pushed his hat farther back in a familiar, reckless gesture.

"Go to the house, Ginny," Lee said, looking back at Cantrell's approach.

"Don't start trouble," Virginia begged.

"I'm letting Cantrell stretch his rope," Lee said ominously.

The feeling of helplessness caught her again as Cantrell, by accident or design, put his horse between her and Lee, at her right. The stolid Eagan pulled up at her left. Ashley Hampton and the other Texan fell in behind them. Cantrell's tired face was stony as he spoke to her. "These your cattle, Miss Bratton?"

"They are."

He spoke to Lee. "Did you buy from a man named Fallon?"

Lee's men were arriving behind them. One could feel the dangerous tension building. Lee's thin grin masked growing temper as he called to his men: "Cantrell wants to know if Matt Fallon sold these cattle!"

They grinned back. They were different from Cantrell's men, Virginia realized. She would have felt safe anywhere with any one of Tom Cantrell's men, but not with these men Lee had brought.

"Lee," she begged desperately. "Ride to the house with me."

"Keep out of this, Ginny."

Cantrell said deliberately: "You'd better go, Miss Bratton."

"These are my cattle. I'll stay."

She never forgot his forbidding look and scornful question: "You know all about them, then?"

"Naturally."

"They were stolen from the Texas settlements in Comanche raids," Cantrell said coldly. "I'm taking them."

"Is this some new trick?" Virginia flared. "All our money is in these cattle! You'll not take a hoof!"

"I buried men because of cattle raiding," Cantrell said deliberately. "I lost Steve Rogers, my partner. I went broke. Now I'll hit every buyer of Comanche-traded cattle. You and your brother are no exception."

Lee was reining his spirited horse away from Cantrell. "You've run your rope, Cantrell!" he said loudly. "Now I'll start giving orders on this ranch!"

Cantrell turned his level regard on Lee. "I had you pegged right, I guess, buster," he said, and it sounded almost regretful.

Ashley Hampton's voice lifted behind them: "Only seven of them, Cantrell. Move the lady away."

Without taking his gaze off Lee, Cantrell said: "This is no

place for you, Miss Bratton. Leave, please. Quick."

"Lee," Virginia begged. "Mister Cantrell." Her voice was unsteady.

A new harsh urgency leaped into Cantrell's words as he watched Lee. "Let your sister get away."

Eagan, at her left, leaned over to catch her reins. And the high, reckless shout of one of Lee's crew knifed the sunlight: "Take 'em like Lee said, boys!"

XVII

Virginia struck her quirt blindly at Eagan's grasping hand and jerked her reins away from him. Behind her, Ashley Hampton's blood-curdling yell filled the narrow draw. Cantrell's horse was wheeling in a fast lunge at the horse Lee rode. Cantrell's heavy revolver was swinging forward in his hand. Gunshots crashed out behind her.

Sick fear for Lee's life sent Virginia's hand to the revolver under her linen jacket. Her frightened gelding pitched and whirled. She lost the treacherous side-saddle support and spun off, her foot catching in the twisting stirrup as she fell. Her hands, head, and shoulders struck the earth as a tumult of shots and yells filled the draw.

The stamping hoofs of spurred horses were everywhere around her as her own horse reared and dragged her. Along the ground Virginia caught a dizzying glimpse of Lee's herd in awful poise before stampeding toward her. A hoof struck her head.

Tom Cantrell did not see Virginia as he drove his horse at Lee Bratton. He pulled his gun fast enough to have killed Lee. Sam Butterworth's remembered jeer mocked—*Soft heart, soft head.*—as Tom shot Lee's horse into a plunging stumble.

Lee was clawing out his gun when the driving shoulder of Tom's horse smashed Lee's horse into its fall. Lee kicked free of the stirrups as he pitched off. Tom's horse careened away, snorting, and Tom heard the agonized shout of Ashley Hampton: "The girl, Cantrell! The girl!"

When Tom looked, her frightened gelding was wheeling toward him, nostrils flaring. Her limp figure was dragging from the stirrup. "Oh, no!" broke from him. A wild impulse to shoot the horse died instantly—the frightened brute might fall on her. Tom spun his own horse around into another tremendous lunge.

Tom left the saddle in a dive at the gelding's head. A hand got the bridle. Both hands clamped on the bit shanks as his feet slammed to earth. He'd never savaged a horse as he did now. He broke the gelding's panic into quivering, agonized quiet with iron hands. With the reins, he iron-handed the gelding's head up and back and worked carefully toward the stirrup.

With one hand, Tom frantically freed her small foot. He shouldered the gelding away, hurled the reins away, and caught her up off the ground. Only when he straightened up did he see the rolling mass of flesh, horns, and sharp hoofs driving at them as the herd stampeded. He glimpsed Lee's prone horse and at least one sprawled man in the path of the stampede, and he ran for the ridge slope with his limp burden, hardly conscious of the continuing gunshots, yells, and increased number of riders in sight. He did glimpse George Sell, gun in hand on a plunging horse, and realized that others of his crew must have arrived. Shaken, gasping, Tom ran with his burden for the side of the draw and stumbled up toward the first brush.

The pounding tide of the stampede passed his very heels, it seemed. A horse screamed. A man's stricken cry lifted faintly. The thundering stampede blotted it out.

Virginia had lost her hat. Her black hair had come unpinned. Dirt soiled her small, pallid face. Blood was oozing from a gash at her hairline when Tom halted beside a scrub cedar. He placed her carefully on the earth and went to a knee beside her.

Gasping, he begged: "Ginny? Oh, Ginny!"

Her head drooped over, twisting her slim neck where the silver earring had lightly rested when she had sat smiling faintly over the roses they would someday plant in the sunny patio. He had lost his hat. Tom pushed his hair out of his eyes and reached for her wrist, and kneeled, motionless, at the miracle of her slow, slight pulse. He held to that reassurance, almost afraid to let go.

The rolling hammer of the stampede faded in the distance. Gunshots and yells died away, and a rider dismounted behind Tom. Ashley Hampton stepped to the spot as Tom carefully tied his kerchief over the gash at her hairline.

"Get my horse," Tom said without looking up.

"Her brother wishes to stop here and see her," the Texan said. "Want him?"

"No. I'll, take care of him later. Get my horse."

When Hampton brought the horse, Tom said: "Easy with her." He settled in the saddle, bent down, took her from the Texan, and wheeled slowly down the slope, holding her carefully. Her head lay limply on his arm. The sun struck her small, soiled face. Tom drew the folds of the kerchief over her closed eyes and held her more closely. He emerged slowly from the jumbled ridges, and sighted home far across the open sweep of grassland. Vaguely he was aware of his crew and prisoners keeping slow pace at a distance, and knew gratefully that Hampton was giving him this solitude. He reached often to her wrist for reassurance. The house was not far ahead when her slightest stir of life came against his body. Tom bent close to catch the flutter of a whisper: "Lee . . . Lee?"

"Lee is safe. We'll soon be home," he said reassuringly.

"Home. . . ." He could feel her relax. He held her more closely and watched Barnaby Polk urge a galloping horse toward them. The old lawyer arrived with a stricken look on his face.

"Is Ginny . . . ?"

"Alive," Tom said.

"What happened?"

"Fell off her horse."

The old lawyer glanced at the armed men escorting Lee and his crew. "There has been trouble?" Barnaby Polk said quietly.

"It's over," said Tom briefly. "I'll not discuss it now, sir."

The keen eyes studied him. Barnaby Polk looked at Ginny Bratton, dreadfully quiet in Tom's arms, her eyes covered by the kerchief. The old man's face was sad as he turned his horse toward the guarded prisoners.

The Mexican woman waited outside the kitchen door as Tom rode slowly into the yard with his burden. Ashley Hampton had gone ahead and was waiting. Hampton's arms reached up for Virginia while Barnaby Polk stood by in silence. Tom dismounted quickly and stopped the woman's distressed Spanish by ordering curtly: "Warm water. Bandages."

Virginia protested weakly: "I can walk."

Tom took her in his arms again, and followed Barnaby Polk through the house to her bedroom. Carefully Tom put her on the bed and adjusted the pillow under her head. "You'll be fine now," he said, and managed a smile. "We'll get you to the doctor at the fort quickly."

"No."

"You need to go. You'll have to go."

Her eyes closed. "You've taken my cattle," she said weakly. "You'll not take me from my home." Tom frowned helplessly, and she said tiredly: "This is my room. Get out."

Tom looked at the old lawyer and met only a stern stare. Silently Tom went. On his way to the kitchen he met the Mexican woman bringing towels and a pan of warm water. She looked at his scowling face and hurried by.

Ashley Hampton sprawled in a chair at the kitchen table, drinking hot coffee. He indicated a full cup waiting. Tom dropped into the chair opposite and gulped half the coffee before muttering: "Who's dead and wounded?"

"Yo' Pete Yancey was shot off his horse and finished under the stampede," Hampton said quietly. "Couple of my men were shot in the meat. They're tough. More of our men busted out of the brush and flustered young Bratton's bunch. One got away. Bratton and three of his men are left."

"Bring them into the patio."

Tom was staring into his coffee cup when the Texan silently went out. Barnaby Polk entered the kitchen. Tom had not seen the tall old man angry. He looked up into icy contempt, stern in every line and wrinkle.

"Cantrell, I misjudged you," Barnaby Polk said in measured words. "I've known Lee Bratton's failings. Of you, I expected better. Even Ginny Bratton, apparently, is not safe around you."

Tom said: "You are entitled to your opinion, sir."

"Lee brought his herd lawfully on land owned by his sister," Barnaby Polk said coldly. "You precipitated trouble by demanding possession of the herd. And you did it with Ginny Bratton there, exposed to any violence."

Restraining his temper, Tom said: "Her brother brought a herd of stolen cattle. And a crew of gunmen looking for trouble."

"There need not have been trouble. There are courts of law for disputes."

"Let Lee Bratton take his case to court, then." Tom swigged at the coffee to control the dark fury working in him. "I've taken the herd and I'll keep it," he said, putting the cup down.

Feet shuffled through the doorway. The surly prisoners were herded through into the patio at gunpoint.

Barnaby Polk said: "You are not the first man to believe himself above the law. In my terms on the bench, I sentenced many such men to hang. You have aroused the country with your illegal actions. By what right, now, do you hold Lee a prisoner in his sister's house?"

Tom laid his revolver on the table. "This," he said shortly. "Men are dead back there because of young Bratton. He brought stolen cattle. He brought gunmen to take over the ranch. Now we'll see."

"I believe you will be shot soon, young man," Barnaby Polk said quietly. "But if not, I promise you justice in a court of law for every illegal act." The old man stalked from the kitchen into the patio.

Alone, Tom drank the last of the coffee. Suddenly he crushed the tin cup in his hand, hurled it across the room, and walked into the patio.

Lee Bratton and his three remaining men stood sullenly against the north wall, covered by revolvers in the hands of Eagan and George Sell. Ashley Hampton stood by the log well curbing, fingering one side of his yellow mustache and impassively regarding the pale anger on Barnaby Polk's face.

Lee's demand was sullen as Tom walked to him: "Do I get to see my sister?"

"Did you buy cattle from Matthew Fallon?" Tom demanded.

"None of your business. You don't scare me, Cantrell."

Tom smashed him on the jaw. The blow slammed Lee's head back against the hard adobe wall. He reeled off and fell, and lay motionlessly.

"Cantrell," Barnaby Polk said unsteadily. "Watch yourself."

"Throw water on him," Tom ordered Ashley Hampton.

The Texan dropped the wooden bucket into the well. He drew it up with the windlass while Tom paced in black silence to the end of the patio and back, and watched the Texan dash the full bucket of water over Lee's head.

Lee shuddered and sat up groggily, pawing at his face. Tom reached down and jerked him upright. "Did Fallon sell you the cattle?"

"Hell with you," Lee mumbled.

Tom struck him down with another blow. Then Tom directed: "More water on him."

Oblivious of the heavy quiet, he paced blackly to the end of the patio again. He saw the Mexican woman peer from the living room doorway and close the door quickly. He wheeled back and watched water again bring Lee to coughing consciousness. Again Tom dragged the dripping figure up.

"Was it Fallon?"

Lee spat in his face. The sober voice of Ashley Hampton cut through the curtains of fury: "Look around, Cantrell."

Gripping Lee's left arm, his fist poised for another smash, Tom turned his head. Ginny Bratton was in the living room doorway, holding the arm of the Mexican woman. She was small, slender, pale, in her belted blue robe. Long, black hair cascaded over her shoulders. Her chin trembled.

"Don't," Ginny said. "We'll leave the ranch. I'll go. He's all I h-have, Mister Cantrell."

"Then God help you," said Tom bitterly. "You have nothing in him." He stepped away from Lee, and told Ashley Hampton: "She must see the doctor at the fort. Get the wagon ready."

"Cantrell," Barnaby Polk said. When Tom faced the tall old man, he heard an icy promise. "There is law. You will meet it, young man."

"Tell that to the men who are dead," Tom said blackly. He walked out of the patio and out of the house, and got a shovel and pick. Alone he rode toward the grassy draw, and the men who Lee Bratton's irresponsibility had killed.

XVIII

Matthew Fallon heard what had happened from Lee Bratton's man who had escaped and ridden fast to the Upper Frío Plaza, where Fallon himself had come. And in the hot sunset, Lee's

three remaining men came into John Hovey's saloon with word
that Lee would follow, after driving his sister and their lawyer to
the fort. Standing at the back end of Hovey's crowded bar, one
of the men told of the savage handling Lee had received from
Cantrell. "Cantrell means to get you," he warned.

"By tomorrow," Fallon promised, "there'll be three or four
men in town here for every man Cantrell has." A barber had
worked on him; he had bought a new suit and eaten well. He
was coolly, arrogantly confident now.

After dark, Fallon was at a table in the back corner of the
saloon when Lee entered. All the swaggering, laughing confidence had vanished from Lee. He ignored the noisy men at the
bar and walked sullenly back to Fallon. Lee caught up a bottle
and glass and poured a drink before he dropped into a chair.

"I'll kill him," Lee said in a shaking voice. "If it's the last
thing I ever do!" He added bitterly: "Like he killed my horse."

"Cantrell is too much man for you," Fallon said scornfully.
"Men are coming who'll take care of Cantrell. Quite a few are
already here."

"Cantrell's house is like a fort," Lee said sullenly. "Even has a
well in the patio. They might get their cattle back, but Cantrell
can hold them off." Lee tossed down the drink and glowered at
the empty glass. "I know how to get him. He'll be in the open,
easy to get. He's coming to town here with his men."

Fallon clenched his twisted hand in the coat pocket. His
sarcasm was barbed. "Cantrell told you his plans, I suppose."

Lee reached for the bottle again, too lost in rage to notice the
sarcasm. "My sister heard Cantrell plan it. He's coming after
the three men who shot his partner."

Fallon's instant question was sharp. "Does Cantrell know
who they are?"

"How do I know? He said he was coming. Ginny begged me
to stay away from him." Lee downed his second drink. The look

he turned on Fallon was hot and sullen. "Out in the open, right here in the plaza, is the place to get him. Shoot him down like he shot my horse."

Fallon carefully poured a drink with his left hand, and held his voice calm. "How many men will Cantrell bring?"

"All of them, the way he talked in front of Ginny," Lee said, sullen and spiteful. "It'd be a chance to take his house, too. Wouldn't be anyone there but the Mexican woman. Ginny ordered her to stay and take care of the boy."

"What boy?"

"Some kid who ran away from the Apaches," Lee said without interest.

Matthew Fallon tasted his whiskey and sat thinking. "You're sure the boy is at the ranch now?"

"I saw him. It'd be a chance to burn the house, only I want that house after Cantrell's gone." Lee dropped a clenched fist on the table. "Cut him off here in town. Take his house. Cantrell won't have a chance."

"If Cantrell did ride into the plaza here with his men," Fallon said slowly, "a few guns could cut him down from cover before he knew what was happening." Fallon sat thinking about it, finishing the drink in small sips. "There's no doubt that Cantrell would leave the boy at the ranch," he said under his breath.

"Why should he bring the kid to town? What difference does the boy make anyway?" Lee said impatiently.

"Forget it." Fallon's own heavy face was flushing from heady satisfaction. "You'd better stay sober," Fallon advised, keeping contempt out of his voice. "I'll post men toward Cantrell's ranch to sight him if he starts to town."

Fallon left Lee there at the table, and wondered scornfully why Cantrell hadn't killed the young fool, instead of letting Lee ride away with information that would destroy Cantrell beyond all doubt now. In the next half hour, to men he could trust,

Fallon gave careful orders. Then, alone, he walked through the night shadows to the feed corral on the west side of the plaza. On the soundest horse available, he rode out of town, rating the horse carefully. This night's ride would be long, and only Matthew Fallon himself could safely penetrate the frowning mountains south of Fort Ross. Only Matthew Fallon could find Senya's band of Apaches.

At Fort Ross, after the dull boom of the sunset gun, Major Alcorn paced the edge of the empty parade in front of his adobe quarters. Lieutenant Fitzpatrick, tired, perturbed, and ravenously hungry tried to turn smartly each time the major swung about.

"Miss Bratton, fortunately, was not killed," Alcorn said evenly. "A good night's rest, the doctor says, will do much for her."

"I hope so," Fitzpatrick said under his breath. "For her sake, and for Tom Cantrell's sake."

Alcorn slapped his gilt-corded hat impatiently against a leg. More disturbed himself than he cared to admit, Alcorn held his even tone. "Tom Cantrell has run wild, and capped it by taking cattle from this girl. The reports you've dispatched suggest the country to the north is up in arms."

"Tom handled them roughly," Fitzpatrick said dryly. "Armed men are gathering in the Upper Plaza to go against him."

"How many men?"

"I can't estimate, sir. They're coming in steadily. I have two men loafing around the Upper Plaza, listening to the talk. I could move the rest of the patrol here to the fort," Fitzpatrick suggested hopefully. "We're on the north bank of the Frío tonight, a few miles out of town."

"Remain there," Alcorn decided. "Before noon tomorrow, send me a report on the situation in town. And another report in the afternoon. If armed men move toward Tom Cantrell's ranch, let me know immediately."

"If they start for Tom's ranch, Major," Fitzpatrick said slowly, "they may kill Tom before they can be stopped."

"He was one of the best men the regiment ever had. Gone completely wild." Alcorn shook his head regretfully. "Return to your patrol. Keep me informed."

Fitzpatrick saluted and walked to his horse, denied the good meal at the bachelor's mess he had anticipated. He toyed briefly with an idea of getting warning to Tom Cantrell. But habit, training, and the thought of Alcorn's vigorous anger at such a breach of orders made Fitzpatrick reluctantly put the thought aside.

Late that night Tom Cantrell paced, bleakly alone with his thoughts, outside the quiet ranch house. Finally, in his room, he slept uneasily on the hard pallet of his pole bunk. Sunlight was outside the window when he wakened and rolled on his side, eyeing the wolf skins on the dried mud floor while his thoughts ranged over the past and the future. Yesterday Eagan and two more men had followed him, and had helped dig graves and do what had to be done. Ginny Bratton had been gone when they returned.

Now Tom knew he hadn't been ruthless enough. Matthew Fallon was the key man in all this bloodletting. Fallon should have been hunted first. When Tom dressed and stepped into the quiet living room, the small walnut organ beside Ginny Bratton's bedroom door had a forlorn, deserted look. Tom remembered that Ginny had ordered the Mexican woman to remain at the ranch with the boy. He decided to let the order stand, and saddled a horse and rode out to the herd. Lee's stampeding cattle had scattered and drifted on to mingle with the other cattle.

Lee Bratton himself remained a baffling problem. Ginny's brother was no sweepings of the frontier settlements. But the years that had shaped Ginny Bratton had put in Lee reckless irresponsibility and hot-headed temper. Tom rode back to the house, tied his horse to a corral pole, rolled a smoke, and stood pondering Ginny's brother.

Eagan leaned against the corral poles in companionable silence. Ashley Hampton came from the kitchen with coffee in his hand.

"Will they come at us today?" Hampton asked.

"Perhaps," Tom said. "Tomorrow at the latest." He was watching the small figure of the boy moving aimlessly between saddle shed and house, scanning the ground. "What's he doing?" Tom inquired.

"Playing Apache," said Eagan indulgently. "Looking for that busted-star heel print you talked about yesterday."

"More sense than we've shown," Tom said abruptly. He called: "Look in the patio, along the north wall, son! The men were standing there! You're the only one who's thought about their heel marks!"

"A smart kid," said Eagan proudly.

The boy heard Eagan's praise. A smile touched his mouth. He ran into the house.

"I'll look, too," Tom said. Eagan and the Texan went with him.

They found the boy kneeling at the damp earth in the patio, where water had been dashed over Lee Bratton. Tracks covered tracks, but the boy was tracing a small circle in the earth with his finger. Tom bent over it and made out the partly obliterated print of a heel plate with a star design in the center. One point of the star was not showing.

"He stood in front of me and I sent him away," Tom said bitterly. He dropped a hand to the boy's shoulder. "Son, thanks!"

The boy smiled happily.

Ashley Hampton was thoughtful. "They all walked here. Which one?"

Lee Bratton had stood here. Had Lee helped murder Steve Rogers, so his sister could buy Steve's half of the ranch while Tom Cantrell was far away in Texas?

"Whoever made this print will be at the Frío Plazas now," Tom said under his breath. "Perhaps the other two men who helped kill Steve."

"Take all the men if you go," Hampton said quietly. "Do it right, or wait."

"Every man," Tom decided. "I want him."

Even Sam Butterworth rode with them, hunched in his old leather shirt, his long buffalo gun cradled across his lap. They were halfway to town when Eagan brought his horse alongside Tom.

"Does the major mean to do anything about the kid's mother?" Eagan asked.

"Not at this time."

"It ain't right." Eagan rode glumly. "I talked too much," Eagan finally said. "I tried to make the kid feel good yesterday while we was up on the butte. Told him his mother would be back before long."

"Your loose tongue, Eagan."

"He believed me, like I was his father," Eagan muttered. "He trusts me. Now I've got to tell him Eagan is a blow mouth." Eagan dropped back, a troubled man.

In surprised sympathy, Tom realized that Eagan was a family man now. Eagan had found something to cling to, and that reached trustfully to him. Eagan's rather barren life had become rich with purpose, despite his worry.

Ahead of them, tall cottonwoods and China trees marked the green oasis of the Frío Plazas. To the south, a rise of dust trailed a rider galloping fast from the Upper Plaza toward Fort Ross. Through the binoculars Tom made out a trooper who must have overstayed his leave. Tom smiled slightly over that reminder of other days. Then, as the flat-roofed structures of the Upper Plaza took shape, Tom checked his revolver and carbine and saw the other men doing the same.

XIX

They pulled the horses to a walk as they entered town. When they rode into the wide, sunny plaza, Tom cast a sweeping look at the adobe structures on the east and south sides of the plaza, and the scoured channel of the Frío along the north side. On his last visit, freight wagons, stamping mules, cursing teamsters had filled the center of the plaza. Lieutenant Fitzpatrick's returning patrol had been watering horses and mules down the Frío bank. Townspeople had been out in the open. Now there were only a few horses and several wagons at the hitch racks. Two indolent men watched them from the shady portal of the Frío Mercantile, where Ginny Bratton had gone to her knees beside her brother's beaten figure.

Tom's narrowing gaze swept past Hovey's saloon to the adobe wall of the feed corral and wagon yard on the west side of the plaza, where they were heading. "Quiet," Tom said to Ashley Hampton, at his right. "Almost too quiet."

The leisurely tramp of their horses reached the middle of the sun-flooded plaza. Tom was squinting at the flat roofs along the south side of the plaza. He sighted a head lifting cautiously above the low adobe roof parapet of Hovey's saloon.

"Get behind the wagon yard wall!" Tom ordered instantly. "We're in a trap!"

The peering man came upright, carbine in hand. He was Lee Bratton, yelling a warning as he jerked the carbine to his shoulder: "Now, Cantrell!"

"Ride for it!" Tom called, roweling his horse.

Tom caught the saddle horn and slid over, Indian-style, behind the horse. The spiteful report of Lee's carbine cut through the pounding rush of their horses. Tom heard a meaty slap as the bullet struck his horse. He yanked the carbine from its scabbard, and lost the gun as his horse plunged down.

Tom landed, sprawling, sliding as the horse fell away from him. A spurred horse swerved violently and barely missed trampling him. The rider and a companion pulled up.

"Keep going!" Tom called thickly. He was scrambling to his hands and knees, diving for his carbine.

Lee's yell had torn peace from the town. Guns opened up around the plaza. Bullets shrilled viciously through the bright sunshine as Tom got his carbine and started a crouching run toward the open gateway of the wagon yard. Men were shooting from the roof tops and doorways. Two men had appeared in the gateway of the wagon yard. They dodged back into the yard as Tom's men rode at them, shooting. One of the men fell. The first riders burst through the gateway past him, and swung right and left behind the shelter of the high adobe wall.

Crouching, Tom ran over to a sprawled man whose horse had galloped on into the wagon yard. It was one of the Texans, shot in the head, beyond help. Tom ducked as lead screamed past his shoulders. Bullets kicked up spurts of dust near his running feet. He heard dimly through the racket of gunfire the challenging Rebel yell of Ashley Hampton, who was waiting in the gateway ahead.

The rangy Texan held a long-barreled revolver in each hand. He was laughing. Already several of the men were firing back over the wall. A bullet ripped across Tom's back and struck dust from the dry adobe beside the gate. Gasping from the frantic run, Tom reached the Texan and levered a shell into the carbine. His hands, he saw, were abraded, bleeding from the hard fall.

"Get yo' wind while we close the gate," Hampton said.

Eagan helped with the gate. As the heavy plank halves swung shut, a bullet splintered through the wood. Swearing, Eagan dropped the wooden gate bar into place.

"Save your cartridges!" Tom called.

Sheltered by the adobe wall, Tom caught his breath and scanned the yard. A row of stalls roofed with boards extended along the inside of the front wall. Open feed boxes occupied the south and west walls. The north side of the yard held an office, harness and feed rooms. The man who had been shot lay on his side, dead. He was one of Lee Bratton's men. Tom jerked up a foot and found no heel plates on the dusty boot. The plate he wanted had to be on Lee's boots then, or on one of Lee's two other gunmen.

Buckboards, spring wagons, and a buggy stood in the wide yard. Snorting, uneasy horses were tied at the feed boxes around three sides of the yard. Tom eyed them and spoke with satisfaction to Ashley Hampton: "We've got most of their horses here."

The boom of old Sam Butterworth's buffalo gun rolled through the plaza. From the board roofing over the front feed boxes, Sam said sourly: "He won't stand on no more roofs with a gun."

"Was it Lee Bratton?" Tom called quickly.

"No such luck."

Ashley Hampton said: "How'd they know we'd be here? Didn't know it ourselves until we started. This was planned."

Tom had been wondering. He guessed, reluctantly: "Miss Bratton knew we were coming to town. Must have told her brother."

Hampton indicated the horses tied at the feed boxes. "Not that many men live in town. Fallon's friends must be here."

"And we're bottled up until dark," Tom said. "And not enough cartridges."

"Got a water well," Hampton said, looking about. "They got to get on roofs to shoot in at us." He grinned again under the yellow mustache, enjoying a thought. "We're minding their horses. They've got to stay for us to shoot at."

Tom grinned, too. Revolver in one hand, carbine in the other, he walked to the office, and then searched the harness and feed rooms. They had the place to themselves.

He saw Ashley Hampton digging a hole through the front adobe wall with a long-handled shovel. George Sell was shooting from a feed room doorway at the men on the roof tops. Men on the planking above the front feed boxes were firing over the wall, ducking down, shifting positions.

Tom ran, crouching, to a spring wagon in the middle of the yard. Screened by the wagon bed, he could see the roof parapets of Hovey's saloon and the Frío Mercantile. Guns around the plaza were firing in fast bursts and slower searching shots. Bullets smashed through the heavy wood gate. Twice splinters struck Tom's face as bullets ripped through the wagon wood. A horse tied at a feed box back of him reared and fell. Minutes later another horse dropped.

Heat pooled inside the adobe walls of the yard. A smell of blood and death crept through the hot air. Blood had caked, dried on the back of Tom's shirt. Presently he made another crouching run from behind the wagon and got the shovel Ashley Hampton had used.

The Texan stood sweating beside the small hole he had dug in the adobe wall. "Makes a bulls-eye to shoot at," he said, indicating the hole. "But a man gets a view out."

"It's the best way," Tom said. He stepped back and called to the men on the board roofing: "Come down one at a time and dig holes in the wall! You can cover the plaza better!"

Tom hacked a ten-inch hole through the hard adobe above a feed box. As the shovel broke through, a bullet ricocheted off the blade, driving shock up the handle.

Eagan was waiting for the shovel. "Been trying to spot that Fallon," Eagan said grimly. "Ain't seen him."

"Don't miss if you do," Tom said.

He peered cautiously through the new hole. A man jumped out of the saloon doorway, bringing up his carbine. Tom's quick shot drove him stumbling back into the saloon. Another man who looked like the large, untidy Ben Poole raised up behind a roof parapet. A fast shot missed and the figure ducked down. Twice in the next hour Tom saw Lee Bratton on the roofs. Each time he held his fire, and Tom knew he was being weak.

Buck Ellis was the first man who called: "Who's got cartridges to spare?"

"You're wasting them!" Tom called. "Take it easy!"

After that they fired less frequently. Gunfire out in the plaza continued heavily. Tom noticed some of his men glancing up dubiously at the slow progress of the sun. Night was long, dangerous hours away. And not enough cartridges.

Another slow hour went by. Tom laid his hot gun on the feed box and walked to the well in front of the office. He was gulping water thirstily from the tin bucket when he lifted his head suddenly, listening intently to a new sound in the endless, slamming gunfire.

A man never forgot the brassy bugle notes, however faint, blasting the charge. Tom put the bucket on the well curbing and shouted: "Stop shooting!" He ran to Ashley Hampton, who had turned, sweating and curious, beside his loophole. "Troopers coming from the fort," Tom said.

"Chance to get some cartridges," Hampton said.

Tom looked out the loophole. "Not cartridges and not help," he said bitterly. "Major Alcorn is moving in troops to take a hand. And they won't be helping us."

The bugle blasts cut the hot sunlight, louder, clearer. And

troopers from the fort entered the empty plaza in a column of twos at a leisurely, disdainful trot. The right file bent toward the Frío bank. The left file skirted the store fronts, guidon whipping, carbines at the ready as the long, blue lines lengthened out and out.

"Have a look," Tom said.

"I have watched too many blue uniforms coming at me," Ashley Hampton said.

The gunfire had dwindled and died away. Only the measured strike of shod hoofs filled the plaza quiet, broken by commands running down the lines.

There were more distant sounds. Tom guessed: "Major Alcorn is drawing a line outside the town, too."

Ashley Hampton said: "What does that Yank major think he'll do now?"

"Whatever it is," Tom promised grimly, "it won't be good for us."

XX

The two long files of mounted troopers lengthened out along the north and south sides of the plaza as Tom watched through the loophole in the adobe wall of the wagon yard. And pride came through resentful bitterness. In the explosive quiet after the racketing gunfire, the measured fall of shod hoofs, the easy creak of leather were the murmuring power of Fort Ross, poised over this lawless part of New Mexico. Tom had shared the lives of those men. Now, apart from them, he watched the two long files of armed troopers enclose the plaza. The vigorous, familiar commands of Major Alcorn were audible.

"Captain French! Disarm and bring out those men in the wagon yard! Captain Weatherby! Clear the roofs and buildings!"

Ashley Hampton disgustedly hurled his carbine out in the wagon yard. "No Yanks disarm me." The rangy Texan stalked to the well and drank from the water bucket.

Eagan unbarred the gate. Lieutenant Fitzpatrick led a detail of troopers in on foot. His black field hat cocked smartly, his revolver in his hand, Fitzpatrick eyed the dead men, dead horses, and sweating, defiant prisoners. Fitzpatrick's relief was visible when he sighted Tom Cantrell.

Fitz walked over to Tom. He sounded almost envious as he said: "Did you have to do it here in town, under the Old Man's nose?"

"They jumped us, Fitz. We didn't know they were here."

"Alcorn thinks you rode in for a fight. He's in a pet, Tom, came himself to handle it."

"What does he think he'll do?"

"Hasn't said." Fitz winked. "He can't court-martial you now. Probably raise a blue fog."

Looking past Fitz's shoulder, Tom said with wry warning: "Here comes Deacon French to blow down your neck."

"Oh, oh," Fitz muttered, turning hastily.

Captain French had ridden his horse through the gate. His critical glance swept the wagon yard. Stocky, usually dour behind his heavy cavalry mustaches, French called with an edge of sarcasm: "Mister Fitzpatrick! The major is patiently waiting your pleasure!"

"Yes, sir," said Fitz, reddening.

Tom called what Fitz could not: "Don't get excited, French. This won't make you a general."

French, a stickler for regulations and rectitude in junior officers, darkened. At Fort Union, French had thoroughly disapproved of joyous young men like Fitzpatrick and Tom Cantrell. He walked his horse over to Tom now and stared with displeasure. "I suppose, Cantrell, you're proud of this," he said, breathing heavier.

"No lectures, please," Tom said wearily. "Take it out on the lieutenants. They have to listen."

Captain French turned his horse away in hostile displeasure. Fitzpatrick looked unhappy. When the prisoners were herded to the gate, Tom moved over beside Fitzpatrick. "Fitz, get my saddlebags off my dead horse out there, will you? Hold them for me."

"Did you have to stir up French?" Fitz said acidly. Tom grinned, and Fitz had to grin, too. "I'll get the saddlebags," Fitz promised.

Troopers were bringing men out of the buildings and off the roofs, and tossing weapons into a growing pile. Major Alcorn, on his horse near the dead Texan, watched silently. Presently Alcorn rode over to Fitz's prisoners. Alcorn's expression was stern.

"You would do it," he said. "I warned you."

"And I told you, Major," Tom reminded him.

Alcorn's—"Yes, you told me."—had a regretful sound. He rode away.

Townspeople were cautiously venturing out. Tom's attention was caught by a two-horse buggy with a dusty, fringed top that was rolling slowly into the plaza. A saddled horse was tied behind, and Barnaby Polk's lank figure sat beside the driver. Judge Augustus Andrews, Tom guessed, had arrived from the Mesilla court term.

The buggy passed the prisoners in front of the stores and turned over to Fitzpatrick's group and stopped. Barnaby Polk stepped out.

Tom addressed the old lawyer civilly: "How is Miss Bratton, sir?"

"That, young man, is no concern of yours," said Barnaby Polk.

Major Alcorn rode over to the buggy and spoke forcefully. "Martial law is in force. Strangers are barred from the plaza for the time being."

The reply from the buggy was testy. "Where did a major of cavalry find authority to proclaim martial law?"

Frowning, Alcorn admitted: "I concede the lack of full authority."

"Or any authority, Major?"

"Major Alcorn," Barnaby Polk said, showing humor, "allow me the pleasure of presenting my old friend, Judge Augustus Andrews, just arrived from Mesilla."

Alcorn had not looked under the fringed buggy top. His chagrin was visible as he regarded the plump, elderly man who stepped down now from the buggy. "Judge Andrews, sir. I had the pleasure at Fort Union last year. You were with the general."

Ashley Hampton spoke under his breath at Tom's shoulder: "In Mesilla, they called that old coot the hanging judge. Don't look it, does he?"

Judge Andrews was in white shirt sleeves. Dignified white burnsides framed his pinkish, smooth face. He was pleasant as Alcorn dismounted. "Waiving the matter of martial law, Major, what do you propose to do now?"

Fitzpatrick had sent a trooper jumping to hold Major Alcorn's horse. "I propose to restore order," Alcorn said flatly. "This man, Cantrell, sir, has inflamed all the country to the north by his illegal actions. Cattle have been stolen. Men have been killed. The young lady who purchased an interest in Cantrell's ranch almost lost her life yesterday when a herd of her cattle was forcibly taken by Cantrell and his men."

"I have talked with Barnaby Polk and Ginny Bratton, Major, while we waited outside of town for this gun battle to stop."

"I can't court-martial civilians," Alcorn said reluctantly. "But I can and I will stop this bloodshed by locking Cantrell and his men in the guardhouse, and ordering all other men to disperse."

"You'll stop nothing that way, Major," Tom broke in with quick temper. "You're aware that all the stock on my ranch will be taken. You must know that when we're turned out of the guardhouse . . . without our guns, probably . . . we'll be shot down within five miles of the fort. Is that your kind of a trial? Is that the way you'll decide who will die? It's murder!"

Judge Andrews turned deliberately. The smooth, pinkish features framed by the white burnsides gave him a grandfatherly look. He sounded pleasant and friendly. "Young man, you have a point there. Any criminal in the territory is entitled to his just court." Judge Andrews pursed his lips as he looked Tom over. "Whatever the outcome of his trial," he added pleasantly. He turned to Major Alcorn. "This, Major, seems to be an unusual situation. I believe that the public welfare presses me to hold court here, and dispose of this trouble lawfully and fairly."

Ashley Hampton muttered: "He's sniffed a hanging."

Major Alcorn frowned. "This isn't a county seat, Judge. Facilities of the law are lacking. Not even a deputy sheriff, let alone a district attorney."

"Major, I'm empowered to hold court in a cornfield at midnight, if I choose," Judge Andrews said. "Barnaby Polk, a learned member of the bar, can be sworn in as special prosecutor. Quite sufficient for such irregular proceedings necessary to the public welfare."

Barnaby Polk glanced coldly at the prisoners. His remark to the judge held regret. "Augustus, it would be a pleasure, but I must decline prosecution of this man Cantrell. I plead prejudice from strong personal feelings."

"You draw a fine line at times, Barnaby." Judge Andrews pursed his lips again. "No doubt some other member of the bar can be located."

Alcorn shook his head. "This part of the territory sees few lawyers."

"Understandable," Judge Andrews said dryly. "How about

your command, Major? Do you have a man with legal training?"

"Not that I. . . ." Alcorn paused, turned, and lifted his voice.
"Captain French!" And when French joined them, breathing
audibly from his haste, Alcorn said: "Captain French, didn't I
hear once that you'd studied law?"

"You did, Major." Some of French's dourness fell away. He
brushed at his mustache. "I was admitted to the Missouri bar,
Major," French stated with gratification. "Quite an honor, I've
always felt."

"Where did you practice?" Judge Andrews asked.

French deflated slightly. "I've never had the chance to
practice, sir. Always regretted it."

"But you were admitted to the Missouri bar?"

"Yes, sir."

"Excellent," Judge Andrews said. "Major, detach this gentleman with orders to assist the court. We'll get him into some
kind of civilian clothes, swear him in as special prosecutor, and
go to trial."

Ashley Hampton muttered resignedly: "He's got us."

XXI

Troopers clattered about and banged chairs and tables in Hovey's saloon while Tom Cantrell and his men sat under guard on
the bar. Next door, in the Frío Mercantile, the post surgeon was
using a store counter for his work on wounded men. On the
mercantile portal dead men lay wrapped in blankets.

Eagan glanced over his shoulder at the bar bottles and spoke
glumly to a raw-boned private, standing guard in front of them.
"Flugie, a man headed for a hanging oughts have a drink."

Private Flugelmeir shifted his tobacco to the other cheek and
said: "Sarge, this here's a courtroom now. No drinkin'."

Tom worked his back muscles gingerly. The raw bullet furrow

was painful. He looked up when voices spoke at the guarded front door. Barnaby Polk stood there. Ginny Bratton was entering the saloon alone. Tom pushed off the bar, tossed his hat beside Ashley Hampton, and ignored Private Flugelmeir as he went to meet her.

A small white straw hat tilted toward Ginny's eye, masking court plaster over the injury at her hairline. She wore a plain white suit, and looked small and slender, pale and composed when they met. Her voice was steady.

"Isabel Alcorn is returning to the ranch with me, Mister Cantrell, to get the boy. She feels it her duty to see that the authorities take charge of him now."

"Best, perhaps," Tom said. "Why doesn't Isabel come here and tell me herself?"

"She feels it would be too painful after what has happened. You have disappointed her." Ginny Bratton's blue eyes were steady. "Barnaby Polk," she said, "assures me that you will have justice."

"They'll call it that," Tom said absently. He was thinking of the dreadful slackness of her small figure in his arms yesterday.

Ginny looked at his cut, abraded hands. She drew a breath. "I'll not watch your trial. I'm going back to the ranch and make my home secure."

"You'll be happy there," Tom said. His faint grin came. "Don't forget to plant roses in the patio."

Ginny looked up, startled. She bit her lip, hesitated, and turned hastily back to the front door, where Barnaby Polk waited with a cheroot between his lips.

Tom rolled a smoke, then forgot to light it as he walked back and leaned against the bar beside Ashley Hampton. He was still lost in thought when the trial opened.

In the back of the saloon, Judge Andrews sat behind a card table. At the judge's right, a few feet in front, Captain French sat behind another card table, tugging nervously at his mustaches as he frowned over scrawled notes. Tom sat behind a card table in front of the bar; his men perched on the bar edge behind him. Rows of chairs were filled with spectators, many of them participants in the gun battle. Armed troopers lined the walls, stood behind the bar, and were posted at front and back of the building.

Major Alcorn and Captain Weatherby sat in the front row of chairs, alert and available, as Judge Andrews used the bottom of a bottle for a gavel. In a black coat now, Judge Andrews still looked grandfatherly, but he was also something else, Tom thought, watching closely. On Judge Andrews had descended the majestic, invisible mantle of the law and a judge's great authority. His assurance dominated the room.

"This court," Judge Andrews said, "is now in session. Any disturbance will be dealt with. The defendant, Thomas Cantrell, will stand."

Tom got to his feet. The coldest pair of eyes Tom had seen in some time surveyed him from under bushy white brows. "The court," said Judge Andrews, "understands that you waive indictment by a grand jury, and formal trial by jury, which right you have."

Tom glanced over the spectators, most of whom had been trying to kill him. "I waive indictment and a jury," Tom said dryly.

"Captain French will stand."

French got to his feet, almost a stranger in the baggy black suit borrowed from the Frío Mercantile next door. A grim, dogged pomposity cloaked French. This, Tom decided, was French's long-suppressed ambition, this hour when he would finally dominate an actual trial.

"For the record, Captain French," Judge Andrews inquired perfunctorily, "are you a member of the territorial bar?"

French cleared his throat. "No, Your Honor. I am here by orders of my commanding officer."

"Are you a member of any other bar?"

"I am a member of the bar of Missouri, Your Honor."

"The court considers your qualifications satisfactory. By powers invested in me, and for the public welfare, I appoint you special prosecutor in the case of The Territory of New Mexico versus Thomas Cantrell, charged with unlawful possession of livestock. The court understands you are best prepared to bring this charge to trial."

"Yes, Your Honor."

"Raise your right hand, Captain, and repeat after me. . . ."

French repeated it: "I solemnly swear I will prosecute the defendant, Thomas Cantrell, without fear or favor. I will not knowingly suppress any evidence for or against him. To the best of my ability I will so prosecute this case that justice may be done, alike to the Territory of New Mexico and to the defendant. So help me God."

And French would try, with pompous, severe doggedness, Tom thought as Judge Andrews said: "Thomas Cantrell, are you ready for trial?"

"As ready as I'll ever be."

"Have you any witnesses?"

"Only my crew. The rest of my witnesses are in Texas."

"Do you have an attorney?"

"No."

"Do you wish the court to appoint an attorney?"

"Not at this time."

"The court reminds you of your right to object to evidence presented. Sit down. The prosecution will open."

French drank from a glass of water. He cleared his throat and glanced about the room. "Your Honor, the prosecution will prove that the defendant, Thomas Cantrell, about midday yesterday, unlawfully took and retained by force certain livestock owned by Lee Bratton." French cleared his throat again. "I place in evidence witnessed bills of sale purchased with drafts on the Santa Fe account of Mister Barnaby Polk, administrator of the estate of Peter Bratton, father of Lee Bratton. I call Mister Barnaby Polk as witness in the matter of the bank drafts."

Captain French stepped over and placed the papers before Judge Andrews as Barnaby Polk rose up from the front row of chairs and took the witness chair beside the judge's table.

Judge Andrews scanned the bills of sale through steel-rimmed spectacles and directed, without looking up: "Take the oath, Barnaby."

Lee Bratton, in one of the front chairs, gave Tom a hostile, satisfied stare as Barnaby Polk gave testimony about the authority given Lee to issue bank drafts against his inheritance for purchase of cattle. Then French put Lee in the witness chair. Coolly Lee told of purchasing cattle from Matthew Fallon.

"Object," Tom broke in. "Did Fallon own the cattle? Put Fallon under oath."

Captain French glowered indignantly. Judge Andrews frowned. "Objection denied. The defendant will not try to direct proceedings. In the absence of conflicting testimony, evidence presented so far will be accepted by the court."

French stroked his heavy mustaches in satisfaction. His questions drew from Lee an injured account of how Tom Cantrell, backed by armed men, had forcibly taken his herd. It sounded convincing. In growing complacency, French said: "I call Joe Sloan as corroborating witness."

Sloan had been in the patio yesterday with Lee. Tom had ignored him to deal with Lee. Now, closely, Tom watched the slouching, hard-faced man take the witness chair and tell his story. In the midst of it, Tom's mind wandered to the small, limp figure of Ginny Bratton being dragged by her horse.

When Tom looked up, he met the cold stare of the grandfatherly old man who would judge him. And the old man was a hanging judge. One could feel the knowledge triumphant in the room, Tom reflected, looking about. What their guns had failed to do, Judge Augustus Andrews would probably do with a lawful noose. French had caught the feeling. He was a righteous man, determined to win this one case of his life. Even if it meant hanging a man, Tom mused, watching French's confident pompousness increase.

"I could call another witness, Your Honor, to repeat the same testimony," French said. "But proof of ownership has been established. Two witnesses have sworn to the unlawful taking of the livestock. I ask Lee Bratton to stand."

Lee got to his feet. French took another drink of water and smoothed his mustaches. "There he stands," French said in solemn, approving tones. "An example of the finest virtues."

Lee modestly dipped his head. Barnaby Polk, his veined hands folded on the shabby stovepipe hat resting on his lap, glanced up at Lee thoughtfully, made a vague, restless sound in his throat, and closed his eyes as French's voice deepened with emotion.

"The only sister of this fine young man needed help. Her faith in her brother was justified. Lee Bratton gladly used his small inheritance to buy the cattle she needed." French clenched a hand and struck the table. "What finer thing could a brother have done, Your Honor? He gave all he had unselfishly. And he was despoiled, and his sister left injured and helpless, by the violent, illegal acts of this defendant. The prosecution asks for justice, Your Honor, and believes justice will be rendered."

French pulled a white handkerchief from his hip pocket, mopped his face, and looked around with satisfaction before he sat down.

Judge Andrews was polishing his spectacles. His glance at

Tom showed no emotion. "In the court's opinion, this makes a *prima-facie* case. Unless the defendant produces conclusive testimony, which will overcome testimony of the prosecution, I will be obliged to rule against the defendant. Thomas Cantrell, the court hopes you realize the seriousness of your situation. The court is reluctant to permit trial to proceed further without asking you again if you wished to be advised by counsel."

"There is only one other lawyer in town, and I'd want him," Tom said. "I ask the court to order Mister Barnaby Polk to defend me."

Judge Andrews peered over his spectacles. "The question," he said, "was a matter of form. I find this most irregular."

"I don't," Tom said calmly. "He's a lawyer, isn't he?"

"Barnaby Polk is a lifelong friend of the Bratton family," Judge Andrews said. "Barnaby represents the two children in all legal matters. He is entrusted with the guardianship of their estates, which you, Thomas Cantrell, are accused of having unlawfully damaged."

"I know all that."

The tall figure of Barnaby Polk slowly unfolded to his feet, shabby stovepipe hat in one hand. He said sternly: "Whatever this scheme, young man, I warn you now that if you are found guilty by this court, the aroused feeling of men you have wronged will undoubtedly result in your being hanged quickly to the nearest cottonwood."

Tom glanced at the rows of seated men waiting for their guns to be returned and for Alcorn's troopers to ride back to the fort.

"No doubt of that," Tom agreed. "They'll hang me and my men . . . or shoot us to save time."

"And yet," said Barnaby Polk, "with that knowledge, you ask me to attempt a perhaps half-hearted defense of your case, which seems lost already by the weight of accepted evidence?"

Tom looked at the tall old man a long moment. He smiled. "There's no lawyer in the territory I'd rather have defending me, sir."

"A sense of duty to the bar," said Barnaby Polk slowly, "forces me to assume your defense. I request the court to grant a short recess while counsel talks with his client in one of the back card rooms."

Judge Andrews looked annoyed and resigned. "Twenty minutes, Barnaby. And during recess, the court will allow one drink per man at the bar."

Tom picked up the dusty saddlebags that had been resting at his feet, and followed the long strides of the old man back to a card room, while chairs scraped and spectators crowded to the long plank bar.

XXII

Recess was over. Bottles and glasses littered the long bar when Judge Andrews rapped on his table for order. "The defense will open," Judge Andrews said. His plump figure sat more alertly as Barnaby Polk stood up beside Tom Cantrell. The old lawyer had removed his coat.

Captain French sat aggressively behind his table opposite and regarded his opponent with dour tolerance. The case, French seemed to feel, was already won. The judge obviously believed so. This old Barnaby Polk, reluctantly defending Cantrell, would make a careless formality of it. This one law case in French's life would be successful.

Barnaby Polk hooked his thumbs under his red suspender straps and stood lost in thought while the last sounds died away in the big room. He looked awkward, and sounded uncertain, as he spoke slowly. "This courtroom holds infuriated men, Your Honor, who allege that my client forcibly took their livestock, too. Men have been wounded and killed because of it. Obviously the angers and enmities in this room will remain unsettled until all the complaints are judged. Obviously, also, if Thomas Cantrell is guilty on one charge of illegal possession, he is guilty on all the charges. Yet, strangely, the prosecution has ignored all these other alleged wrongs and injuries."

French got hastily to his feet. "I resent the implication, Your Honor. The other injured parties did not have their bills of sale with them. It would take days to produce them. Lee Bratton had his proof." French slapped a heavy palm on the table. "Guilt in one charge is sufficient."

"The court," said Judge Andrews, "was informed of these facts and agreed. And continues to agree."

"The defense," said Barnaby Polk, "will accept sworn testimony of ownership and injury, subject to contrary proof."

Judge Andrews frowned. "Counsel for the defense will place his client in greater jeopardy if he adds further counts to the charge. The court warns that sentence will be passed on each count."

"The defense understands, and will yield, Your Honor, while the prosecution brings all other charges against Thomas Cantrell."

"So directed," said Judge Andrews grimly. "But the defense has been warned."

Wrinkle by wrinkle, a benign smile spread across Barnaby Polk's face. He sat down.

Captain French flushed. Then he said: "I will call every man present whose stock was taken by Cantrell. Ben Poole, come forward and take oath. Describe what was taken from you."

"And tell where the stock was purchased," added Barnaby Polk benevolently. "The defense will make a record of all livestock described, and requests the court to do the same, in the interests of impartial judgment."

"This court is always impartial," Judge Andrews said testily.

Captain French, vindictive now, put the glowering Ben Poole through his testimony against Tom Cantrell. Man after man, angry and resentful, came forward and described his losses, and where his cattle and horses had been purchased. Finally French said with challenging satisfaction: "The prosecution again rests."

Judge Andrews flexed a plump hand that had been scrawling copious notes with a pencil. The judge's comment was edged. "The court hopes that counsel for the defense can justify all this."

"Counsel will try," said Barnaby Polk. He stood up. Sad and thoughtful, he looked at Lee Bratton. Lee's grin back was confident.

"Your Honor is aware," Barnaby Polk said in a musing tone, "that as a young man I attended school in Tennessee with the grandfather of Lee Bratton. We sparked the same young ladies. Counsel for the defense recalls that he was the better man at it."

Judge Andrews bristled slightly. "Barnaby," he ruled, "your wild oats have no connection with stolen livestock."

"Counsel for the defense takes note of the court's rebuke," said Barnaby Polk apologetically. "I was trying to make clear a great reluctance to oppose Lee Bratton and his sister in these proceedings."

"You made that plain earlier," Judge Andrews said tartly.

"An old man's memory," said Barnaby Polk, "is inclined to wander. Nevertheless, it has been a happy obligation of remembered youth to serve in *loco parentis,* almost a father, to Lee Bratton and his sister." Barnaby Polk stroked his chin. In the quiet courtroom, his voice grew reflective. "But having put a reluctant hand to the plow, counsel for the defense is obliged to open an unsavory furrow to the just eyes of this honorable court."

Judge Andrews sat straighter. His plump figure seemed to

brace inwardly, and warily. "Plow, Barnaby," he directed.

"This court," said Barnaby Polk calmly, "and all men present are aware that issues greater than the theft of livestock rest upon the outcome of this trial. More violence will be done if full justice is not rendered today."

"Justice," said Judge Andrews, "will be given."

Captain French nodded with rising satisfaction. Barnaby Polk gazed reflectively at him. "In good faith," the old lawyer said, "this court has accepted bills of sale issued by one Matthew Fallon, who does not seem to be present to testify. The sworn testimony of livestock purchases has repeatedly reached back to this same Matthew Fallon. But a stock brand is not proof of ownership. Merely notice that proof will be offered."

"This court, and also the defense," reminded Judge Andrews testily, "have accepted the bills of sale and the sworn testimony."

"Subject, Your Honor, to contrary evidence," said Barnaby Polk calmly.

Slowly the old lawyer reached a veined hand into the depths of his upended stovepipe hat and brought out a sheaf of papers. He lifted a thumb to his mouth and moistened it. In silence, as a man might deal a poker hand out on the table, he dealt the papers, one at a time.

Judge Andrews stirred restlessly. He seemed fascinated. Finally he cleared his throat and spoke an acid warning: "In appreciation of counsel's undoubted talents, the court warns that only four aces had better appear in this deck."

"Counsel notes the court's long memory," said Barnaby Polk benignly, "and submits respectfully that no drawing to wild flushes will occur."

Judge Andrews flinched at some stab of memory. He watched warily as Barnaby Polk again reached into the depths of the hat and brought out two leather-bound tally books and a brown envelope. The old lawyer laid them on the table.

Captain French was watching with increasing uneasiness. Now he stared like a man partly hypnotized as Barnaby Polk slowly selected several papers from the table and fanned them out in lean fingers like a prized poker hand.

"Your Honor," said Barnaby Polk, "from the sworn testimony of Ben Poole, I am now selecting five three-year-old steers branded JV on the right shoulders, and purchased from Matthew Fallon. These five steers are now allegedly in the illegal possession of Thomas Cantrell."

"The court," said Judge Andrews cautiously, "has made note of those steers."

"Next," said Barnaby Polk, "I offer this notarized affidavit, executed at Five Springs, Texas, by one Will Seabright. The gentleman attests that on or about the Tenth day of August, last year, Comanches raided his ranch. Some sixty two-year-old steers, branded JV on the right shoulder, were run off by the Comanches. Will Seabright further attests that his was a new ranch. He had never sold or given away livestock branded JV on the right shoulder."

"Never?" said Judge Andrews sharply.

"Never," said Barnaby Polk. "Next, Your Honor, I submit this notarized power of attorney, which authorizes Thomas Cantrell to recover for Will Seabright all livestock branded JV on the right shoulder, wherever found. In sworn testimony, the prosecution has admitted that Cantrell came upon these steers, now three-year-olds, on the open range. Counsel for the defense submits that Thomas Cantrell could not unlawfully have taken what had never passed from the legal ownership of Will Seabright. This Matthew Fallon sold what he did not own. And on this table before me," said Barnaby Polk blandly, "are other affidavits and powers of attorney covering all the rest of the livestock, which allegedly was illegally taken by Thomas Cantrell."

Judge Andrews drew a long breath. "Barnaby," he directed, "bring me that mess of papers." Judge Andrews's chagrined mutter was barely audible. "I might have expected aces all over the place."

Barnaby Polk carried the papers and the brown envelope to the judge's table. He remained standing by the witness chair, looking directly at Major Alcorn, in the front row of spectators.

"It is common knowledge," said Barnaby Polk evenly, "that men of New Mexico have traded profitably with the Comanches and other plains tribes for generations. But the times are changing. Men like Thomas Cantrell are settling in the remote parts of the territory. They mean to develop the wild land and build for the future. They are entitled to protection, not harassment, by the law or by the military."

Major Alcorn's mouth was a tight line as Barnaby Polk continued: "The defense in this trial has smoked out, and put into sworn testimony, the illegal transactions of the man named Matthew Fallon, who is not present in the courtroom. The defense will now cross-examine Lee Bratton."

Lee's triumphant confidence had gone. He was slightly sullen as he took the witness chair. For a long moment the tall old lawyer looked down at him. Then something chill and rather terrible entered the old lawyer's question.

"Young man, what kind of heel plates do you wear on your right boot?"

Captain French lunged to his feet, protesting: "Objection, Your Honor. The question is not relevant."

Judge Andrews, intent on the papers, and still chagrined, did not look up. "Objection denied," he ruled absently.

Tom Cantrell's thoughts had gone to the callous murder of Steve Rogers. That fiercely demanding question by Barnaby Polk could hang Lee Bratton. Could break the heart of Ginny Bratton. And could, Tom suspected, bring enduring sadness to the tall old man who stood waiting, while Lee's sullen stare dropped to his boots.

Lee's answer was hostile as he lifted his right foot to his knee. "Take a look," Lee said. "I never wear heel plates."

Barnaby Polk closed his eyes a moment. No expression touched his face. "Excused," he said evenly. "The next witness I will call is Red Kane."

This was the second gunman who had been in the patio with Lee. Red Kane had not testified. In a surly tone he took the oath while Captain French pulled nervously at his mustache. Not knowing what was happening, French was flustered.

"What heel plates do you wear?" Barnaby Polk asked the witness.

Red Kane lifted his right boot. "How do I know? They was tacked on last month in Las Vegas."

Barnaby Polk looked. "Quarter-moon in the center of the plates. Witness excused." Calmly now, Barnaby Polk said: "Joe Sloan, take the chair. And counsel for the defense asks the court to read the contents of the brown envelope."

Slouching, belligerent, Joe Sloan sat in the witness chair. His statement was rough. "Save your wind, old man. Here's my boot." He brought the right boot to his knee.

Barnaby Polk said: "A worn heel plate which has a four-pointed star cut out of the center. One side of the plate is broken away, leaving a three-pointed star."

"Make you feel any better, old man?" Joe Sloan asked as he dropped the foot heavily to the floor.

"The witness will remain seated," said Barnaby Polk.

Judge Andrews had been intently reading the sheets he had taken from the brown envelope. His smooth face was flushed as he looked up.

"Barnaby," said Judge Andrews coldly, "in my courtroom, under my nose, you diverted my attention. After doing so, you dealt off the bottom of the deck, and introduced evidence in another matter. You dared do this, Barnaby, to the dignity of the court."

"Counsel for the defense was examining the credibility of witnesses," said Barnaby Polk meekly. "Only justice in the trial of Thomas Cantrell is expected. Other acts of court are outside the province of this bewildered and respectful counsel for the defense."

"Barnaby. . . ." Judge Andrews shook his head and removed his spectacles. He cleared his throat, cast an accusing look at Barnaby Polk, and said: "The court will rule in the case of The Territory of New Mexico versus Thomas Cantrell."

Spectators bent forward intently. The room was completely silent.

"After impartial consideration of all testimony and evidence," said Judge Andrews, "the court finds Thomas Cantrell not guilty on all counts, therefore lawfully possessed of the livestock he now holds. The men who purchased from Matthew Fallon have no recourse, save to recover from Fallon, if possible. Furthermore, this court deems it necessary to request Major Alcorn to include the person and the possessions of Thomas Cantrell in military orders to protect all settlers. The court will communicate this request to the general in command."

Arms folded across his chest, Alcorn said calmly: "That is not necessary, Your Honor."

"Very well, Major. And since this court is using the protection of the Army, and is now issuing a bench warrant, the court requests the Army to secure the person of Joe Sloan, for action of the grand jury in the matter of the murder of Steven Rogers."

Joe Sloan sat motionlessly in the witness chair while the meaning entered his mind. Then his lunge out of the chair met the grabbing arms of Barnaby Polk. Sloan's furious fist struck the old lawyer's middle. Barnaby Polk grunted painfully and clung. Tom knocked his table aside as he dived to assist him.

He caught Sloan as the man broke away. Armed troopers rushed to them and took Sloan. Judge Andrews hammered his bottle on the table. The flurry of excitement died.

"Court," said Judge Andrews, "is adjourned."

Tom called out: "I'll speak now!" He looked over the room. "You've heard it's legal. You know now you've been jobbed. You'll never be safe again trading with Matthew Fallon, or men like him. I'm going to comb your ranges for stolen livestock. I'm going to break the thieves among you and help the honest men. Think it over, because my ranch is here to stay." Tom turned his back to them.

Barnaby Polk had dropped into the witness chair. He was rubbing his middle as he glanced up at Judge Andrews, who had hurried to his side. "We grow old," said Barnaby Polk. "Old and helpless, Augustus."

"I wouldn't have missed it, Barnaby," said Judge Andrews. "You grunted like a boar hog when he hit you." The two old men were smiling at each other. "Barnaby," said Judge Andrews, "get me out to your girl's ranch, and put a hot toddy in my hand."

XXIII

All of them traveled together back to the ranch, in the late afternoon. Major Alcorn had ordered Lieutenant Fitzpatrick and troopers to escort Judge Andrews to the ranch, and remain there during the judge's visit. Barnaby Polk had told Tom: "I want Lee Bratton at the ranch while I'm there. He'll behave."

Tom rode the old lawyer's horse. Plans for the future pushed through his mind. Dubiously he eyed Lee Bratton, who was riding apart, lost in sullen moodiness, unrepentant. The mass of the Lizard Butte was ahead when Barnaby Polk caught Tom's eye from the buggy seat and beckoned.

When Tom came alongside the buggy, the old lawyer spoke thoughtfully to him. "I'm aware now how you saved Ginny Bratton's life, and how the trouble really started. I don't believe Ginny knows the real facts."

"She'll not be interested."

"Ginny is a fair-minded young lady," said Barnaby Polk. "It should be possible to exist on the ranch with her, on some sort of business-like basis."

"Possible," Tom agreed dubiously. "You might suggest it to her."

"I will do so."

They crossed the immense draw where the cattle were scattered out for miles. Tom was riding beside Ashley Hampton. "Isabel Alcorn's buggy is still here," Tom commented as they neared the house. "Too late for her to start back to the fort today."

"Two young ladies and some organ music would make a party to celebrate," Hampton commented.

Tom chuckled, and lapsed into thought again. But when they rode into the wide yard behind the house, he dismounted and looked around alertly.

"Where are Isabel's horses?" Tom said, eyeing the empty corral. Then sharply: "Something wrong here!"

A movement on the ground beyond Isabel's buggy drew Tom's attention. He ran around the back of the buggy and found Sarina, the Mexican woman, on the earth. Her wrists and ankles were tied. A towel was bound around her face.

Ashley Hampton's shout was bringing troopers and the crew galloping into the yard. Tom kneeled beside the woman, barely noticing a keen-bladed little stiletto thrust into the earth. Her hand held a crude wooden cross, which had evidently hung about her neck, inside the bright, gaudy apron. The broken cord dangled as her rigid fingers clutched the cross. Her black eyes, which had smiled so often, were haunted, frozen in an agonized stare as Tom bent over her.

Men were running to the spot. Lee Bratton, one of the first, looked down at Sarina and said thickly: "Apaches!" Lee dropped to one knee, demanding harshly: "What happened to the girls?"

Sarina's black, tear-swollen eyes looked back at Lee as Tom unfastened the towel about her face.

Lee demanded again: "The girls! Where are they?"

Tom stared at what he had uncovered. His eyes went to the stiletto thrust into the earth. Tom said: "She can't answer. Apaches had their fun with her tongue."

Lee stumbled to his feet and stared wildly around. Cords in Tom's neck went rigid as he lifted the woman in his arms and started toward the house.

Ahead of him, Lee was already running, calling: "Ginny! Ginny!" He vanished into the house.

Tom could have told him that all the big house would be silent. If mercy had been granted, Ginny Bratton would be there. But Lee would not find peace if he found her.

Somewhere behind Tom, Eagan was shouting, "Hey, kid? You hiding, kid?" But there was no belief in Eagan's stricken calls.

The kitchen had been looted. Flour covered the floor. Moccasins had tracked through it. And Ginny Bratton's bedroom was a shambles. Drawers had been pulled out and thrown to the floor.

Tom laid his mute, agonized burden on the bed, and looked again at the cross, clutched desperately in her rigid fingers. "Fitz! Fitz!" broke from Tom. "Ah, Fitz! How did they know we'd be gone this one day?"

Lee Bratton was standing at the foot of the bed. Some great, haunted knowledge bloomed and grew to conviction in Lee's stare. Lee wheeled and ran from the room.

"We'll have to get her to the doctor, and get word to the

fort," Tom told Fitzpatrick. "But first I want to question Lee Bratton!"

The drumming rush of a departing horse came through the open bedroom window. Tom stepped to the window and saw Lee slashing with the rein ends and spurring away from the ranch—heading south, back toward town.

"The fool! We need him!" Tom shouted. He bolted from the room and ran back through the patio.

Sam Butterworth was in the kitchen. Tom panted: "Is your rifle loaded, Sam?"

"Yep."

"See if you can stop Lee Bratton."

Sam's long buffalo gun was leaning beside the open doorway. Sam caught it up and limped outside. He gazed after the receding rider. "Want him kilt?"

"The horse, Sam! Can you stop him without hitting Bratton?"

"Can try," said Sam. "Ain't got my rest sticks." Sam's eye stopped on Eagan. "Get down on your hands and knees, and gimme a rest for this gun."

"Do it, Eagan," Tom ordered sharply. "Quick!"

Eagan got down. Sam wet a finger in his mouth and tested the wind, and sat down stiffly on the ground beside Eagan. Sam's wispy, iron-gray beard moved in little jerks as he munched tobacco and rested the buffalo gun across Eagan's back. Sam peered calmly at the receding target. Absently Sam spat past Eagan's cheek. Eagen flinched.

"Hold still!" Sam said irascibly.

Eagan bowed his head and held rigid, muttering under his breath. Sam was cool as he peered through the sights. Slowly he squeezed the trigger. The heavy report slammed through the taut quiet.

Tom thought he heard in ringing ears the big .50-caliber bullet, almost half an inch through and two inches long, sing its vicious shrill into the distance. Nothing seemed to happen. It was agonizing. A miss was disaster. And Lee might be killed. Then suddenly Lee's furiously galloping horse flipped into a somersault and Lee pitched clear and sprawled on the ground.

Lee staggered to his feet and stood helplessly. "Bring him back!" Tom called. "He knows something about this!"

Ashley Hampton rode fast toward Lee, leading a saddled horse. George Sell followed. Tom turned to Sam Butterworth. "You're the best tracker here, Sam. Where'd they head? How much start on us?"

Barnaby Polk came to Tom's side. Lines had deepened in his face. "Not Lee," he said sadly. "Not this."

"Let Lee say it," Tom said. Fury filled him like a sickness.

Sam Butterworth started a limping circuit of the house. Fitzpatrick, white with anger, came out into the yard. "The woman will live," Fitz said. "I'll start word to the fort."

"Hear Lee Bratton first," Tom said.

Lee rode back between the two men. They had his guns. Lee's head was bowed. He dismounted in silence. Dirt from the fall covered him. He looked older.

Lee swallowed hard before he could speak. "Should have shot me, instead of the horse." Lee struck a fist desperately into a palm. "I did this!"

"Why?" Tom asked. "You were all your sister had."

"You told her she had nothing in me," Lee said. He had to stand a moment and get control. "I wasn't running away. I was heading to find Matt Fallon and kill him."

"Why Fallon?"

Lee looked at Tom from haunted eyes. "I wanted to kill you yesterday, Cantrell. The way you ran over me, and shot my horse. That horse hadn't done anything to you."

"It was the horse or you," Tom said. "You went for your gun.

I still regret the horse. He was a beauty."

"Wasn't he?" Lee said. He sounded like a man years older, turned inward to conscience and grief over his sister. "It was me, last night in town. I told Fallon the way to get you was when you came to town, looking for the men who'd killed Steve Rogers. Ginny had told me you meant to go."

"Did you tell Fallon about the heel plates?"

"Ginny hadn't mentioned heel plates. She wanted me to keep away from you. Matt Fallon kept asking if the boy and the Mexican woman would be alone here at the ranch if you rode to town. It didn't mean anything. Fallon didn't speak of Apaches. All I wanted was you, Cantrell, if you rode to town."

"And all I wanted," said Tom, "when I left the ranch unguarded, was the man wearing that heel plate. Both of us played fools for a smarter man." Lee's haunted look was grateful for any understanding at all. "Fallon," Tom said, "wasn't in town today. Do you know where he is?"

"The man at the feed corral said that Fallon picked the best horse they had last night and rode away," Lee said. "I can guess where he went. He deals with the Apaches, too."

"We met him up the trail, coming from the Apaches," Tom remembered. "Fallon admitted getting his horse from them. He knew about the boy then, evidently. And last night he found out from you where the boy was." Tom drew a breath. "We'll need fresh horses," he said to the men. "Then we'll find Fallon."

Fitzpatrick protested: "Tom, the girls come first!"

"We'll lose the trail at dark," Tom reminded. "Tomorrow we'll never catch up. Fallon found these Apaches last night. He can take us to them tonight. Get word to Alcorn, Fitz. Tell him to meet us at the Black Butte with help. We'll plan from there."

Lee's question was humble: "Can I have my guns and go with you?"

"If you'll take orders like a responsible man."

"I will," Lee promised. He walked over to the horse he had ridden back, and leaned against the saddle, his head on his arm.

Barnaby Polk looked at him. "His grandfather and his father were good men," the old lawyer said to Tom. "There should be hope for him."

"We'll see," Tom said. He turned to the waiting men. "We'll spread out and comb the country on our way to the Black Butte. Fallon should be somewhere near town. Major Alcorn can have the town and the fort searched for him. We have to get hold of Fallon before dark."

XXIV

Matthew Fallon had turned aside at the Black Butte in the blazing midday and ridden leisurely through the foothills to Fort Ross. He needed a shave and wanted to make a check on military patrols. This visit to the fort could also account for his absence from town. In the barbershop, at one end of the sutler's building, Fallon relaxed under a hot towel.

"Heard how the big gunfight in town went?" the barber inquired.

"Gunfight?" Fallon exclaimed under the towel.

"The Old Man himself moved out in force to stop it," the barber said cheerfully.

"I hadn't heard," Fallon mumbled. He lay excited under the hot towels. Cantrell must have ridden to town with his men. Probably Cantrell was dead. "Haircut, too," Fallon said. "Everything. If there's trouble in town, no use hurrying into it."

Later Fallon strolled about the fort, and talked with smiling assurance to Adjutant Blount. Blount knew only that Major Alcorn had moved out fast, taking most of the garrison.

It was late afternoon when Fallon rode from the fort, down the twisting little valley of the Frío, toward town. He had never felt better. With Cantrell dead, all the future was secure. Now, more than ever, the Apaches would be friendly to Matthew Fallon. He was thinking of the Apaches in scornful amusement when a detail of eight troopers and a sergeant approached on the rough road at a leisurely trot.

Fallon pulled up, smiling, to hear what had happened in town. Then he saw Joe Sloan, a prisoner of the troopers, and braced himself for some unpleasantness. "What happened in town?" Fallon inquired cautiously as the detail met him and halted.

The grinning sergeant said: "Big fight, big trial. Got one here they're holdin' for murder."

"There's no court nearer than Mesilla," Fallon said skeptically. "And the Army can't court-martial civilians. What sort of a trial?"

"Today there was court," said the sergeant. "Judge Andrews come in from Mesilla, and tried Lieutenant Cantrell for stealin' cattle. Cantrell got turned loose. The judge told the men whose cattle Cantrell took to look to some fellow named Fallon for their money."

In his shock, Fallon realized that these troopers did not know him. Joe Sloan's baleful expression confirmed the sergeant's story. Sloan spoke from his horse malevolently: "The men aim to get their money from Matt Fallon, soon as they catch him. And the judge is holding me for the grand jury, for killing Steve Rogers."

"On what proof?"

"I ain't rightly sure," Sloan said. "But if I ain't helped outta this mess, I'll tell that grand jury just who paid for that killing!"

"A man," Fallon said, "is usually helped when he needs it." The crippled hand in his coat pocket was sweaty as he waited for Joe Sloan to take the hint.

"I better be helped."

Stunned disbelief held Fallon as the troopers went on with

their prisoner. Cantrell was alive, and backed now by the law and the Army.

A little later Fallon sighted dust rising ahead, and turned his horse up the slopes. Beyond the valley crest, out of sight, he watched a column of troopers led by Major Alcorn pass on toward the fort. About half the garrison, Fallon estimated. Troopers must have been left in town.

The sun, slipping down the western sky, was still hot. Fallon felt cold as he rode on. Men at the Upper Frío Plaza were not friends now. Cantrell might be there. The law and the Army were there. When Fallon reached the Black Butte, he rode around to the towering north side and pulled up, thinking hard.

Papers and money he needed were at his ranch on the Gallinas. He could stop at the ranch, and then disappear to Santa Fe, and in comfort and safety shape his plans. Fallon reined his horse north.

The sun slid from sight in a red blaze. Indigo shadows crept over the silent earth. The click of hoofs against rocks sounded loud. Fallon had the strange, uneasy feeling of gradually being engulfed and made small in the brooding twilight. He rode down into a gouged arroyo and out of it, and skirted the base of a rocky dike that looked like a raw backbone in the deepening shadows. Where the dike pinched off, Fallon's horse pricked up its ears and nickered. Nerves tensed as Fallon saw a silent, motionless figure on a motionless horse, not a hundred yards away, at the end of the rock dike. He had to fight the impulse to snatch for the revolver under his coat.

In the fast fading light, Fallon saw that the stranger was an old man in a leather shirt, balancing a long rifle across his lap. Some harmless old drifter evidently. Fallon pulled up. "Who is it?" he called.

The reply was idle: "Name's Sam Butterworth. Light, Fallon, and wait comfortable."

Memory came to Fallon in a tide of horror. He recalled that hunched figure on the seat of Cantrell's trail wagon, and the anger of the men in Largo Cañon, where this old man had helped Cantrell.

"I don't understand," was all Fallon could think of to say.

"We'll talk about it," said the motionless figure idly. "I figgered 'twas you when you topped a rise couple miles back, with that right wing tucked in your coat pocket. Git down."

Fallon realized that the muzzle of the rifle covered him. Thinking desperately, he estimated the swiftly fading light. He kept the talk going. "What do you want?"

"You."

"Why?"

"I git lonesome. Light."

Fallon calculated how many jumps a spurred horse could make before the heavy buffalo gun could be brought into action, and how uncertain a racing target would be in this light. "Over there by you?"

"Don't matter."

The old man would be slow, Fallon decided. He drew a breath. "If it'll make you feel better," he said agreeably. He gathered the reins tightly in his sweating left hand and drew the twisted right hand from his coat pocket for better balance. His shout at the horse, his savage rake of spurs launched the startled animal into a bolting run. And nothing happened, as he had calculated. Half a dozen strides—a dozen. The old man was too slow. When Fallon heard the bellow of the big rifle, his horse was already hurtling down.

Fallon struck hard and rolled. He fought dizzily up to one knee. The loop of a rope dropped around him, jerked tight, yanked him down again.

"Rest easy," the old man's idle voice said. " 'Twon't be long." He fired two revolver shots in signal. Two distant shots answered. The old man dismounted and limped along the taut rope. "Gonna tie your ankles and fists. Don't git nervous. It's only Tom Cantrell coming."

The run of a horse drummed through the gathering night to them. From the earth where Matthew Fallon lay helpless, Cantrell's figure loomed, tall and gaunt, against the sky as he swung off. Cantrell stepped close and looked down silently. When Cantrell spoke, his voice was quiet. "Almost lost him, didn't we, Sam?"

"He was heading north, Tom. I ain't told him nothing."

Cantrell looked down. "Tonight, Fallon, you're going to guide us to that Apache camp."

"I don't know what you mean," Fallon said.

"Today, while we were in town," Cantrell said, "Apaches hit my ranch. They took the boy. They also took Miss Bratton and Major Alcorn's daughter."

Fallon could have cursed in despair. Those girls should have been at the fort. He had planned carefully, and this had happened. In all the West, there was no safety for a man who admitted a part in it. "I don't know anything about Apaches. I haven't been near your ranch. I've been at the fort."

"Will you guide us?"

"Cantrell, I'm a crippled man. I'm helpless here. I can't tell you something I don't know."

Sam Butterworth chuckled. "Ain't he throwing lies in a sweat? Tom, I seen the Utes make a big trapper talk. Half mile away you c'd hear him screaming it out."

Cantrell's quiet voice said: "How, Sam?"

"Tied him on an ant hill, Tom. Them big ants'll eat to the bone in a few hours. They's an ant hill back there a ways."

"I'm not a Ute," Cantrell said.

"You got a soft heart. And a softer head. Y'only got tonight, Tom. And all your life waiting ahead to think about what a soft heart'll cost you tonight. Lemme handle him."

Something colder and more terrible than Fallon had ever heard in a man's voice came now from Cantrell's gaunt, looming figure. "I'll do my own dirty work, and live with it. Drag him over there. I'll get stake pins and a rock."

Fallon knew how it would be. They would frighten him, thinking he would talk. He closed his eyes and suffered the ignominy of being dragged by the horse and rope.

He felt the soft mound of an ant hill tear open as his body was dragged on top. He locked his jaws. Near his head, Cantrell drove a stake pin into hard earth with a rock. Cantrell's hand pulled Fallon's wrists overhead. Cantrell lashed the wrists to the stake. Already the vicious, stinging bites were on Fallon's neck. Life flowed up on his face.

Suddenly Matthew Fallon realized the full fury and relentless purpose of this man Cantrell. Fallon's control broke. He screamed as the crawling wave moved over his face toward his eyes. He kept on screaming.

XXV

The dark mass of the Black Butte bulked ahead as their horses splashed through the shallows of the Frío. Beyond the sandy south bank a sharp challenge lifted.

"Cantrell and five men!" Tom called.

The two other men had been in the spread-out line of their search for Fallon. Signal shots had called them in. One man had given his horse to Fallon and was riding double. They rode past the mounted sentinel into deeper shadows under the butte steeps. A horse sneezed ahead. Bit chains softly chinked. The night came quietly alive with shadowy lines of horses and dismounted troopers. A man could feel the held-in emotions of those silent, waiting men. Anger came off them in a physical wave, as it filled Tom. Isabel Alcorn belonged to the regiment.

A horse approached. Major Alcorn's vigorous voice shouted: "Cantrell?" Tom answered. Alcorn rode to them. "The man Fallon was at the fort this afternoon and left. He's not in town."

"We have him," Tom said.

"Which one?"

"Back of me." Tom turned his horse back as Alcorn rode close to Matthew Fallon's horse.

Several sulphur matches sputtered and flared together in Alcorn's fingers. The bursting yellow flame showed the startled expression on Alcorn's drawn face. Matthew Fallon huddled loosely on his horse. A rope around his middle ran to George Sell's hand. Fallon's heavy face was blotched with livid little bites. His crippled claw of a hand pawed aimlessly at the puffy face as the light died.

"What happened to the fellow?"

"I'm not an officer, not a gentleman," Tom said. "I tied him on an ant hill. He'll help us tonight."

Alcorn's silence neither approved nor condemned. But as his walking horse came alongside Tom, Alcorn's words were introspective: "And I put off going after that boy's mother."

"A man's own home has to be hit," Tom said. "I'll need a small fire and some smooth dirt to draw a map. These nights are short. We can't delay."

Alcorn's order cut through the night, and as they rode on another hundred yards, Tom said: "Lieutenant Fitzpatrick left three men at the ranch and put his other men in our line of search for Fallon. Judge Andrews and Barnaby Polk stayed at the ranch with the Mexican woman. We decided not to move her."

"The post surgeon should be nearing your ranch now," Alcorn said. "Fitzpatrick did right. Here we are." As they dismounted, a small pile of dry twigs blazed up, gouging a red hole in the dark.

"The boy," Tom said, "drew plans of the Apache camp for Eagan yesterday morning. He thought men were going after his mother. The boy wasn't sure how to reach the camp, but Fallon knows." Tom called to Eagan. "Draw a map of that Apache camp on the ground by the fire."

"The two girls might not have been taken there," Alcorn suggested.

"Then we've lost them, Major."

They took that thought with them to the small group forming by Eagan. The fire was crackling, throwing increasing light. On his knees, with a small stick, Eagan was drawing in the sandy earth a plan of the distant Apache camp that none of them had ever seen. Only Fallon had been there.

As Eagan scored the earth with his stick, he said: "The kid says they's only about eighteen, twenty fighting bucks in this band. A sub-chief named Senya runs it. This here X I'm marking is Senya's wickiup. It's about halfway back from where the rocks drop off, according to the kid."

"Let me have the stick," Tom said. He kneeled beside Eagan. "The camp is on a large shelf, on a shoulder of the mountain, as Eagan says. The wall of a small cañon drops straight down from the north edge of the camp. East of the camp, and south of it, wooded slopes lift higher. The cañon bends around south and will block quick escape to the west." Tom looked up at the intent faces. "Surprise has to be complete, or they'll scatter into the trees, and have time to kill any captives."

Tom could feel the possibility of that torturing Alcorn, as it knifed Tom himself when he thought of it.

"They'll have guards posted, of course," Alcorn decided.

"Perhaps not," Tom said. "They'll expect pursuit and probably break camp at daybreak and scatter back into the mountains. Tonight they should feel confident they can't be tracked in the dark."

"How many hours to the camp?"

"Six hours or more from here," Tom estimated. "We go in through a cañon about fifteen miles east of here. Then up through a higher cañon to some fairly level land. At the first water, we turn upstream, keeping in the water. There's no other way. Rocks pinch in to a narrow cut. Beyond the cut is a thirty-foot waterfall, with a trail around it. Then a reasonably safe horse trail works up the side of a cliff. At the top, a swing right through brush and trees will bring us down an easy slope into the camp. A dozen good men and horses could go ahead for the surprise."

"Not enough to deal with twenty good Apache fighters," said Alcorn flatly.

Old habits almost made Tom defer respectfully to the major's decision, but he said: "That's only half of it, Major I'm taking my men into this side cañon, directly under the camp. The boy told Eagan that the Apaches climb up and down the cliff. They keep a few horses in the cañon. We'll climb to the cañon rim, and be at the edge of their camp before daybreak. When your men come in from the opposite side, we'll try to reach the prisoners fast."

Sam Butterworth said; "Mostly they'll shoot high. A man who keeps low is safer."

"He's right," Alcorn said. "All of you remember that." Then doubtfully Alcorn said: "Suppose this Matthew Fallon leads us wrong?"

"He won't, Major. George Sell will be close to him."

Alcorn stood in silence as Tom tossed the stick to the ground and stood up. A man could only guess the despairing surges of Alcorn's doubt. Isabel's life was at stake, if she was still alive. Tom knew what the man was struggling with. Tom had lived with it for hours.

"I see nothing better," Alcorn said slowly. "Captain Weatherby, pick your twelve best men and horses. Prepare to mount in ten minutes."

It was hours later, well after midnight, when Tom and his men turned their horses aside and watched the shadowy file of silent troopers pass quietly on through the faint starlight. Fitzpatrick had reached the Black Butte before they left and was in the advance detail. A small wind brought a chill down off the high peaks as Tom led the way into a small cañon.

The booming howl of a mountain wolf drifted across the cañon. Tom listened and decided it was not an Apache signal. The walls of the cañon were lifting higher. Brush and trees at the top showed blackly against the serene stars. The pale sands of an almost dry streambed wandered up the cañon at their right. A shod hoof struck rock with an audible clink and Tom felt his nerves tighten. In Apache territory, a man never knew.

In these brooding, pre-dawn hours, this plan Tom had insisted on was beginning to seem reckless. He was only guessing that the Apaches had returned to this camp with their prisoners. The soft creak of Ashley Hampton's saddle drew close. The Texan's quiet voice said: "We will get them."

Tom said—"Yes."—grateful for the reassurance.

They were following Sam Butterworth. Reluctantly Sam had agreed he could not climb the cañon wall with his bad leg. But Sam's instincts had been honed by forty years of this. The boy had said the Apaches kept horses in this cañon for convenient use. Sometimes they tied horses at the foot of the cliff trail. Just beyond that point stood a dead oak tree. Farther on, the cañon bent south. Finally a horse snorted ahead of them.

Sam Butterworth dismounted. Tom did the same. Reins in one hand, carbine in the other, Tom moved to Sam's side. "Smell 'em?" Sam muttered.

Tom tried the air. "Don't seem to."

"Smoky kind of stink," Sam said. "Cold air's bringing it down here off their camp. We'd best tie the horses and walk."

They moved cautiously forward on foot, skirting brush along the foot of the cliff. More horses snorted in the dark ahead and moved clumsily in hobbles. Tom presently smelled corral odor.

Sam halted as the hoot of an owl mournfully floated through the cañon. Small life rustled mysteriously in the nearby brush. Tom looked up at the sheer cliff overhead. It was worse than he'd expected.

Sam gave a perfect owl hoot and listened. "Wait here," he muttered. He vanished without a sound. It seemed a long time before he returned. "Looks clear," Sam said. "Better'n a hour before light."

They were a battered group, Tom was thinking. Buck Ellis and Ashley Hampton's three remaining Texans had been wounded, but they were here. Sam's leg was bad. Tom moved over to Lee Bratton. "Going to follow orders?" Tom asked.

"I'm trying."

Tom dropped an encouraging hand on the younger man's arm. He could sense Lee's gratitude. Tom's low orders to the men were brief: "Hampton will follow me. Eagan next. Then Lee Bratton. We're the most able-bodied."

No one argued. In single file, they followed Sam Butterworth's drifting advance to the foot of the trail, which would end, if they had luck, at the cliff rim high above. Tom led off, along a visible path threading the brush that cluttered the steep talus slope. The climb steepened. The path faded out above the brush.

Their boots made faint, grinding sounds on the rocks. When Tom paused, his deep breathing sounded harsh. Sweat lay clammy on his skin. In daylight, the way might have been plain. This blind groping up in darkness was guesswork. Halfway up,

Tom guessed wrong. A vertical sheet of rock blocked him. They had to back down. Dirt and gravel slithered from under their boots. A small rock bounced down some yards before it stopped.

Tom made another try along a small ledge, and sighed in relief when the stars silhouetted rocks above that could be climbed. The faintest gray was touching the sky. Tom looked down and could make out the Texan and Eagan. Presently the way to the rim could be seen. Tom motioned the others to wait, and went up alone, a careful step at a time.

Rock had split off the uneven cliff rim, leaving a sloping shelf some feet below. Tom crouched on the shelf and cautiously peered over the rim, through a fissure between two slabs of rock. He was looking down a slight slope, directly at the Apache camp on level ground beyond. The thatched side of the first wickiup loomed not thirty yards away, silent and unreal. There was enough light to see other wickiups, some seven feet high, scattered along both sides of an open clearing. Trees stood behind them. Tom gestured for the men to come up. When he looked back, a pup had ambled out of a wickiup. A tan cur at the far end of camp got up from the earth, looked toward the pup, and turned toward the nearest trees.

Moments later an Apache ducked out past a deer-hide door flap. Eagan had edged over beside Tom, and saw the Apache. His suck of breath was audible. The buck wore a breechclout. Red and yellow symbols were painted on his bare chest, black stripes on his face. The Apache scratched under an arm and watched an old squaw emerge from the opposite wickiup and shuffle around back.

Some moments later another Apache emerged from the nearest wickiup. Long moccasin leggings were folded loosely around his muscular calves. His chest and face were painted in black and red. Lazily the Apache scratched his chest and studied the sky.

Children, squaws, other paint-daubed men began to emerge from the wickiups. Guttural voices spoke back and forth. In the gradually increasing light Tom could sight horses tied back among the trees.

Every crouching man on the shelf had drawn his revolver. Tom moistened his lips as the nearby Apache wandered idly toward the cañon rim, still scratching himself. Back somewhere among the trees a dog began barking.

Tom wet his lips again as he peered through the narrow fissure at the Apache idly approaching them. The yawning figure moved up the slope toward the cañon rim. Tom tightened his grip on the revolver. Back in the trees, the dog's barking took on intensity. In the camp, a man called out in sharp gutturals. The Apache reached the rim and looked down into Tom's gun muzzle.

XXVI

The Apache's widening eyes showed complete amazement. He made no sound as a convulsive leap carried him back. He was twisting around in the air when Tom shot him. The slamming report reverberated through the gray dawn as they burst over the cañon rim. The Texans gave high Rebel yells, more blood-curdling than war whoops when a man remembered the ferocious Rebel charges in the late war. The other men took it up.

Only Ginny Bratton was on Tom's mind as he ran past the writhing body of the Apache. Ginny was in the rising, screeching confusion ahead, and Isabel, too, if a little mercy had been given them—and now they might have short minutes to live.

A barrel-chested Apache in breechclout and paint catapulted out of a wickiup ahead, clutching an iron-tipped lance. He saw Tom running at him and hurled the lance in a lithe explosion of movement. Tom wrenched to the right; the sharp iron point of the slender lance ripped through his left jacket sleeve. He shot the man with his revolver and halted in a crouch, trying to judge which wickiup belonged to Senya, the chief. This first night, at least, the prisoners might be under Senya's control.

Women, children, and fighting men were spewing out of the wickiups. Like hornets from a kicked nest, Tom thought. The bucks clutched carbines, revolvers, shields, lances, and through the tumult the great yells of Eagan were recognizable.

"Kid! You here, kid?" Eagan was shouting.

Tom looked back. His men had formed a loose square, advancing deliberately now, their guns smashing out shots as Apache fighters were sighted. Tom thought he heard gunshots east of the wickiups, back among the trees. Tumult around him cut off most of the sound. Then, ahead, Tom saw a squaw darting from a wickiup. She held a hunting knife. Other figures half hid the squaw, but the sash around her loose deer-hide dress caught Tom's stare. The sash was exotic-looking material, patterned in bright gold and silver threads. He had last seen it over Ginny Bratton's small shoulders. Tom knocked a frightened Apache boy aside as he ran recklessly toward the squaw.

A buck leaped around another stumbling squaw who carried a burden basket by its leather strap. A carbine muzzle swung up at Tom. Behind Tom's shoulder another carbine crashed a shot. The Apache's carbine sagged down. A visible hole in his chest was bubbling red froth as he reeled backward.

A look back showed Lee Bratton levering in another shell. Over to the left, Ashley Hampton was stalking forward with a long-barreled revolver and carbine. The Texan's yellow mustache half screened a grin of ferocity. Farther back one of the wounded Texans had fallen.

The squaw saw Tom running at her. She darted back into the wickiup. Tom's shoulder hit the deer-hide door flap. He burst into the dim, smoky interior. Grass pallets lay around a small depression in the center of the wickiup, where embers smoldered. Ginny Bratton and Isabel Alcorn lay on the pallets. Their arms and ankles were lashed with skin thongs.

The squaw had turned with the knife. Tom jerked the carbine up, flat side to her, as she struck with the long blade. The knife slipped over the carbine and slashed Tom's arm. His jab with the flat of the carbine struck her chest, driving her violently back. The squaw stumbled back over a saddle and household gear. Her body broke out through the thatched side, half into the open. She scrambled on out and vanished.

The girls were trying to sit up.

"Keep down," Tom panted. He swung around and almost shot a man plunging after him into the wickiup. It was Lee Bratton. "Watch them," Tom ordered.

He was gasping for breath, his left arm bleeding as he ducked back outside. In the pallid dawn, Tom glimpsed a mounted trooper among the trees east of camp. Bent low, revolver in hand, the trooper was riding a weaving charge at the camp.

A crouching, coppery figure retreated around the wickiup opposite, turned, and saw Tom. Red cloth circled the Apache's forehead. A red cloth streamer dangled from his left arm. Tom remembered that stocky figure looming in the binoculars the first day, sitting a dun horse on the foothill crest. There was Senya, who dealt with Matthew Fallon.

Senya's hard-breathing jump toward Tom had a sinuous flow as he whipped up a Spencer carbine. Tom fired with his revolver. He missed. The gun clicked empty on his next try. Tom dropped it. Sam Butterworth had said: *Keep low.* Tom squatted clear to his heels as he now brought up his carbine.

The Spencer carbine blasted muzzle vapor almost in Tom's face—and missed. Tom forced steadiness as his sights lined on the painted chest. He squeezed the trigger and saw the bullet tear through a painted black bar on the chest.

Still crouched, Tom looked past the falling Apache and saw

Lieutenant Fitzpatrick gallop into the camp ahead of three troopers. Major Alcorn rode recklessly between two wickiups, firing his revolver at some target. The major pulled up and looked anxiously around.

"Here!" Tom shouted. When he came upright and turned, he saw that a bullet hole had pierced the deer-hide door flap at shoulder height. Sam Butterworth had been right; they shot high. "Anyone hurt in there?" Tom called.

Lee's hard, confident voice replied: "All right in here!"

"Major Alcorn has arrived!"

Apaches were fading back among the trees to the south and west, still shooting. The troopers charging into camp were making them retreat. Tom's men, their guns cocked, were looking into wickiups and finding them empty.

Eagan broke into a run. The boy had stepped out of a wickiup. "Get back, kid!" Eagan shouted. He dived into the structure after the boy.

Fitzpatrick rode his blowing horse to Tom. "They'll all be up in a few minutes," Fitz said. "How is it?"

"The girls are safe in here," Tom said. "Look after them, Fitz."

And when Fitz swung down and took over, Tom walked slowly toward the south end of camp, reloading his revolver. Blood was oozing down his left arm and over his wrist. He entered a wickiup and found a length of red calico. He carried the cloth out to a dismounted trooper and said: "Help me bandage this arm."

Afterward, Tom moved on to the south end of the camp and sat cross-legged on the ground, watching the full command come through the trees in a rush, and the clean-up start. The gunfire retreated south and west, growing sporadic. After a time, sullen women and children began to drift back.

George Sell's calm, disgusted voice broke into Tom's

thoughts: "What'll I do with this thing?"

George Sell sat his horse, holding the rope that ran to his prisoner. Matthew Fallon sagged on his horse. His swollen, blotched face was bent low. He swayed loosely. The claw-like right hand dangled at his side. The man was broken, not even interested in what was happening around him.

Tom stared at the sight, thinking of the grief and injury this one man had caused. "Get him out of my sight," he said. "Hold him for the law."

George Sell sounded flinty as he yanked on the rope, and Fallon swayed in the saddle without protest. "I'll tie you to a tree," George said.

Tom looked away as they departed. Troopers were setting fire to the wickiups. The dried thatch blazed furiously and fell off in sparks and smoke. From where he sat on the earth, moodily smoking a cigarette, Tom could see Ginny Bratton and Isabel out in the open now. Lee was with them.

Men paused to speak to them and hurried on. After a time the rising sun found this smoke-hung mountain shelf, and presently Lee Bratton walked through the smoke haze to Tom. Lee looked ill at ease.

"I told Ginny everything," Lee said. "I'll take my medicine, whatever it is."

Tom regarded him a long moment. "You've been taking some of your medicine," he said.

"Ginny wants to see you."

Tom sat undecided, then got to his feet, flipped his smoke away, and walked through the camp, carrying his carbine.

He saw the small boy standing between Eagan and a slender squaw. The boy was holding the squaw's hand and looking up at Eagan. Sunlight fell on the squaw's brown hair. Her tanned face had a cast of sadness, but her features were not unattractive as her gaze stayed wonderingly on Eagan's red, bristle-covered face. Eagan was grinning widely as he talked to the boy and mother. Something like a smile hesitantly touched her face.

Tom faintly smiled himself over this thing that had entered Eagan's barren life. The mother would go where the boy went, Tom suspected. Eagan's life would be warm and full, and the ranch would have them all in the years ahead.

Lieutenant Fitzpatrick was talking to Isabel. Hat smartly canted, his kerchief and yellow leg stripes catching the sunlight, Fitz seemed in rare form. Isabel was regarding Fitz with a familiar look, a possessive look. They would continue with the regiment, Tom knew, both of them knowing it was right.

Ginny Bratton was sitting alone, her feet over the edge of the rimrock at the cañon drop. A tightness caught Tom as he neared her. The opposite wall of the cañon was not so high as this south wall. Past Ginny's slender figure, Tom could look out to the north, where Ginny was pensively gazing. Morning mists hung about the purple masses of the distant Secundos. All the great land to the north was brilliant in the new sunlight.

The crisp white suit Ginny had worn yesterday was now wrinkled and soiled. Her black hair had come down. The loose braid she had made fell over her left shoulder. She looked up as Tom paused beside her on the cañon rim. Her face was smudged and tired. Her hands rested listlessly on battered binoculars in her lap.

"Lee said you wanted to see me." Tom sat down at Ginny's left on the rock, his legs over the edge.

Ginny gazed into the north again. "Lee has told me everything," she said slowly.

"Everything is good now," Tom said. He eyed the binoculars in her lap. "Can you see the ranch through those glasses?"

"I tried," Ginny said. "Something seems broken inside. They were in the wickiup, stolen in some raid, I suppose." Ginny sat pensively, and then said: "I'll take your note for my half of the ranch."

"Doesn't fit my plans now," Tom said after a moment.

"Your plans? Who cares?"

"You own half of a good ranch. Why sell?"

"I don't want it," Ginny said, looking into the north. "The court gave you our cattle. We haven't much left. I'll not try to live fighting an angry, ruthless man, and worrying about Lee's safety. I'll take your note."

Tom shifted closer and reached for the binoculars. "Lee," he said casually, "won't be any trouble. Lee has grown up. And your Sarina will laugh again and be happy she's alive." Tom put the binoculars to his eyes. "Barnaby Polk suggested some sort of a partnership could work."

"It can't!"

"I can see the ranch," Tom said. "Try again." He had to put an arm around her shoulders to hold the binoculars to her eyes.

"I can't see a thing," Ginny said.

"It's the way you're looking." Tom had to bend close to adjust the binoculars. Smoky fragrance was in Ginny's black hair. Her small shoulder was stiff and uncompromising. "See the corral?"

"No!" Ginny said.

"I'm changing the focus. See the patio? And the roses on the new trellises? And the lady standing there?"

"Isabel," Ginny said, "might not like roses."

"Who cares? This lady likes roses." When Tom looked, Ginny's eyes were closed behind the binoculars. "She has the blackest hair," Tom said.

"Black hair?" said Ginny faintly.

"The softest hair." Tom put his cheek against Ginny's hair, and it was soft. "Not one rose half as pretty as she is. Ah, Ginny, can't you see our house?"

Smoke drifted about them. A small smile was curving Ginny's

smudged cheek, as it had in the patio that day. "Now I see it," Ginny said. Her eyes were still tightly closed as Tom tossed the binoculars into the cañon. "So nice," Ginny said. "So lovely. Tom, let's go home."

ABOUT THE AUTHOR

T. T. Flynn was born Thomas Theodore Flynn, Jr., in Indianapolis, Indiana. He was the author of over a hundred Western stories for such leading pulp magazines as Street & Smith's *Western Story Magazine,* Popular Publications' *Dime Western,* and Dell's *Zane Grey's Western Magazine.* He lived much of his life in New Mexico and spent much of his time on the road, exploring the vast terrain of the American West. His descriptions of the land are always detailed, but he used them not only for local color but also to reflect the heightening of emotional distress among the characters within a story. Following the Second World War, Flynn turned his attention to the book-length Western novel and in this form also produced work that has proven imperishable. Five of these novels first appeared as original paperbacks, most notably *The Man from Laramie* (1954) that was also featured as a serial in *The Saturday Evening Post* and subsequently made into a memorable motion picture directed by Anthony Mann and starring James Stewart, and *Two Faces West* (1954) which deals with the problems of identity and reality and served as the basis for a television series. He was highly innovative and inventive and in later novels, such as *Night of the Comanche Moon* (Five Star Westerns, 1995), concentrated on deeper psychological issues as the source for conflict, rather than more elemental motives like greed. Flynn is at his best in stories that combine mystery—not surprisingly, he also wrote detective fiction—with suspense and action in an artful balance.

The psychological dimensions of Flynn's Western fiction came increasingly to encompass a confrontation with ethical principles about how one must live, the values that one must hold dear above all else, and his belief that there must be a balance in all things. The cosmic meaning of the mortality of all living creatures had become for him a unifying metaphor for the fragility and dignity of life itself. *Gambler's Odds* will be his next Five Star Western.